MW00643169

SHELL HOUSE

Foreword by **KATHLEEN SHOOP**
Edited by **DEMI STEVENS**
Mindful Writers Retreat Authors

Copyright © 2022. All Rights Reserved
"Flora & George," "Frannie & Eli"– Kathleen Shoop
"Wren and the Sea Captain" – Stephanie Keyes
"Time Share" – Larry Ivkovich
"The Gazebo at Silver Lake"– Larry Schardt
"The Inheritance of Courage" – Jennifer D. Diamond
"The Heart of the Home" – Hilary Hauck
"Lifting Fog" – S.M. Kraftchak
"A Shell for a Shell" – Lorraine Donohue Bonzelet
"Molly's Magic" – Denise Weaver
"A Seashell of Love" – Carol Schoenig
"Love Dawns at Shell House" – Cindy Moldovan
"Say Hello to Henry" – Amy Morley & Michael Morley
"Hope in Flames" – Gloria Bostic
"A Sunday Séance at the Sea" – Kimberly Kurth Gray
"Life in the Mirror" – Madhu Bazaz Wangu
"Mystery at Shell House" – Lisa Valli
"Seashells and Cockle Tales of High Magic" – Michele Savaunah Zirkle
"See You Around the Cosmos, Sweet Cheeks!" – Phil Giunta
"Vacation: It's a Family Affair" – James Robinson, Jr.
"Slaughter Beach" – Deborah Hetrick Catanese
"Summer Memories at Aunt Mabel's Place" – Judy England-McCarthy
"Queen Anne's Amulet" – Demi Stevens

Print ISBN: 978-1-64649-254-1
Ebook ISBN: 978-1-64649-255-8

Shell House contains nonfiction and fiction pieces. Many of the works are set in a Rehoboth Beach, Delaware, home known as "Shell House" that once stood along the shore near Silver Lake. However characters and incidents are the product of the authors' imaginations or are used fictitiously.

Proceeds benefit the
Marine Education, Research,
and Rehabilitation Institute of Delaware
MERRinstitute.org

CONTENTS

FOREWORD

Welcome to the fourth installment of the Mindful Writers Retreat Anthology Series. We are so grateful for you and your enthusiasm for our collections. Just to remind you, we are a group of authors who meet for retreats at the Ligonier Camp and Conference Center in Ligonier, Pennsylvania, in order to enjoy uninterrupted writing time. We use sitting and walking meditation as tools to inspire and focus on the work at hand. Each anthology provides retreat writers an opportunity to submit stories, essays, poems, recipes, and more—all centered on a particular theme. The three previous collections lent themselves to different seasons and holidays so we thought a summery beach read would be a solid addition.

To further narrow the beachy theme, author Kimberly Kurth Gray sorted through endless photos of beach houses and beach towns where we could set our stories. When she found the historic Shell House of Rehoboth Beach, Delaware, our collection was born. Though the main requirement was for our chapters to be set on a beach, we wanted fiction to include Shell House as part of its core story. Choosing the historic Shell House allowed us to write stories set anywhere from 1920 when the home was built to 2020 when it was razed.

The stories in this collection draw from a variety of human experiences—new love, old love, family love, and friendship... even love of a house that has played host to generations of special events. Stories feature bootlegging, fantasy, science-fiction, architectural conservation, and more to explore all the ways people love and lose each other over time.

In addition to their imaginations, authors have drawn from the history of Rehoboth and Shell House to shape their stories. Some have been inspired by local mythology and lore or invented their own to create a compelling tale. Some stories are linked by more than the town, beach, and house. Keep an eye out for reappearing characters and mentions of elements such as recipes. We hope these loose connections create an even richer reader experience.

As this collection demonstrates, beach living and vacationing is a vital part of life, often what means the most to those who are lucky enough to spend time waterside. Beautiful, low-key Rehoboth is the perfect setting for big, life-changing events. It also invites inner transformations that occur under the hush of letting some things go and grabbing tightly to others. The Rehoboth tides and shifting sands lend themselves as backdrop and impetus that mirror life itself. Beach memories are held dear and passed on to relatives as though precious jewels or hidden treasure.

As always, we've chosen a charity to receive proceeds from anthology sales. This time, we selected the MERR Institute—Marine Education, Research and Rehabilitation Institute of Delaware. Because Rehoboth's coastline and its waters provide food, recreation, housing, and opportunities for millions of people, all of this use means we need to take even better care for the environment that lends romance, inspiration, joy, and relaxation.

From their website:

> *The Marine Education, Research and Rehabilitation Institute, Inc. is a nonprofit stranding response and rehabilitation organization dedicated to the conservation of marine mammals and sea turtles. MERR Institute, Inc. is authorized by National Marine Fisheries Service and the State of Delaware to be the official stranding respondents for the Marine Mammals and Sea Turtles of Delaware.*

Proceeds from your purchase of this anthology will be donated to the MERR Institute. We hope that you love the collection, and that the funds we raise help to preserve the gift that Rehoboth is to all.

To learn more about the fabulous work that MERR Institute does, find them at www.merrinstitute.org

See you next time with all new stories and a great new theme to explore!

—Kathleen Shoop

FLORA & GEORGE

Kathleen Shoop

June 21, 1925

Flora Daniels and Rachel Platt slept on chaise lounges by the sea, waves crashing in mesmerizing rhythm, salt and jasmine perfuming the air. Flora stirred, the wooden slats digging into her spine. The rising sun warmed her cheeks. Without opening her eyes she groped the sand for her hat and pulled it on. She swallowed anxiety and reminded herself that this would be the last time she took such a risk. The Shell House Soiree would bring enough lettuce for her to buy back her father's farm, pay for her brother's attorney, and more. She'd even begun to grow her hair out so she could easily return to boring old farm life without sparking the least curiosity from her old neighbors.

If only the booze had arrived on schedule she would feel as carefree as she needed to appear. Every other non-alcoholic detail for the party had been executed. She cheered herself with reminders that she'd never failed before. Yes, the boozy delivery was delayed. But better safe than stuffed away in the Big House and made an example of how bootlegging could go bad in a quiet, resort town like Rehoboth Beach.

"Morning." The Shell House cook Molly's voice and the scent of coffee came from behind Flora. She gestured to a third chaise. "Sit. Have a cup. What's new?"

"Thank you," Molly said, "but no. My family reunion."

Flora swung her legs around and put her feet in the sand, reaching for a mug. "Oh, right. Yes. You leave this morning."

"The servers you hired are already organizing in the kitchen, fluttering about the house, moving furniture for the band and..." Molly's knuckles whitened as she gripped the second mug tightly.

Flora understood Molly's concern. She was the primary caretaker of the mansion nestled between the Atlantic Ocean and Silver Lake. "Mrs. Carpenter knows you're not responsible for anything this weekend. Everything will be all right."

Molly sighed and set the second mug in the sand near Rachel who sat up.

"You little rosebud, you, Molly," Rachel said. "You're saving us with the best joe I've ever smelled in my life."

Molly nodded. "It was lovely to meet you both. Thank you for promising to be gentle with the house and for, well, I baked something special—not elegant like the foods you've selected for the soiree but... I felt the need to make one humble thing. Just some canned fruit and flour."

Flora smiled, wishing she had more time to spend with Molly, the kind of friend she used to have. "You didn't have to do that."

"Well, looooooky there," Rachel said.

Flora ignored Rachel, wanting to reassure Molly.

Molly continued. "I'll stow it in the pantry for when you need something different, when, you know, when a need reveals itself. I don't know. It's silly."

"Sounds fabulous." Flora wasn't sure what Molly meant, but the lady had been so sweet and hospitable that she took the gesture to heart.

Rachel shook Flora's arm. "Seriously, look at those jelly beans."

Flora lifted her hat brim to see what Rachel was harping about.

"I think my heart stopped," Rachel said.

Flora's breath hitched. "I think the condition is catching."

Two men in deliciously immodest bathing costumes sauntered toward them like jungle cats, wet skin glistening.

Flora forced her breath to even out, confused, energized, curious as the gaze of the tall, dark heartthrob turned her inside out.

George Wilk and Nelson Nickel completed their sunrise swim and headed toward the women lounging by the sea. George shook his head, spraying ocean water from the ends of his hair. The lounging doll with bobbed, blonde hair slid on sunglasses with splayed fingers, clearly studying him and Nelson. The other beauty was all hat, brim flopping out six inches from her head. And legs—long, slim, sunned, and better than that—exposed. She didn't move to adjust the fringed dress that had ridden up her thighs. He'd met a woman like her before. And lost her. But he'd never forgotten.

"Can we help you?" The bob-haired bearcat pushed her tortoise shell sun cheaters back on her head and sipped coffee.

"We've come about the soiree," George said. "That *is* the Shell House behind you, right?"

The hatted one removed the straw monster. Cinnamon-colored hair dropped around her shoulders. She shielded her green eyes with one hand. "Invite only."

His stomach fluttered then he froze as her steady gaze gripped him. He felt like he'd been tumbled by a mammoth wave.

George glanced at Nelson then patted his hips and chest as though searching for his invitation. "The morning swim has left me without pockets."

"Your name then," the redhead said. "It will ring a bell."

George got down on one knee and extended his hand. "George Wilk."

She shook her head, but slipped her hand into his. Electricity shot through him, her green eyes reeling him in.

"I think I know you," he said. He would have bet his house on it.

"No."

"The *third*," Nelson chimed in, breaking the spell between the woman and George.

She pulled her hand from George's and sipped her coffee, studying the black liquid as it sloshed against the lip of the mug like tidewater. "Oh, well, George Wilk *the third*. That clears everything up. Another tomcat with *the third* tacked onto the end of his name. Joy, joy."

"You really don't remember me?"

"You've slithered in from the water like a footed eel and planted yourself inches from me. I see you perfectly well, and no. We've never met."

"Where're you boys staying?" the one with bobbed hair asked.

"Tent house," George said. "Down the way."

Red looked him up and down. He knew she'd like what she saw.

"You don't look like tent house people," she said.

"We're simple men."

"*With* invitations." Nelson shifted his weight. "Met a fella on the train. Said he's cousin to the man who founded the resort fifty decades ago... said he was great pals with the current Shell House folks and so it would be fine."

The woman dressed in cook's clothing stared, looking intrigued.

The blonde got to her feet, hand on hip, chin out. "That's how you think this shindig works? A party like..."

"Looks like you've already had a party." Nelson scooped up two bottles—whiskey and champagne, shaking them by their necks.

Red craned, surveying the beach. It was littered with bottles glinting in the sun. She put her lid back on and stood, the fringy hem of her dress falling to her knees. Beautiful knees. George almost reached out to touch them. He got to his feet, towering over her.

Red crossed her arms. "That foot juice isn't ours. We weren't zozzled. We had dinner and watched the sunset and... I happen to take great pleasure in snoozing in the sea air." She held her palm out to Nelson, wiggling her slender fingers.

He handed her the champagne bottle. She ran her finger over the label while Rachel eyed Nelson, biting her lip.

The cook shrugged. "Bottles wash up all the time."

Red looked queasy. Perhaps she wasn't as fun as she appeared. Perhaps the party wasn't what George thought it would be.

Molly opened her arms. "Seems like there's always room for more guests at a soiree, Miss Flora."

Flora glared.

"*Flora*," George said. "Oh my, a stunning flower in the form of a sea goddess."

She rolled her eyes.

George wanted to be welcomed to the party, needed access to do his job. "How about Nelson and I clean up the bottles in exchange for an invite from *you*? We're a dependable good time." He winked.

Flora dug her toes in and out of the sand, red nail polish hinting that she indeed must be more fun than this. "Fine. But please behave as though you've been issued a proper invite. We can't have people just waltzing in like... It's not a church picnic. We aren't in the business of saving souls. And this property isn't mine. I have standards to uphold."

George grinned. "My soul's in good stead. Promise."

"Mine's not," Nelson said making Rachel dissolve into giggles.

George pushed his hand through his hair. "We'll be our best selves until the moment we board the train to Los Angeles."

"Big shots. Movie stars." The blonde snapped her fingers. "Knew it."

"Yes. Actors," Nelson said. "You got it."

"Splendid." Molly cleared her throat, drawing the attention of all of them.

Flora raised her eyebrows at the cook.

"Pineapple upside down cake. In the pantry." The cook took Flora's hand.

"I *love* pineapple cake." George's eyes lit up.

Flora drew back. "I do... I do too." She barely said the words aloud.

The odd sense of knowing Flora pulsed through George again. He hadn't been lying.

The cook backed away, brushing her hands over her apron. "Well. That explains it, then."

"Explains what?" Flora asked.

A crashing wave camouflaged Flora's question and with that, invite secure, George's heart sped up, insides quivering. If he'd been a romantic at all, he'd swear he fell in love with Flora the moment she looked up from under her hat. Yet he had a job to do. If the booze hadn't been dropped already, he would have time to catch them in the act. The most notorious bootleggers on the Atlantic coast were supposedly tasked with drenching tonight's soiree in the best booze money could buy. And he was there to make an example and launch his career.

Flora spent her day with the servants and her extensive list. Periodically she would saunter to the edge of the brick patio that overlooked the ocean to be sure George and Nelson were collecting the bottles. She witnessed them playing catch as though they were amassing footballs, not the remnants of illicit whiskey and champagne. But they were making progress. She didn't need ministers and Rehoboth families plucking contraband from the sand, knocking at the door with questions or accusations. She hoped the beached bottles didn't mean her full delivery had met its demise.

Inside she ordered the men to angle the piano and one bandstand near French doors. Staging for the dancers and circus acts, who were coming with a polar bear and cheetah, had been constructed on the patio that stretched between the house and swimming pool. Tables were clustered between the pool and Silver Lake, making use of every inch of the property. Fireworks would be set off by the lake throughout the night.

A champagne fountain, awaiting its bubbly, sat in the middle of the buffet table. Silver trays on wooden lifts would showcase shrimp, scallops, steak, lobster, and jello salads. Tarts, tortes, cookies, petit fours, and truffles would surround the chocolate fountain for revelers looking for something to soothe boozy bellies.

Pointing here, directing there, Flora focused on every detail but the booze. Despondent by five o'clock with its absence, she took a quick bath. She styled her hair so it scalloped along her face and was tied in the back to create the effect of having bobbed locks. Clad in gossamer, the ivory fabric as light as butterfly wings, she sparkled with silver and gold appliqued stars and never felt more beautiful.

Tick, tick, tick. Pacing the foyer, Flora's stomach filled with acid. Merrymakers would storm the castle soon. They'd be greeted with zero champagne, malty beer, wild gin blossoms, or highballs. They'd demand refunds amid angry chaos.

A server tapped her shoulder, explaining that the special delivery had arrived and she was needed in the cloakroom. This wasn't how the drop-off normally went. She never met with the delivery men. They knew where she'd hidden the money and they knew where to leave the drink. Later she'd check that the cash was gone and she'd be able to breathe, knowing that no one would be taking payment in broken limbs or worse.

But she couldn't be coy and risk the party not starting on time. If she needed to just hand the money over in person she would. So when she entered the cloakroom, she stopped short at the sight. Two chubby guests, a man in a fedora and dark suit, and a dame in a silver evening gown, stood in the middle of acres of drink. They introduced themselves as Aunt Marjorie and Uncle Stu—distant Carpenter relatives and proud owners of the personalized invitations Flora had made herself.

The hefty woman and stocky man's arrogance dripped as thick as the diamond necklace snaking down Aunt Marjorie's bodice.

The hair stood up on the back of Flora's neck. It couldn't be. It was so obvious it was absurd. Clearly the woman was a man dressed in disguise. Flora inhaled sharply. This was the game of the most notorious prohibition agents in America—Izzy Einstein and Moe Smith. The blood rushed from her head. She grabbed the door jamb, forcing herself to stay upright. It couldn't be.

"Seen a ghost?" the man said.

She pressed a hand to her throat. "Just two guests in the back room of the kitchen where they don't belong. It's quite embarrassing for you to witness the sausage being stuffed into its skin. Unsightly, to say the least."

The man held one elbow out to his "woman friend" and the other out to Flora. "Well, then."

She knew how this worked. They were waiting to see her pass payment to the delivery men or charge money for the booze when guests arrived. That was when they could pounce. She swallowed hard. The party was too good to be true. Why, oh why, had she gotten greedy for one more cash infusion?

She forced a swallow and reminded herself that she knew her share of paths through prohibition weeds. People could privately consume alcohol that had been purchased before prohibition began. "Surely you're familiar with the host family's stores of alcohol. The labels show the date to be long before 1919."

The man winked at her as they headed into the foyer and toward the pool patio where hired dancers were already spinning, charming, and mesmerizing. Though still daylight, the electric lights strung along every elevated surface and flowering shrub reflected off of silk and tulle table coverings. "Very familiar, yes."

"Well then, enjoy and let me know if there's anything missing from the evening."

She slipped her arm out of Stu's and backed away, right into George.

Flora felt him take her elbow. Did George know his grip was the only thing holding her up? The sultry June night and the stress of Izzy and Moe being at the party caused her to sweat. George dabbed his hanky against Flora's brow. She didn't have time to sort through a complicated plan. No time for nuance.

She grasped his wrist. "I need your help. Please."

George cocked his head and a smile lit his lips.

She let go. "Not that kind of help." Well, maybe that kind of help, but not until later.

He lit a cigarette and handed it to her. "I couldn't have imagined that you would look more ravishing than this morning, but here you are, *more* stunning, draped in stars, as though you've been harvested from the moonlit sky itself."

Her face grew hotter still. She snatched the hanky from him and patted her cleavage, his eyes following her movements. Good. He was interested enough to stay close.

"You look dressed for improv, if you will," she said.

His wiry, muscular physique propping up a creamy linen suit made his actor status even more evident. He moved with magnetic, liquid grace.

The band shifted from rehearsal to performance, adding to the atmosphere.

Flora pulled George by the shoulders and whispered, "See those two out there?"

He turned his head.

"Be casual."

He grinned, a glint in his eye showing he was game. "A mystery? Well, first off I can tell that woman is a man and—"

"Yes... yes. Isn't she?"

"To each his own. I can tell you're of that same mind."

"Well, yes unless..."

He narrowed his gaze on her and held her hand, caressing the back of it with his thumb. He took her breath away for the second time that day.

"Unless what?" he asked.

She noticed the couple watching so she traced one hand around the back of George's neck, pulling him closer. He bent in, his spicy clean scent thrilling her. She brushed her lips over his then whispered, "That's Izzy Einstein and Moe Smith."

He flinched then froze.

She drew him in by his tie. "You know. They're prohis! They infiltrate parties and arrest the hosts and... they're always in the papers. Please, I can't get caught."

He shook his head, confused. "But you're not..."

The prohis moseyed toward Flora and George. She looped her arms around his neck, leading him to dance. Just as Izzy and Moe were steps away, the music soared and the front doors flew open. Revelers flooded in, women glimmering in sequined gowns of every hue, couples spinning past waitresses, emptying trays of champagne flutes without even stopping.

The crowd separated Izzy and Moe from Flora and she dragged George into the back hall.

"I need you to stand guard while I make sure the payment was made. I can't let those two see me and..."

His face crumpled in confusion.

"Please. As soon as I know all is settled we can dance the night away."

He hesitated then nodded, following.

She entered the pantry and hustled to the back wall. She hauled the few stacks of china that hadn't been laid, flour and sugar bags, and coffee tins to the table. With a deep inhale she slid the bolt on the tiny door and exhaled at the sight. The money was gone and a receipt marked paid in full was set with a bottle of champagne.

She turned with bottle and receipt in hand. The sight of George filled her with joy. It was over. All was well. She could leave this life behind. She lunged toward him and he scooped her up, spinning. He sat her on top of the work table, stepping in between her legs. She set the bottle and receipt aside. With slow purpose, he caressed her thighs and she took his cheeks in her hands and led him in for a kiss. He expertly worked around her mouth, trailing down to her neck, sending chills through her, kissing for what felt like hours. She pulled him tight, then leaned back to let him trace toward her cleavage. Her hand knocked into something as she shifted. "Look."

"Special cake. Humble cake," George said, kissing the glaze from her hand.

"I guess this is the moment Molly mentioned," she said realizing she hadn't eaten all day. She read the note aloud. *"Sometimes cake is more than cake. Enjoy the journey."*

George smiled. "Shall we?" He cut into it and fed her, his fingers brushing over her lips, making her want his hands everywhere. He popped the champagne and they sucked back half the bottle while they scarfed down cake. With a final swig she pushed his coat over his shoulders, slipping it off.

And that was when she saw it. A badge. Her heart thudded against her chest. She went dizzy, unable to make sense of the man she'd been ready to help disrobe. She was so confused. Izzy, Moe...

George looked horrified.

She pushed him away and slid off the table, straightening her dress with an exhale. "That's not Izzy and Moe out there, is it?"

He shook his head slowly. Without looking she groped the table for the receipt.

Gone.

He held it up. She bolted through the pantry, rushing onto the brick terrace, skirting along the hedges and boardwalk that led to the ocean. The band's music lifted and fell with fast and slow tunes. Laughter floated into the heavens and Flora felt as though she'd lost everything for nothing. How could she have been so stupid? *Actors*. Fakeloo artists. George and Nelson had as much admitted they were undercover that morning on the beach. But she'd been too taken with George to think it through.

She raced to the water's edge and stopped when it hit her knees. She eyed the horizon, the moon's reflection gyrating on the ocean's surface. She could swim... to where? How far? If she died, did it matter?

George sidled up to her, his arm brushing against hers. She heard the tinkling of federal bracelets, the metal glinting in the starshine.

She tried to use her best, big voice. "You could say she swam into the horizon. Gone forever."

He furrowed his brow, making eye contact.

"I could make it."

He took one of her hands then the other, both engulfed in his large grip. "I don't doubt it."

This was it. This was how it all ended. Now she wouldn't even have money for her own attorney, let alone her brother's. The farm would be gone forever. She'd shed her innocent persona for nothing. Nothing.

The water splashed against them. This moment could have been so spectacular. If she'd only paid more attention. Beautiful, regular men didn't roll up on beaches like bootlegged champagne. Yet she hadn't even questioned it.

He didn't let go, but hadn't cuffed her either.

"I could make it if you just let me go."

He held her hands tighter and looked away. "Or..."

"Or what?"

George couldn't get past what he was feeling. The cuffs were poised. This arrest would make his career. He and Nelson had been wrong all along, not suspecting a woman had been the one coordinating the bootleg Summer Soiree Party circuit. And he could not have guessed that there was such a thing as love at first sight, that everything would change the instant he met this woman, the instant he realized who she was.

"Or what?" Flora repeated.

He looked deep into her eyes. "Or we make a clean sneak. Right now. We'll invent a story about where *she* went while we're on the train."

"Why would you do that?" Fear swept over her face. She must have wondered if his offer hid something cruel or unusual.

He tried to explain, but his words sounded crazier than what he felt stirring inside. "I can't really say, I mean, I know it's lunacy and I can't believe I'm doing this but... I don't want you in the cooler. I want—what I *want* is..."

"What?"

Her breathless words grasped at his heart.

"*What* do you want?" she asked.

He realized she could be swindling him. If they got on the train, who was to say she wouldn't slink away into the great plains of America while he slept? He clutched at his chest, the mix of pain and excitement as intoxicating as the drinks back at the house. His thoughts ran wild, but one thing was clear. It was time for him to take a risk. "You. Us. Take to the winds."

Her breath hitched and her frightened expression seemed to change to relief. She reached up and pulled him into her, talking in between her kisses. "I want that. Yes. It doesn't make any sense, but... *yes!*"

The first set of fireworks erupted, spilling into the sky behind the house.

He pulled her closer, each grasping the other tightly, urgently, as he wished every bit of them could meld, disappearing from this world and reappearing in a new one. "I'm serious."

"I want this. I do," she said.

This was no weak sister and he needed to act fast. They would have to pull leg to make the night train without Nelson noticing. "Stay here," he said.

She shook her head. "I need my handbag, the ice, my cash and..."

He rubbed his chin.

She pointed at the house. "We'll sashay back inside, act like nothing's changed. I'll gather my bags and meet you back in the pantry. I can't leave the only things I own, the money. Just one suitcase. I'll come down the back staircase."

"Okay. I'll be sure Nelson's occupied with Rachel and..." His voice cracked. This would mean he wouldn't speak to Nelson again? He hadn't thought that far.

"Are you sure? I can run on my own. You're a nice man doing a nice thing. You don't have to handcuff yourself..." they both chuckled at that, "to me just because you want to do a nice thing."

He brushed the backs of his fingers along her cheek, hoping they could spend the rest of their lives exploring each other. "I only want to let you go if I go with you."

She looked relieved and convinced. She got up on her toes and kissed him hard. "Meet you in ten."

And they trailed back to the house and went their separate ways. She disappeared up the front staircase while Uncle Stu and Aunt Marjorie cut George off on his way to the kitchen.

Stu gripped his arm. "You better hightail it out of here."

George halted. For a moment he thought this was indeed Moe and Izzy and the agency had doubled up on prohis because of the importance of this bust. But no. He would have recognized them this close up.

"Why?"

"That big blond man dancing with the doll named Rachel? He's a prohi. And he's going to take this place down. So you better tell that sweet Flora to take a powder before the next set of fireworks."

Now George was perplexed. He started to ask more questions, but Stu shoved him toward the kitchen. "You've about five minutes."

George nearly went to Nelson, to explain that he was sorry but it had to be this way. But when he saw Nelson scanning the space, he knew Nelson would never turn away from the bureau. He would never betray the badge. This was it. George was either stealing away with Flora or staying to fail at the capture of her. Would she even show as planned?

He jogged to the pantry and was placing the bottle of champagne and all of Flora's lists and receipts into the two-sided vault when she walked in, suitcase in hand, makeup scrubbed off, dressed like a killjoy ready to extinguish a party.

"I want to leave a note," she said. "To seal the end of one life and the beginning of another."

He lifted his shoulders. He wasn't so sure about this.

"Just a short one. No one will find this vault. But I don't know. I feel better explaining in case they do. I had the vault put in myself the other day."

And so they signed their intentions onto paper sealing their new start in intertwined handwriting.

They added it to the vault and bolted it, sliding a panel over the door. They replaced the china and other items so no one would notice the door unless they were looking for it.

He checked his watch. Three minutes. Voices in the hall indicated the fireworks were going off soon.

When the people passed, Flora and George started down the hall. More voices. They spun around and snuck back upstairs. From Flora's bedroom, they exited via the balcony. They tossed the suitcase and purse then took turns sliding down the pillars that held up the balcony. George helped her onto the ground, light as a feather, then took her hand. The fireworks started. "You ready for this?" he asked. "You can back out."

She looked stunned for a second then smiled. With a great exhale she tugged his hand. "Ready and willing." She dragged him to the path that led to the road that snaked along the back of Silver Lake. And with that, a new life was born.

WREN AND THE SEA CAPTAIN

Stephanie Keyes

Some people are born to be in love—possibly even for their whole lives. They find their person and there's a connection that leads to some defining moment others never see, and they're inseparable. Soon, they've woven lives for themselves that resemble rich tapestries, with trips to foreign lands, house moves so terrible they're laughable, afternoons of combing forgotten bookstores and reading the hours away as rain sends droplets pattering on the roof, all threaded in a series of bright golds, vibrant reds, and stunning oranges. As their creations grow, they'll add more threads—for children, families, legacies...

Then there are others who seem destined to be alone, those of us forever searching for threads we can weave into love. No matter how many potential someones they meet, the relationships fail. There is no connection, no genuine spark. After a time, they doubt the existence of the phenomenon people call "love" and the ever-elusive concept of a lifelong partner.

"You'll find love again, I promise." Though Aunt Ruth swore this with all the solemnity of a Girl Scout, I wasn't certain I believed her. Even my name implied I was incapable of such things: Wren. Like the bird, I was small, plain, and evicted from the nest far too young after my parents' untimely death. Then she delivered her last-minute invitation—a night's stay at the famed Shell House in Rehoboth Beach (her treat). I could never say no to Aunt Ruth.

Which was why I packed my suitcase and left before I could even begin to process my husband's betrayal. Jeremy hadn't noticed. He'd simply continued packing his belongings into tidy, P-Touch-labeled banker's boxes so he could move from our apartment and into the home of my once-best friend.

The late-August air was swollen with humidity as I drove the last few miles to my home for the night. Memories returned to goad me as light glinted off the one thing my meticulous husband had left behind: the shiny gold band we'd once picked out in a flurry of kisses in the middle of a snowstorm. Yet there was no fighting the memory of discovering him devouring her—that terrible moment had destroyed the rest, like a virus.

A string of lightning whipped across the sky. My attention darted from the GPS on my phone and back until I spotted Penn Street. I rolled the car to a stop in front of #2 and sat in the driveway, staring up at the imposing three-story manor, covered in shingles bleached into twenty different shades of gray from the persistent salt air. Shell House's darkened panes gave it a forgotten look, as though it remained stuck in the past.

Movement caught my eye. I could have sworn the curtains twitched.

One fat drop splattered the windshield and then another. "You're seeing things." Muttering, I closed the windows and grabbed my overnight bag from the passenger seat before running up the weathered steps to the covered front porch. In moments, I'd opened the lockbox and freed the key. Soon, the doorknob twisted under my direction.

Setting my bag on the floor, I flicked the light switch, illuminating walls bathed in cheery floral paper. The quiet of the house should have felt unsettling, but a peace slid over me. I locked the door behind me and began my tour from the entryway to the living room, and finally into a large, semi-circular kitchen, where wide windows overlooked the dunes.

Switching on more lights, I wandered to the refrigerator and opened it. Inside, I found a bottle of wine and a plate of cheese, along with several containers of food and a single note card.

Welcome.

"Aw." Warmth rose in my chest, only to catch in my throat as the overhead lights bounced off my wedding band. In that singular moment, it felt tight, as though shrinking on my finger, strangling me from the inside out. Before I could stop myself, I tore from the cheery kitchen and raced outside.

The slow-building rain slapped my skin, stinging me with its intensity as I raced up the wooden walkway that led to the sea. Waves roared with my approach, leaving the impression that I climbed toward the eager mouth of a hungry beast. As quickly as it began, the path crested and drew in a sharp breath. The barren beach stretched before me without a soul in either direction.

The sea resembled a cauldron of white-tipped waves, its water shaded in that ominous, dirty color that preceded a storm. Lightning flashed in a crack of white across the navy-blue, velvet-like sky, thick with an undercoat of clouds that tumbled over one another as they built. The surrounding air crackled with an indescribable energy.

I stalked to the spot where the tide touched the sand. Seizing my left ring finger, I easily yanked off the ring. It had always been a little too loose—as though I'd held a tenuous grip on my marriage from the beginning. Biting back tears, I flung the band as hard as I could until it disappeared into the foamy water.

For several moments afterward, I simply stared, unmoving, at the place where it had gone into the water. In the aftermath of my impulsivity, a sharp pain filled my chest, and my heart contracted in mourning. The one reminder that I once had a life, a love, was lost forever. Jeremy would never be mine. We would never have a future, a family, or grow old together. We'd never have anything together now.

The bubble of grief that had been building in my throat for days seemed to expand, and I gasped. The rain let loose, pouring down so that the already-weakened dam holding back my emotions gave. I fell to my knees, finally letting the tears go as rain soaked me to the skin. For more moments than I found myself capable of counting, the weather and I were one.

It wasn't until the empathetic rain softened into a steady mist that my tears ebbed and my teeth chattered. Wrapping my arms around myself, I struggled to my feet. I trudged up the beach and back up the walkway. I'd made it over the threshold to the kitchen when I came up short.

A man stood at the counter pouring a glass of wine. He was tall, at least six foot four, with cheekbones that belonged on a supermodel, muscles that pressed through his clothing, and short-cropped black hair that curled at his earlobes. He wore all black—from his cloth jacket to his worn work pants with patches at the knees, and thick black boots he wore on what seemed like generous feet. Yet an indescribable tension vibrated underneath that outward calm.

That memory of shifting curtains rushed back to me. So I'd been right—I wasn't as alone as I'd thought.

The stranger's eyes widened more by the second, as though he were just as surprised to see me. "Hello."

The air conditioner kicked on and a shiver ripped through me. I knew suddenly that I must look like a wet dog dripping puddles on the hardwood. "I thought my aunt rented this place for the night. Are you the caretaker or something?"

His eyes seemed to see through me as he offered me a glass of red. "You seemed... troubled. Perhaps you could use something to calm your nerves." He frowned at the open wine bottle. "I would have offered something with a little more weight, but we're out of whiskey." He didn't meet my eye, as though giving me space to collect my thoughts.

"Thank you." Embarrassment crept over me, my face flaming. This man was the caretaker, and I'd come into his place of business and had a meltdown or an epiphany.

"I'm Wren." I offered him my hand, and he took it. A sense of bone-deep familiarity rushed through me, as though we'd met before.

He broke contact, though the impression of recognition lingered on my skin like grains of sand between my toes after my big oceanfront moment.

"I'm Samuel. It's nice to make your acquaintance." His cheeks pinked as he allowed himself to meet my eyes once more. "You must be famished. Can I prepare a meal for you?"

Wow, this was going above and beyond in the customer service department. "Don't you have to be getting home? I don't want to keep you from your family."

His smile grew wistful as he slid off his jacket, revealing a dark green sweater that lit up his brilliant irises. It was chilly, but a sweater seemed like overkill. "I'm always here."

Samuel rolled up his sleeves, then headed to the kitchen and opened the fridge. He paused, surveying the offerings. "We have a lovely chicken dinner, or I could prepare some eggs and breakfast meats. The choice is yours."

I didn't want chicken, but I also didn't want to put him to any trouble or let food go to waste. "The chicken would be nice, thank you."

Samuel reached for the meal but paused, turning back. His eyebrows dipped. "But you'd prefer the eggs." He turned and pressed his hands to the countertop, splaying impossibly long fingers out before him. "You're settling."

Equal parts curiosity and horror filled me that this stranger should be able to read me so easily. "How did you know?"

"In these few minutes since we've encountered one another, you've maintained eye contact with me. Yet one question about the menu and you're averting your gaze. So... the eggs?"

A smile tugged at my lips. It felt foreign, as though it didn't belong to me. Maybe I'd forgotten how to smile amidst my silent battles with Jeremy. "Please."

Samuel waited until I met his eyes again, then nodded and went about the business of getting a pan. "The rooms are upstairs in case you'd like to freshen up."

"Thanks." Swallowing hard, I turned from him and left the kitchen in a rush of relief. Why did the caretaker have to be so good-looking? Of course, his level of attractiveness didn't matter. This situation would have been awkward no matter the man.

My lips curved as I climbed the stairs, and I noted the informal library at the top, comprising several columns of built-ins crammed with books. There were seven bedrooms to pick from. Though some were massive, I chose the smallest with a slanted ceiling, one gabled window that looked out to the sea, and a twin canopied bed that I would have loved to sleep in as a girl.

Floral-patterned wallpaper adorned the space, as well as every other room in the house, leaving the impression I'd stepped into an indoor garden. It put me in the mind of my grandmother's home and soon sent the tension draining from my shoulders.

By the time I returned to the kitchen, my favorite aroma of breakfast for dinner filled the room. Samuel placed the bowl of scrambled eggs, chopped sausage, and bacon before me, sending my stomach rumbling.

"You're not eating?" I asked as he took the seat opposite mine, making no move to serve himself.

A whisper of a smile tugged at his lips. "I'm not hungry at the moment, but perhaps you'll eat and talk a bit while you're doing it." He crossed his arms as though waiting for me to entertain him.

Biting into the concoction, I almost moaned with pleasure as the spices from the sausage and bacon somersaulted over the flavor of buttery egg. Yet the satisfaction didn't last.

What could I say? My life had imploded. All I had to show for it was an empty house that I never quite got around to decorating. "I'm not used to talking about myself."

"I'm not surprised." Samuel's steady voice cut into my mind, chasing the thoughts aside. "I don't know you, still, I can sense that you've not thought about yourself for a long time."

He was right; he didn't know me. Yet he'd already shown more insight than Jeremy had in all our years together. Samuel set a small pot of tea between us, steam wafting from its spout, forming a thin veil that separated us like the lattice in a confessional. Perhaps that's why my story came tumbling out—about Jeremy, his cheating, and how I'd desperately wanted him to love me, though I wasn't sure he'd ever tried.

"He doesn't seem a kind man." Samuel traced the pattern on the mosaic tabletop, his voice neutral despite the painful truth.

"No one's ever said that to me before." I swallowed the last bite on my plate, half trying to remember the last time I'd eaten an entire meal. "Why couldn't I see it? I guess I just..."

"Wanted to be loved." His statement didn't seem designed to rush my response.

The truth hit me with the brilliance of a sunrise peeking over the horizon. In seconds the world became a different place, the lights harsher, as though I'd been living beneath a shroud of unreality.

I'd spent years married to a man who'd never learned how I liked my coffee, and this stranger had gotten to the root of my problems in a matter of minutes. "How did you know?"

He faced the now-darkened windows. Lights winked in the distance from houses farther up the shoreline as more thunder rumbled—the storm declaring it wasn't done with us.

"My wife. I loved her. She didn't love me. I thought she would... in time." He continued to stare into the blackness that only the sea can create, lost in his memory. "We had a son. I hoped he would bring us together."

When he didn't continue, I leaned across the table. "What happened?"

"My boy lasted three brilliant days before he left us." Samuel brought his too-bright eyes to mine. I imagined as much as his unshed tears wanted to fall, he'd never let them go. "One night my wife left our bed and took her life in the sea—let the tide carry her away."

"Samuel. I'm so sorry you lost them." I cupped his hand and again, something stirred within me. Right place. Right time.

Grief gave way to gratitude in his eyes. "No one has tried to console me in what feels like a hundred years or more."

"That must be difficult."

"That it is." He nodded solemnly, seeming to remember times beyond this one and people I couldn't see. "What will you do when you go back? Will Jeremy have gone?"

I drew my hand away and sipped my tea, letting the brew warm me. "He's already left me for her." I swallowed hard, remembering again that I'd lost a husband and a best friend in one go, though many would argue they should have been the same. "He'll have erased any evidence of himself from our house. That's why I was so mad for throwing away my wedding ring. It was the only proof the marriage happened, that I was once someone's wife."

Samuel didn't judge—or at least there was nothing in his eyes that showed it. "Do you suppose you never settled in because you expected him to leave?"

His unfiltered question startled me, leaving me with a million questions of my own darting from the darkened corners of my mind where I'd shoved those fears. "Part of me must have known. We eloped. I didn't have a big wedding with a registry... I didn't even take his name—I kept mine. Whenever Aunt Ruth wanted to visit, I always went to her... I kept us closed off from the world as a couple."

A sinking feeling centered on my gut then. "I settled. I didn't marry him for love, but because he was the first person who asked and I suppose..." I swallowed hard, unsure if I wanted to say this next part, but knowing I had to, "... I didn't want to be alone."

"Don't begrudge your choices, Wren. You wouldn't be the first to marry for companionship." Samuel seemed to blur around the edges as we sat there, rain pelting the windows and cocooning us in the cozy kitchen. I stifled a yawn, my limbs suddenly feeling forgotten and out of use. "And I have a feeling Jeremy wasn't the one for you."

A warm ball formed in my gut. "You mean, I haven't lost all hope then?" The question sounded logical in my brain, but came out garbled from my yawn.

A slow smile spread over his face. He rose and held out his hand, which I took. "You need sleep. It's late."

"Is it?" I glanced about the room and located the clock on the wall. I'd arrived before the dinner hour, but now it was just a few minutes shy of midnight.

Slowly, I stood, awakening muscles that had taken a beating from my moments on the beach. I stretched, closing my eyes, and reached for the ceiling. When I opened them again, Samuel stood before me. He took my hand in his, raised it to his lips, and pressed a kiss to my knuckles. "Wrens are small creatures, but they're also a symbol of rebirth. You'll begin again."

A sense of peace rushed into me. "Thank you." My throat clogged up as though this were some sort of goodbye, though it was only temporary. "Good night, Samuel." I turned and climbed the narrow stairs that led to my room. Despite the howl of the wind and the growl of the sea outside, I'd never felt safer.

The next morning, I awoke to a cloudy day and no trace of Samuel. Disappointment filled me, but it quickly dissipated. I'd let go of too much last night to feel sad. It was as if I'd dropped ten pounds, but instead of from my hips, the weight I'd let go had wrapped itself around my heart. Adventures lie ahead—I'd need to find a new home, one that didn't remind me of my soon-to-be ex-husband, new friends, a new life for Wren.

After packing up, I moved to the entryway and prepared to leave the keys behind me. That's when the painting caught my eye. It dominated the sitting room I hadn't had a chance to explore—a stunning likeness of a familiar green-eyed caretaker. I sucked in a breath as I read the small plaque beneath.

Samuel Wright (1847-1887)
Captain, The Mariner

🐚

One year later...

I replayed my night at Shell House often. Not just because I'd spent the evening conversing with a spirit, but because Samuel had given me a gift. Not the tangible kind wrapped in a neat bow, but one of understanding. After that, the pain of losing Jeremy eased with startling swiftness.

It was a glorious fall Saturday as I wandered through my still new-to-me neighborhood. A street sign caught my eye, and I strolled into my favorite bookstore. I breezed past the stacks into a large, open area filled with cushy chairs and sofas dotted with over-plump pillows.

That's when I saw him.

He'd spread history books I recognized from the used section in the back across the nicked coffee table. *The Great Captains of the Sea*, *New England Sea Captains and Legends*, and *Lore of the New England Coast...* It was definitely him. He had the same dark hair and high cheekbones—the same infallible posture.

I forced my voice and knees steady. "Samuel."

The familiar, kind smile filled his face. "I'm sorry. Have we met?"

He didn't remember me, but no, that wasn't it. There was something different about him. His eyes weren't the deep sea green, but an intriguing blue.

"I'm sorry. You look so much like Samuel Wright, the sea captain."

The stranger's eyes lit with curiosity. "You know about Samuel?" He thrust out his hand. "I'm his great-great-nephew, Evan. Evan Wright."

Without hesitation, I took his hand and a sense of rightness shot through me. Only with Evan I'd sensed I wasn't just in the right place, I was with the right person.

That was the moment I realized some people were meant to be in love. Even me.

TIME SHARE

Larry Ivkovich

Celine Vranic stood at the window in the second-floor bedroom of Shell House, the doomed Carpenter mansion. The huge master suite's luxurious furnishings, including a four-poster canopy bed, hardwood floor, twin bathrooms, and wood-burning fireplace, held no interest for her. She'd studied and sketched all the rooms multiple times in the last three days. Now, only the view of the moonlit coastline between Delaware's Rehoboth and Dewey beaches riveted her attention.

She turned as soft footfalls behind her broke the spell. "Ready, love?" Julia Boisseau stood at the doorway of the bedroom. "It's time."

Time, Celine thought. *That's the irony, isn't it?*

The historic house and its acre of beachfront property had been for sale for over a year with no takers. A shame and a tragedy, everyone said, yet no individual or organization had been able to come to the mansion's rescue, which was now slated for demolition.

So it was up to Celine and Julia. Celine had come up with a fantastic, unbelievable plan but, with Julia's mystical help, Celine was sure it could work.

"Not having second thoughts, are you?" Julia said. She and Julia married in 2013 when same-sex marriage became legal in their state. Julia was agelessly beautiful, despite her middle years. Her dark-brown skin was flawless, her youthfully trim, tall figure graceful beneath a long, blue sundress. Black hair tumbled about her shoulders in thin braids.

Second thoughts? Celine ran a hand through short, graying, auburn hair. She glanced at the jeans, sneakers, and T-shirt she wore over her own still-slim body. Her "traveling clothes," as it were. She dressed for comfort because, as Julia said, no one at the party in the 1941 timeline would even know Celine was present.

She'd be an astral-projected observer out-of-time, an unseen temporal traveler, one not trying to alter the past in order to change the future. Or inhabiting the body of someone in that timeline in order to act. Or trying to find out who really assassinated JFK, stopping 9/11, or discover the identity of Jack the Ripper. As tempting as all that was, they could only perform this ceremony once, the numinous energies being site-specific.

Celine was determined to find something which had been hidden within the labyrinthine depths of Shell House decades earlier. A phone conversation with her grandmother six months earlier had been the spark...

"Why haven't you told anyone before, *báka?*" Celine had asked.

She visualized Estella Vranic shrugging. "The time was not yet right. To every season, *da?*" An intake of breath. "Do you remember the death of Zachary Smith Reynolds in 1932?"

"Sure, at the Carpenter North Carolina home." Celine, like most Rehoboth residents knew of the infamous scandal. "They never discovered if it was murder or suicide." Reynolds, heir to his family's tobacco fortune, married actress and singer Libby Holman, who also happened to be the Dupont heiress Louisa d'Andelot Carpenter's not-so-secret lover. Louisa, along with her husband, John Lord King, owned Shell House and frequently entertained there. But Reynolds owned a home in Winston-Salem where he'd died under mysterious circumstances.

"Just so." Estella's voice became softer. "But realize, *unuka*, the story passed down to certain family members is that Reynolds possessed a valuable jeweled amulet, a piece of treasure rumored to be part of the sunken *Queen Anne's Revenge*."

"Blackbeard's ship? The one that sank off the Carolina coast? But the wreck wasn't discovered until the '90s."

"Indeed. Nevertheless, that is the story. This amulet is rumored to still be hidden somewhere in Shell House."

Celine startled. "I've never heard this before."

"I did say it was a secret, did I not?" Estella said. "You doubt your old *báka*?"

Celine grinned. "Of course not, Grandmother. Please, continue."

Estella cleared her throat. "It's said Reynolds gave the amulet, supposedly encrusted with diamonds and rubies, to a trusted servant of the Carpenters for, perhaps, safe keeping. The reason has always been unclear. What is suspected is, for whatever reason, the servant hid the amulet somewhere in Shell House and there it resides to this day."

"Wow." Celine didn't know how else to respond.

A chuckle. "I know, my *unuka*, the story *does* sounds like some cliched paperback whodunnit with many plot holes, does it not? But I feel you may be able to puzzle this out before the house is destroyed and hopefully before I pass on."

Sudden tears blurred Celine's eyes. Estella had been the first family member to welcome and accept Julia as well as always encouraging Celine to practice her art. "But *báka*, if no one's solved this yet, how can I do it in so little time?"

"I have faith in you, child. You have always been strong and steadfast throughout your life. I have been so proud of you for that."

That was it then. If for no other reason, she'd do this for Estella. "Thank you *báka*. I... I got that from you. I'll do my best."

No pressure, Celine thought with a sigh. *Damn.*

Celine felt the warmth of Julia's sudden closeness, the subtle, woody scent of her perfume.

"No, no second thoughts," Celine replied to her earlier question with a nervous laugh. "It's now or never, right?"

Julia's occult and curio shop on the boardwalk had been a popular and successful attraction for years. Only a select few of her clientele knew the Mystic Emporium's owner was herself a practitioner of the thaumaturgic arts.

But this ceremony Julia and Celine would undertake *had* to be performed that night. Unlike other rituals which required the power of the full moon, this one needed to be done during the *new* moon, where darkness held sway. In another month, Shell House would meet its sad fate.

"I just... I wish, Jules, we didn't have to go through all of this," Celine said. "Lying to the real estate company that I wanted to do some drawings of the house and research for a book before the liquidation and demolition began. Which, I know, is true enough, but..."

With Celine as a popular local artist and Julia as a longtime successful entrepreneur, the pair weren't without a certain amount of cachet in the beach communities. The agency and the house's seller agreed to their request.

"I'm nervous too, Celine," Julia said. "But I have faith we can do this. If what Estella said is true, this amulet's value may be able to save Shell House."

True, but it would be the most complicated and intense conjuring Julia had ever attempted. The study and practice had culminated six months after Celine had first asked Julia about the possibility. "If only we could have had, you know, a practice run, say, traveling a week back or so," Celine protested weakly for the millionth time, knowing full well all their energies needed to be concentrated for this to work.

"I'll be monitoring you, love, keeping the temporal portal open." Julia smiled, laugh lines crinkling the corners of her brown eyes. "It's okay. You, we, *will* be okay."

Julia was right but Celine wished they weren't attempting this alone. It would just be the two of them. No one else knew; it was doubtful anyone would believe them anyway, even the members of Julia's conjure community. Mindful time travel? Ha! But Julia was adamant about not allowing anyone else to put themselves in possible jeopardy. It was a gamble, they both knew, but one worth taking, fantastic as it sounded.

Celine nodded, took Julia's hands, and squeezed. "Okay. I'm ready."

They knelt on an area rug between the two living room couches. Exposed wooden ceiling beams loomed above the room's ornate furnishings and tiled floor, shimmering in orange candlelight.

The sprawling, two-story mansion stood between the ocean in front and freshwater Silver Lake in back. A confluence of earth and water energies, Julia said. Conducive to conjuring. A momentary breath of cool summer wind whispered in from the seaward windows, causing the candles to flicker.

At this early hour after midnight, the beach community, even its rowdy summer crowds of students, slept. The COVID-19 pandemic had a lot to do with that, keeping many tourists away, shuttering some businesses, curtailing others, like Julia's.

But other forces, those of the numinous kind, were at play. They gathered around Shell House, as if expectant, eager to participate in this singular ceremony. The power within and without was palpable, boosting Celine's confidence.

Celine took a long sip of the special herbal tea Julia had made. Its hypnotic effect was immediate, bracing Celine for what was to come. Julia touched a drop of spiced oil onto Celine's forehead and lips. The spell would be a variation and hybrid of a number of cultural rituals, enhancing its power to open the temporal portal. At least, that was the hope.

Celine closed her eyes, assuming a meditation pose, back straight, hands in her lap, thumbs touching. Julia began to chant, softly, slowly, her voice gently rising and falling. She murmured the words to an old slave song of safe travels.

The lilting sound of Julia's voice filled Celine's head, the potion and oil already having their soothing effect on her. The sound of the sea began a calming accompaniment, enveloping Celine, the slapping of the waves against the rocks, the hissing of the surf drawing back from the sand. A comforting warmth caressed her, beckoning, tugging.

Celine gasped...

And opened her eyes.

She stood in the living room but this was a room decades removed from the one she'd... *left.* Besides different furniture and décor, a raucous party was in full swing. Loud phonograph music, people in formal attire talking, laughing, dancing, drinking, snorting cocaine. Though Celine had been prepared for the wild revelry the Carpenters were famous for, she still had to take a moment to adjust.

My god, she thought finally. *It's 1941. I'm really here!*

She had to work fast. No telling how long Julia could maintain this temporal connection. Celine had memorized the layout of the house through her sketches and multiple walkthroughs and knew where to go. She moved through the crowd, not like a ghost, but weaving her way as people parted before her, allowing her passage as if instinctively sensing *something.*

Arm in arm, two laughing women walked by. Celine recognized Louisa d'Andelot Carpenter from old photos.

Short hair, dressed in a man's suit, wine glass in hand, Carpenter accompanied raucous friend and frequent Shell House guest, actress Tallulah Bankhead. And over there, was that dapperly dressed man Noel Coward?

Go, go! Celine admonished herself. *Can't be distracted.* Despite the effects of the tea, she felt her doubts returning. Could she really do this?

She made it to the outer hallway, stopped and refocused. Of course she wasn't there physically. Her body was back in 2020 with Julia. But, incredibly, she still felt physical sensations so she had to concentrate, getting in and out as quickly as possible.

She blinked in surprise. One of the servants stood several feet away looking in her direction. A tall middle-aged black man, formally dressed, white gloves, held a tray of drinks, expertly balancing it among the jostling throng. One of the servants. Surely he wasn't looking at her...

But, as Celine continued toward the winding wooden staircase, a tingling between her shoulder blades made her turn. The servant had moved closer, his gaze still focused in her direction. A puzzled expression marked his handsome features.

What the hell? Celine turned and hurried off. Had to be a coincidence.

She reached the stairs, wondering at the decorative rope tied to two wooden stanchions which blocked off the steps. For some reason, access to the second floor had been declared off-limits. Celine moved around the obstacle and started up to the second floor. If they'd gotten the timing right, if their determination of where the amulet had been hidden was correct...

The master suite, Celine thought. The question being, would she get there in time to find out where the amulet was hidden?

She reached the second floor to see cans of paint, a wooden stepladder, and various tools arranged in the carpeted hallway. A large drop cloth covered a floor-to-ceiling bookcase. Apparently some renovation was in progress. Hence the rope barrier.

Just then Celine heard a loud string of curses, bangs like that of drawers slamming shut. She moved toward the end of the long hallway. The door to the master suite stood partially open, the noises coming from within the room. The cacophonous sounds of the party drifted upward, momentarily drowning out whatever was going on in the suite. Though a window at the end of the hall was open, Celine realized she couldn't hear the surf because of the noise. For a moment she paused, unsure, then started to enter the room.

"Who are you? Why are you here?"

Celine turned. The servant who'd seemed to be looking at her moments before stood a few feet away, holding the empty tray at his side.

What...?

"I know you're there," the man whispered, moving closer, squinting as if that would help him to see her. "I sense you."

Celine stood still, not sure what to do. He *sensed* her?

"You've a touch of *mojo* about you," he continued. "I feel it."

Oh my god! The guy must possess abilities like Julia, whose magical essence had to be clinging to her. How else could he know?

"Think your words carefully," he said, only a few inches from where she stood. "I'll hear them in my own mind. I believe you're the one I've been waiting for."

Are you kidding me?

He smiled. "I assure you I am not."

Celine's jaw dropped.

At that moment, the door to the master suite opened fully and a man stepped into the hallway. "Bertram!" he barked. "What are you doing up here, man? Who were you talking to?"

"My apologies, Mr. Henderson," Bertram said with a short bow. "I too heard voices and, knowing this floor is to be closed for the evening, came to investigate. May I ask what *you're* doing here?"

Celine stared. Who was this guy?

"Yes, yes," stammered the somewhat disheveled and suddenly nervous-looking Henderson. Bow tie askew, suit jacket rumpled, brown hair mussed, dark eyes wide, the man looked like he'd run a race. "Well, uh, look..." He beckoned to Bertram. "I need your help."

"Sir?"

"Come on, come on!" He grabbed Bertram's arm and practically dragged him into the suite, but not before the servant cast a sidelong glance in Celine's direction. Celine followed before Henderson closed the bedroom door. Part of the large room looked ransacked, dresser drawer and bookshelf contents spilled onto the floor, the bed's mattress askew, closet doors open, a bedside table overturned.

"By the Saints, sir," Bertram said. "What has happened here? I must notify the Carpenters."

"No! We can't... Don't you see? They've already been involved in one scandal. You know, that thing with

Reynolds. This mess will further complicate things for them. Just help me out and then we'll put everything back in order and say nothing, right?"

Celine looked at Bertram, more interested in his reaction than Henderson's. Judging by the servant's dubious expression, it was obvious he didn't believe the man's otherwise reasonable rationale. It was Henderson who'd ransacked the room and was only interested in protecting himself. Celine was certain of it.

"Mr. Henderson, I believe you've had too much to drink. I don't think..."

"Do as I tell you!" Henderson became more agitated. "There's something in this room I need and I wager you know where it is."

"And if I do know, why would I help you search for this behind my employers' backs?"

You go, Bertram!

Henderson reddened. "You hid it here without their knowledge, am I right? So I can easily blame you for this mess. Do you really think they'll believe the hired help over me?"

Bastard.

"I see your point... *sir*," Bertram said, a grim expression on his face. "I gather you're referring to the amulet?"

"Yes, yes! Reynolds gave it to you, didn't he? I finally figured that out but why would he give it to *you*?"

"Mr. Reynolds and I had an understanding..."

"Oh well, never mind, where is it?"

Bertram's eyes flicked toward Celine then back to Henderson. "Yes, I do know where it is, but I doubt you'll be able to retrieve it."

Bertram, Celine realized, was the "trusted servant."

"God damn it! Show me." Henderson slapped a fist against his thigh. "I'll... I'll make it worth your while."

Bertram hesitated then moved toward the fireplace, knelt down, and placed a hand on a portion of the wooden floor. "Here. I placed it here while the new floor was being installed." He stood up. "You'd have to pry up the floorboards to get to it. I doubt the Carpenters would approve."

"You're lying! Where is it? Tell me! I need it to pay off my debts! What good is it hiding here?"

Bertram pierced Henderson with a steely gaze. "Is that why you killed Mr. Reynolds, sir? Because he wouldn't give it to you then?"

Henderson's features screwed up into an enraged mask. He stepped toward Bertram. "You piece of..."

No! Celine instinctively reached out a ghostly hand and grabbed Henderson's arm.

Henderson jerked as if shocked and looked around wildly. "What was that? What..." He ran his hands through his hair. "I... I..." He turned and stumbled from the room.

Bertram squinted in Celine's direction. "Well done," he said. "My thanks."

I... how did I do that?

Bertram chuckled. "He felt your *mojo* and became confused and afraid. Your conjurer is a strong one."

Who are *you?* A sudden tugging sensation, like a tether pulling her back, abruptly gripped Celine. The temporal connection was weakening.

Bertram arched an eyebrow. "I sense you don't have much time left. You saw where I indicated the hidden spot? Take that knowledge back with you. Tell your conjurer the amulet's value won't help to save Shell

House. But it can do some good in other ways. Use it wisely."

How do you know that?

"I have some prescient talent. Shell House *will* fall but the amulet's power will live on. It's why I hid it rather than turning it over to anyone. I knew someone with a noble purpose, *you*, would come for it in time."

Noble? Celine hadn't thought of it that way. *What will happen now to you?*

"I will survive. Mr. Henderson isn't held in high esteem in this household, believe me." An approving nod. "You are very brave to have done this. I wish I could have known you, Celine."

And I you, Bertram. Thank you.

He reached out a hand in her direction as if to touch her. Then, just before Bertram and the master suite vanished, Celine realized she'd never told him her name.

Celine gasped and slumped forward, instinctively holding out her hands to right herself. Her vision blurred, her head spun. She heard the surf, the blessed, comforting surf, gulls cawing over the dissipating roar in her ears. A trace of a familiar perfume...

She looked up. Julia lay on the floor, eyes closed. "Jules!" Celine crawled to her side and gently placed Julia's head in her lap. "Jules..."

"Oh," Julia murmured, eyelids fluttering. "Celine, are... are you all right?"

"Me? Yeah! What about you?" Celine helped Julia to a sitting position. Julia was covered in sweat, her hands cold as ice. "What happened?" Sunlight streamed in through the living room windows. "It's daylight?"

"Yes, yes. You were under for hours. I was worried but didn't dare interfere. It was hard keeping the portal open that long. I... I guess I passed out."

"But you got me back." Celine hugged Julia hard. They both supported themselves as they got shakily to their feet. "Jules, to me I was only gone a few minutes, maybe half an hour."

"Really?" Julia shook her head. "Interesting. But you know, Celine, I felt something right before I blacked out. An extra jolt of power, energy, something, came through the portal. It... it helped me to keep it open at the end." She stared at Celine. "It wasn't just me."

Bertram, Celine thought. "Yeah, I've got a lot to tell you and I know where the amulet is. It'll take some minor destruction to retrieve it but the demolition will cover that." Celine grinned. "And I have a message for you."

"A message?" Julia cocked her head. "For me?"

"For both of us. But first let's get those hammers and pry bars out of the van." Celine paused, smiling. "And then I've got to call my grandmother."

The Gazebo at Silver Lake

Larry Schardt

Liam...

The her first time he saw her, Liam fell hopelessly in love with Angie. It ended almost as fast as it began. He never understood why, but did understand the harsh words her father spoke. "Don't show your face here again or I'll have you arrested." Was that her father or was it Angie chasing him away? He never knew.

The question gnawed at him for five years. Now he was on his way back to Rehoboth Beach for the first time since he'd left. He hoped to see her. He hoped she wasn't married. He hoped he'd get an answer.

He held the steering wheel with one hand. In the other he clutched the blue sapphire starfish that dangled from the chain around his neck. It was a cherished relic from Angie. A reminder of love and passion. The magnificent gems were a perfect match for her dazzling blue eyes.

Liam kept his word and wrote the book. The book he promised her. Because his story took place in Rehoboth Beach, his publisher made arrangements with the local bookstore to promote it to kick off the summer season.

The closer he got to Rehoboth, the more his thoughts drifted back to 1973, the summer he graduated from high school. At that time, he hitchhiked to Rehoboth on a whim. His only plan was to earn some money and live life. This time he had a car, a book deal, and a plan.

Liam's publisher told him, "Memorial Day weekend will be the perfect time to promote your book. The beach will be crowded. A summer beach read. Perfect!"

To Liam, *perfect* would be if Angie showed up. Liam didn't know if she still lived in the area but the possibility made him feel like he hadn't taken a full breath of air in a week.

Once he wheeled into town, and before he checked into the hotel, he turned down Lake Drive. When he got to his old haunt, he pulled over and stared up at Shell House on his left, then turned to his right and looked down at Silver Lake. His mind was on overload with memories of that summer when he had been the groundskeeper, and when he reveled in the bliss of intense love with Michelle Angela Kennedy... his beloved Angie.

And that dreadful day when her father threw him out and threatened to have him arrested if he ever trespassed. Liam didn't even get a chance to say goodbye. Unanswered letters and phone calls intensified the sting. His mind raced with love, hurt, and betrayal.

Liam looked through the woods at the Lake, and the white gazebo peeking through the trees. This was their special place. Their hideaway spot where they danced and loved the nights away... Passion ignited by the music of the Beatles, Moody Blues, Procol Harem, and other magical melodies of the summer of 1973.

Liam shuddered back to the moment, pulled away, and headed toward the Henlopen Hotel. Since it was a holiday, the line at the front desk was long, but it moved fast. The clerk checked him in and motioned Liam to his room. Liam walked to the balcony instead and looked out across the Atlantic. The same ocean view he'd shared with Angie long ago. Ah, sweet love!

Maybe she would have seen the posters or the advertisements about the book... maybe she would show up... maybe she still cared. Little chance of that, but he clung to the possibility. She'd never once tried to reconnect. Never returned his calls. Never wrote back. His hopes ebbed and flowed with the waves.

Traveling through his old stomping grounds elevated his anxiety. To calm himself, Liam walked through town and down the boardwalk to reminisce. When he passed Browseabout Bookstore he was astonished at the publicity... posters, pictures, and even a newspaper article, "Former Resident Writes About Love in Rehoboth." Blood rushed to his blushing face when he saw his image on a poster in the window. If Angie was in town, she would surely notice.

When he got to Dolle's Candyland he headed straight for the chocolate counter. He gazed at the dark chocolate starfish... a reminder of their young innocent love. He daydreamed back to when he saved enough to buy one for Angie. It was all he could afford, but her smile and the melting chocolate sneaking out of the corner of her mouth was worth every penny.

"May I help you?" a young girl's voice startled him.

"Uh... No, thanks," he said, without looking at her. His focus was on another woman who was heading toward the door. He only saw her face for a split second.

Was it Angie? She wasn't alone. A lanky, preppy sort of guy in a yellow polo shirt stepped in front of her and walked out. Liam saw the huge diamond sparkle on her left hand when she grabbed the door to keep it from slamming in her face. Liam's heart sank to a new low.

He watched the prep put his arm around her. They looked happy, like a wholesome Ken and Barbie couple. Liam's heart continued to plunge.

"Pardon me a second," he said, interrupting the young salesgirl who was still talking. He bolted to the large display window. There they were walking and holding hands on their way toward the beach. Liam watched as the man pulled her close to plant a kiss on her cheek.

Liam's heart crashed. His worst fears confirmed. The floor felt like it was moving. Watching her walk away was torture. The voice in his head screamed... *Move on, man! It's over.*

Michelle Angela (Angie)...

Steve's fake smile fooled the old ladies and aristocrats. In the beginning he'd fooled Michelle Angela, too, but as time passed she recognized his phony smile as a pretentious smirk.

Her dad loved Steve and assured her he was perfect. The kind of man who would show her what's important in life. Steve did his best to keep his composure when out socializing and hobnobbing at the country club or at an uppity-up party.

But when they were alone, Steve's enraged outbursts were out of control. He insulted her on a routine basis. She hated herself for loving this guy but knew it was best for her family. Michelle wanted to please her father. She wanted to uphold the precious family name.

It was difficult walking on proverbial eggshells. Michelle never knew what would set him off, or when he would explode. Every time he hit her, she blamed herself. He always convinced her it was her fault so she'd cover the bruises with cosmetics or wear long sleeves. She reminded herself it was only temporary. After all, he'd always apologized and confessed his love later. *He doesn't mean to get mad.* She told herself tomorrow would be different.

Michelle didn't enjoy his parties. She enjoyed the beauty of a sunrise, walking on the beach, riding the Ferris wheel, dancing in the gazebo, or simply laughing with Liam. Everything she had done with Liam was what made her happy. She would give anything to hear his laugh once more. But those days were long gone. Those were all things that Steve didn't like. She wasn't even sure if Steve ever laughed, except a sinister snicker at someone else's expense.

But this must be real happiness. Her dad had introduced them. Steve was well groomed, polished, rich... an elite member of the Rehoboth Beach Country Club. He was arrogant, narcissistic, and unkind, especially if he didn't get his way. But her dad approved.

Steve was everything Liam was not... or at least everything she used to believe about her teenaged sweetheart. Even though Liam left her years before, she still wanted to believe he was the idealistic man of her dreams. But he'd left without even saying goodbye. He never called. Not even once. He never took the time to write a letter. She was sure he never wrote that book he talked about either. Talk was indeed cheap.

Her father's biting words replayed in her mind. *"See, I told you he was a worthless hippie. The least he could have done was try to call or take the time to write. He was more interested in our money than you."*

Those words stung... and she replayed them thousands of times. She didn't want to believe Liam could ever have been so terrible. He seemed so genuine. How could she have been such a fool?

Now she spent their evenings mingling with the country club crowd over cocktails. How she hated it... the same boring conversations... golf, yachting, talking in labels, and gossiping about those who weren't there.

At one party she even suggested, "Let's run barefoot in the sand."

"Why? Don't be so childish," Steve snapped and turned to his chums. "She used to be friends with one of those hippie free-spirit freaks. He fed her head with all kinds of foolish ideas. Thank gawd I found her in time to teach her what's really important."

Uncontrollable laughter erupted from their so-called friends. Her self-esteem plummeted. To hide her tears, she turned and darted outside.

That night, when they were alone, he gave her a good talking to. "Don't you ever embarrass me in front of my friends again. I'm not some damn hippie. Get it? Do you hear me?"

Michelle didn't say a word.

He slapped her across her face. "I said, do you hear?"

"Yes," was all she could muster.

One afternoon Michelle and Steve had been on their way to the club when they passed the bookstore. She did a double take at the window display highlighting a new summer beach read, titled *Angie*.

Angie! A name she hadn't heard in years, except in song. The name woke something inside her... Her heart stopped. Could it be possible? She turned and stepped back. The author was Liam Wolf.

Liam! There he was... his picture on a poster. More handsome than ever. Her belly filled with butterflies and her face flushed. *He's doing a book signing, here? When?* In bold letters the sign read: Author signing—Saturday, May 27.

It can't be! That was yesterday! She wanted to cry. She stared at the sign as if the date would change.

She'd missed it. She'd missed her opportunity to ask him why. Why had he left all those years ago? Why hadn't he ever called? Why hadn't he ever written? Why didn't he keep his promises?

"Come on. We'll be late," Steve barked.

"Just one second. I want to look inside. I'll be right out," Michelle Angela said.

Steve clutched her wrist and pulled. "No! We're going. Now!"

"No, I want to check out this book." She held her ground.

He didn't have to say anything. From the look of his familiar scowl and beet-red face, she knew he was boiling with rage. He seized her arm with crushing brutality. Agonizing pain shot all the way through her fingers.

Michelle Angela gathered her courage. "Don't make a scene. Go! Get the hell out of here. I never want to see you again." She winced, broke away, and turned to rush into the store. But not fast enough.

Steve pressed down on her shoulder and stopped her. He swung her around and blocked her from moving. Then he buried his fist into her stomach. She groaned and buckled over with excruciating pain. She refused to let him see her cry.

After gaining her balance, she pushed him with strength she didn't know she had, and headed toward the bookstore. She clutched the door, held on, and struggled to keep her footing. Michelle Angela forced herself to go inside, but Steve followed.

More furious than ever, he said under his breath, "What the hell's gotten into you? Bitch."

With people around she found her bravery. "Leave me alone." She went over to the book display. "Go away! Now!"

Steve shouted an obscenity and flipped her off. Every eye in the store watched his childish rage as he stormed out the door.

She breathed a huge sigh of relief. Staring at the book display, she picked up a copy. She held it close. Liam's book. *He kept his promise!*

The cover showed a gazebo on the shore of a lake. In one corner was the drawing of a blonde teenager. It looked just like the photo she'd given him back in the day.

She turned the book over to read the summary. Her finger ran over each word... *A summer beyond compare... tender love... innocent love... never-ending love.*

She looked inside. On the second page was the dedication...

To my Angie. Thank you for showing me what love is. You will always be the one... Now and Forever. Love, Your Knight, Liam.

Tears streamed down her face. She held the open book to her heart.

Angie cried harder. He'd slipped away again. Her opportunity was gone.

She bought the book.

Liam...

Liam was flying high. The book signing was great. There was a line for most of the day. He saw so many wonderful people and shared the story of his love... of Angie. Some of them might even know her but no one had any idea that Michelle Angela Kennedy was his Angie.

All day long, every time he looked up he hoped he'd see the girl he'd unwillingly left behind. He hoped he could tell her his story. Since she never called or wrote, maybe she'd believe it once he saw her face to face. But his chance never came.

He left a few signed copies with the owner and said his goodbyes.

The next morning he packed up his things, as sad as he had been on the day he left all those years ago. One final walk on the boardwalk. One final trip down memory lane. One final trip in the town he knew he'd never see again. His last hope was gone. Forever! He said a sad farewell to the Atlantic, the boardwalk, and his foolish romantic dream. It was his ultimate goodbye. Now Angie would be a dream forever... and a fairy tale in his book.

Liam hopped into his car and headed out of town. At the last second he decided he needed to see Shell House one last time. Since he had been the groundskeeper, he knew the secrets and hideouts, if they were still the same. He wanted to take one last reminder with him. He loved that old house, the land, the beach, and the Gazebo at Silver Lake.

Liam parked and followed the old familiar path through the woods and down the steps to the gazebo. He sat on the bench along the edge and gazed at Silver Lake. He placed his hand on the space next to him and shut his eyes. The vision of Angie sitting close, wrapped in his arms, was as vivid as if it had happened yesterday.

He'd been so naive and scared when their lips met for the first time. Yet it was a moment carved into the granite of eternity... that oh so tender moment where life transformed forever, until he discovered that forever wasn't as long as he'd hoped.

In his mind he never left. Once again they danced. Once again they laughed. Once again they made the most tender love. While he replayed every magical scene, he got lost in time. He was seventeen again.

He took out his journal and wrote line after line of inspiration. Melancholy words flowed like a river. He spent hours lost in thought.

Finally, he bade Silver Lake goodbye, goodbye to the gazebo, goodbye to his fair princess Angie.

For the first time since he'd left Rehoboth, he removed the starfish chain from around his neck. He laid it on the picnic table. It had been his good luck charm the whole time he wrote the book, a token of hope he clung to. Now the book was completed and she was gone. So was his dream.

He blew a kiss across the lake and walked up the steps. He turned one last time and waved goodbye.

Angie...

Pride welled up inside of Michelle Angela. *Liam did it.* She felt like a kid again. She felt like "Angie" again. She was elated. Happy tears flooded down her cheeks. He kept his promise. He wrote his book. But why had he broken his other promises?

Her mind raced. She searched for answers, like she had a million times before. All along, something just hadn't felt right. Now it felt more wrong than ever.

She hustled home down the beach to Shell House. She burst into her father's sacred Cigar Room Bar. When she saw him sitting with Steve, laughing and smoking, her fury surged through the roof.

"What the hell are you doing here?" she shouted at Steve.

"What do you mean barging in here like this, young lady?" her father yelled. "Steve is my guest and he is welcome here any time. I understand you had a meltdown in town. You ought to be ashamed of yourself."

"Dad, look!" She fumbled as she pulled her blouse out from her pants. She raised it just enough to expose her stomach, revealing a fist-sized bruise. "This is what your great friend did to me today." Her chin quivered.

Her father's jaw dropped. He choked out a blast of smoke. His cigar fell into the ashtray.

Steve quickly played into the role of her doting boyfriend. "Oh honey, I'm sorry. You know I just lost my temper a little bit. It won't happen again." Steve shrugged and held out his arms.

"That's what you said the last time... and the time before that. Never again!"

"Come on, honey," Steve chuckled, trying to envelop her in a hug.

"Get the hell out of here. You will *not* control me anymore. I am a free woman, not your slave. Get out now!" Angie ripped off her ring and hurled it out the window onto the beach below.

"What the hell did you do that for? I'll send you the bill, you ungrateful bitch."

Her father jumped up and growled, "You heard my daughter. If you don't leave now I'll throw you out!"

"You'll regret this. She'll never find another as good as I am," Steve snarled. He took a puff from his cigar and blew her a mocking, smoke-filled kiss, then slammed the door.

She turned to her father and threw the book on the table in front of him. "You lied to me."

"Calm down, dear. What are you talking about?"

She pointed to the cover. "Look who the author is."

"I don't recognize the name," he lied.

"Well, dear Father, remember the groundskeeper, the one I fell in love with, and will always love! That's him!"

"You mean Mr. Peace and Love Flower-Child Hippie?"

"That's exactly who I mean." Angie paused. "I need you to be honest with me. Did he ever call? Did he ever send letters? What did you say to him? Why did he leave?"

Her father gulped. "Yes, he called. I told him never to call again. I didn't want you wasting your life with some beach bum."

"But it's okay to have me almost marry an abusive, spoiled bastard!" Her blood boiled.

"I only wanted what was best for you."

"Don't you think I should know what's best? Liam was kind and sweet. He made me feel special. He made me happy." Angie sighed... "I loved that man. I still love him."

Exhausted from yelling, she paused and inhaled a deep breath. "Dad, what about letters? Did he ever write to me?" she asked in a softer tone.

His face glowed red. He stuttered. "Yes, he wrote. He wrote a lot. I picked the letters up at the post office and hid them."

No longer calm, Angie shouted, "*Why?* You let me suffer all these years. You let me think he didn't love me. That he left me! You're as bad as Steve. How could you?"

She rushed out of the house, ran across the yard, and bolted to the gazebo.

When she started down the steps, she noticed something glisten on the table inside. It was the sapphire starfish. She picked it up and rubbed the smooth blue surface with her fingers as if discovering a genie lamp.

Her legs weakened, she fell to her knees, and with moans of agony the tears flowed.

Her mind drifted back to the night she'd given it to Liam. He'd promised to call... and he did. He'd promised to write letters... and he did. He'd promised to write a book... and he did.

Through the haze of tears, she saw a book on the gazebo bench. She recognized the leather cover. It was just like the journal she gave Liam to start his book. *Is it his? Is he still here somewhere?*

Angie eyed her surroundings at a glacial pace. To her disappointment, there was no one in site. She flashed back to the boy she had danced away the hours with. The boy who showed her how to be a free spirit, how to live the richness of life, how to be a gypsy wildflower. Her heart tangled, full of love and sadness. Angie, now weary and light-headed, sat on the wooden floor in silence.

He was gone again. Forever.

Liam...

Liam headed north on Highway 1. After ten miles he turned east to Cape Henlopen State Park to collect his thoughts.

When he pulled into the parking lot he hunted for his journal, but couldn't find it anywhere. It wasn't on the passenger seat where he usually left it. He was sure he grabbed it from the gazebo, but did he? He looked under the front seat and in his suitcase. After rifling through his things, he slammed the trunk, put the car in reverse, and rushed back to Rehoboth.

When he arrived, he parked his car down the street and charged toward the gazebo steps.

When he looked down, he saw that someone was there... crouched on the floor.

Angie looked up. "Liam!" She stared at him for a moment, then pulled herself up.

He sped down the steps and wrapped his arms around her.

Her puffy red eyes told him she'd been crying. Liam's heart melted. He pulled out his handkerchief and gently wiped her face.

She tilted her head back, looked into his eyes, and shined her bright smile.

A great blue heron spread its wings and soared across the pond. Wild geese squawked their welcome.

"Liam, I bought your book! You wrote about me?" Her long suppressed gypsy heart resurrected. She burst into giggles.

Liam followed. They filled the air with laughter neither of them had experienced in a long, long time.

"I never knew you called or wrote... until today," she sighed.

"You mean you didn't get my messages? How about my letters?"

"My dad destroyed them. I thought you forgot about me. I was heartbroken. I am so sorry."

Liam's spirit soared. "Thank you. I'm sorry, too. I thought I did something wrong. A million times I questioned where I went wrong. I love you. I have always loved you, Angie!"

"Angie! That name is the sweetest music to my ears. No one else has ever called me that. Thank you, Liam. I love you, too."

He pulled her closer and wrapped her in his arms. Their hearts beat as one.

They held each other tight. Angie laid her head on Liam's shoulder. He pulled her chin ever so gently upward and kissed her with the passion he'd been saving up for five years.

She eased from his embrace for a second and put the starfish necklace back around his neck.

The hours evaporated... They danced until the stars twinkled.

Soon the waning moon shined its glow across the water, and welcomed the young lovers back to the magical Gazebo at Silver Lake.

Thank you so much for reading!
Jennifer D. Diamond

THE INHERITANCE OF COURAGE

Jennifer D. Diamond

Tilly attempted restraint. She bit her tongue so hard it might sever. Would her picture-perfect mother even notice if Tilly's tongue plopped right out of her mouth onto the foyer steps? Not likely. *That woman* could ignore a nuclear blast if it didn't threaten her comfort. *No wonder Dad took off in the middle of a downpour.*

"Chantilly, where is your father?" Mommie-Dearest-Sylvia demanded.

"You know, Mother, Dad wouldn't have ditched me if you'd just kept your judgments to yourself." Tilly's wet palm squeaked up the polished handrail. She walked straight toward her petite mother who looked like a sad couture mannequin standing at the end of the hallway.

"When's he coming back?" Sylvia stepped in front of her.

"I don't know." Tilly brushed past Sylvia while shaking her head. Rain splattered off Tilly's frizzy hair onto her mother's designer blouse.

"What do you mean?" Sylvia's heels clicked on the hardwood.

Without looking back, Tilly shouted, "I told you. I. Don't. Know." She didn't give a crap about sounding like a spoiled brat because she was soaked through, shivering, and needed a hot shower.

The madwoman followed her across the entire house—through the sitting room, the sunken den, all the way to her bedroom. Tilly whipped around, stiff-armed in the doorway. "Jesus, Sylvia, back off."

Mother came to a grinding halt, fists on her hips. Tilly assessed Sylvia's mental state while looking down at the coiffed hair, those iceberg eyes, past the always-lacquered lips, to a dainty, jutted chin.

"You tell me right now." Sylvia poked Tilly's chest with one red fingernail.

Tilly slammed the door. *I'm not taking your garbage anymore.*

It had all started earlier in the day. During the entire drive to Rehoboth, Sylvia grated on Tilly's nerves. All *that woman* could talk about was the wedding. Off-and-on hiccups had tormented Tilly ever since the engagement became official, so when Sylvia mentioned reciting the vows, Tilly's stomach squeezed. To her horror, she threw up in the back seat of the car.

"Oh Chantilly, really? You couldn't control yourself?" Sylvia asked in her high-and-mighty tone.

Tilly's cheeks burned as hot as her throat. She hadn't gotten carsick in over fifteen years, not since the sixth-grade field trip.

"You okay, Tilly?" Dad asked.

"Sorry, I'll clean it up." She couldn't meet his eyes in the rearview mirror.

While Tilly took care of her mess, Sylvia whispered, "Is it morning sickness, Chantilly? Are we going to have to let out your wedding gown?"

"No, Mother. I'm not stupid."

At least the woman left her alone for a while, a small victory in Tilly's world. By the time she finished scrubbing the carpet of Dad's Mercedes, the autumn wind had smelled like rain.

Tilly kept quiet for as long as humanly possible because Dad had asked her to be nice. And she'd almost passed out from holding her breath to avoid blurting the truth when her mother whined about the closed-up swimming pool.

"Seeing the back garden winterized makes me melancholy for summer. I miss it already."

"Now, hon," Dad cooed as he wrapped his arms around Sylvia's waist, "you're just a little house cat afraid of the water. How could you possibly be missing the pool?"

Sylvia made a breathy Marilyn Monroe impression, "I'll have you know, Leo, I am neither a 'house cat' nor afraid. On the contrary, I'm an elegant Egyptian goddess."

Tilly snorted, and a little bit of beer-foam went up the back of her nose. *What a cliché. She can't swim because she doesn't want to mess up her blonde updo.* The alcohol fueled an indignant pride in herself for stifling those remarks. *See, Mother? I can control myself.*

Dad nuzzled his face in Sylvia's neck. "Of course, hon. You're my jeweled queen who protects her pharaoh."

"I need a nap," Tilly quipped and retreated to her bedroom.

The final straw was Sylvia's complete disgust over one tiny burp.

After dinner—and her fifth beer—Tilly let a resonant belch slip. Her mother took offense. No way Tilly could hold her tongue any longer. Ten minutes into the fight, she could tell Sylvia was just getting started.

"I don't appreciate your tone," Sylvia chided.

"Well, I don't appreciate—"

Dad cut Tilly off mid-sentence with his glass-breaking whistle, the one using his thumb and index finger. "Enough," he yelled, "I won't spend another second refereeing you two," and he walked away.

"Dad?" He never snapped at her like this. She followed him all the way to the foyer.

"I should have put my foot down years ago." He put on his bomber jacket. "This feud stops now." He jammed a driving cap over his jet-black curls and left.

"Leo?" Mother screeched from the end of the hallway.

Tilly ran through the pelting rain in time to watch his taillights disappear into the darkness. She stood in the driveway with her face upturned, allowing the freezing rain to cool her hot eyelids. *You trapped me here with that woman. How could you leave me stranded?*

Only after her teeth started chattering and her bones ached with cold did she go back into Shell House.

Now, Sylvia had chased her across the house, and Tilly had no way out—unless she wanted to go back outside. The knob started turning, so Tilly locked it. Sylvia kept jiggling it while yelling, "Open the door this minute, young lady." Tilly pressed her palms on the wooden door and leaned as if stretching her calves before a run.

Years of experience taught her there was no good response to Sylvia's tantrums. Her arms turned into sandbags, and her head weighed a ton, so she rested her forehead. The cool, painted wood didn't abate the pounding in her skull, especially with Sylvia continuing to yell and twist the doorknob. Then it grew quiet. Eventually, Tilly's ragged breaths steadied.

"Is Leo very upset with me?" Sylvia asked through the keyhole with such exposed vulnerability it cracked Tilly's resolve. It would hurt Dad if he knew her mother was this distraught.

"I don't know. He just took off." Tilly sighed and unlocked the door.

Thankfully, Sylvia walked across her bedroom, pretending to look out the French doors, while Tilly changed into a silky robe. She picked up a pillow and sat near the head of her bed.

Sylvia perched at its foot, with stiff shoulders and rod-straight back, like an austere schoolmaster.

Tilly said, "You know—" at the exact moment her mother said, "Well—"

The abrupt silence prickled Tilly's skin, so she said, "Go ahead, Mother."

Sylvia smoothed out nonexistent wrinkles from her tailored slacks.

"Your grandmother never talked to me about men or wedding nights, so I don't quite know what to say to you, Chantilly. But if there's anything you want to talk to me about, anything at all… you can."

Sylvia's words were as close to an apology as Tilly had

ever heard. A ribbon of homesickness—for a place she couldn't remember—tugged at her core. But Tilly couldn't believe her mother spoke with sincerity. *Is she for real?*

"You wouldn't understand."

"How're you so sure?" Sylvia asked with a genuine, curious tone.

Tilly stared at her for a dozen fluttering heartbeats.

Glancing down, Tilly picked a loose string from the pillowcase. How could she explain the shifting lump plaguing her since they booked the wedding date? It caused round-the-clock headaches and rolled around in her stomach. Whenever she considered telling her fiancé about her misgivings, it clogged her throat shut. The worst was when it lodged in her chest like a boulder on her heart.

Tilly watched her mother's expression closely, expecting the typical thin-lipped scowl donned during past tirades. But the softness in Sylvia's face was unreadable, so she let thoughts of making Dad happy give her the courage to share.

"You were a virgin bride, so how could you understand what I'm feeling?"

Sylvia threw her head back and laughed, "You think what?"

Tilly sat up straighter against the upholstered headboard. "It's what Grandma Warren told me. She said I was a honeymoon baby."

"Chantilly, Grandma Warren was a liar."

Sylvia's girlish giggles filled the space between them. This wasn't the shrill, artificial laughter she used around Dad's potential clients but a tinkling, natural sound.

"She would have said anything to keep up appearances." Sylvia covered her mouth while the giggles continued. "Oh my." She took a deep breath and fanned her face with her hand. "I can't stop..." She gasped, hid her face with both hands, and bent over at the waist. Her shoulders shook.

Is she crying?

Tilly scooted closer and reached out as if to place a hand on her mother's back.

"Are you okay, Mom?" Tilly asked.

Sylvia sat up and swiped at her wet cheeks with the pads of her pinky fingers. "When was the last time you called me..."

"What?" Tilly pulled her hand back.

"You haven't called me Mom since you were like ten years old."

Tilly hiccupped and hugged the pillow tighter. Sylvia didn't know she had already started calling her future mother-in-law "Mom."

"Anyway," Sylvia waved her hand dismissively, "your grandmother told that lie so many times she actually believed it." She pulled a delicate handkerchief out of her pocket but stopped, holding it midair. "I guess it's why I hated her for all those years." Sylvia sounded out of breath and stared blankly. She batted her clumpy eyelashes, coming back from wherever she'd gone. After dabbing at her nose, she cleared her throat. Unexpected eye contact made Tilly squirm. "You know I love your father, right?"

Tilly studied Sylvia's mascara-streaked face. Openness in her mother's sky-blue eyes bloomed warmth throughout her body. She shook her head to break from the intense gaze. "Sure, of course."

"He was perfect, your father," Sylvia said in a reverent tone. "I had to fight for him, you know? Every girl in school thought he was the catch. But he chose me."

Sylvia pushed herself back until only her feet hung off the edge of the bed. "But then he went off to college and left me alone. Just seventeen, a year behind him in school, I was worried he'd find some coed who was more experienced. I was determined to keep him and I did... right before fall term started." Sylvia raised her eyebrows and leaned back with her hands flat on the quilt behind her.

"Mother," Tilly said as she crisscrossed her legs, "how risqué." For the first time she could remember, she actually *wanted* to hear what her mother had to say.

"Then a beautiful boy moved across the street."

"Who?" Grandma Warren had never told this story.

Sylvia pulled her shiny patent leather heels off just enough to let them dangle from her toes. "He was a bit younger than me and came from California. Hung a surfboard on his bedroom wall." The soft, dreamy sound in her mother's voice suspended time. Tilly couldn't move a muscle even as a cold raindrop rolled down the back of her neck.

"His hair shined light as corn silk, and his smile lit up the world. Everything shimmered when we were together." Sylvia laughed. "We shamed the sun into believing it didn't burn bright enough." She shrugged her shoulders. "And then I graduated high school and started college. He visited me once, on campus, right before heading back to California. Asked me if I wanted to go on a road trip." Sylvia put her hands up, kicked her left shoe off so it flipped into the air back toward her, and she caught it. After doing the same with the right one, she tossed them both on the floor and giggled. Tilly couldn't help but chuckle.

"You have your father's laugh." Sylvia slid down onto her side, her right hand propping her head. "I know I gave birth to you, but did I have anything to do with making you?" She sounded like a little girl asking if Santa Claus was real. "You are 'all-Leo,' there's no doubt about it." She plopped onto her back, staring at the ceiling. "When you were born with a full head of thick, dark hair, I knew." She covered her eyes. "I wasn't sure until then, but after you came out, there was no question."

A fresh ember of fury sparked in Tilly's chest. "Does Dad know?"

Without looking, Sylvia shook her head and patted Tilly's knee. "Your father always does the right thing. He said he'd marry me, and he did. But... what if?"

The heat flared and rushed up Tilly's neck.

Sylvia kept talking. "What if you'd been born with wispy-blonde hair and your eyes stayed ocean blue? I didn't have the courage to choose, so life chose for me."

Tilly pushed her mother's hand away and launched to her feet.

"So, you didn't want *me* because you wanted a love-child with some surfer dude?" Acid splashed up Tilly's throat.

Sylvia sat up. "Not at all, Chantilly."

Rage boiled over. The air scorched around them as Tilly breathed fire.

"I always knew you never loved me."

Tilly kicked the pillow and stumbled over Sylvia's shoes, then stomped across the room. She paced in front of the French doors while shaking out her hands and balling them into fists.

Sylvia stood. "Let me explain."

"No." Tilly put her hand on the brass door handle. "I mean it, Mother. Don't..."

"Chantilly." Sylvia stepped toward her. Tilly yanked open the door.

Shock waves traveled up Tilly's body when she jumped onto the rough stone walkway. The bottoms of her bare feet stung as they smacked across the wet brick patio. Splintered wooden planks running across the low dunes didn't slow her. When she got to the sand, she ran straight toward the ocean and stopped where the frigid water brushed her toes. Tightening the sash of her silk robe provided no protection against the unforgiving wind. Fast-moving clouds zipped across the bright white half-moon. Crashing waves swallowed the sound of her screams, "I knew it!"

The wet sand softened her fall. She wrapped herself in a ball and rocked. *He wants a family. I could never be a decent mom. Not with that woman as my role model.*

"Chantilly, wait. Chantilly!" Sylvia's screeches cut through the wind.

Tilly stood with her back to the ocean. Sylvia bobbled in the sand, kicked off her shoes, and ran with arms waving.

Like a traffic cop, Tilly put up her hands. "Stop." But her mother kept coming. Tilly looked right, then left, but knew Sylvia would chase her up or down the beach.

There was one place her mother wouldn't follow. Tilly turned and walked into the Atlantic. Her feet prickled with the fire of ice-cold water before going numb. When the water reached mid-thigh, Tilly's breathing stuttered, but she moved deeper. A series of waves crested over her belly, and like a kick in the gut, they knocked the breath out of her. Shocks of electric pain seared her skin. She turned around and saw Sylvia standing at the water's edge, still waving her arms.

"Just leave me alone!" Tilly screamed and punched the water.

A wave swept Sylvia off her feet, then the swell lifted and dragged her sideways. Tilly lunged, reaching, right before a wall of water pummeled them.

The current pulled Tilly deeper. Salt burned her eyes. She sucked in water as she kicked and clawed. The iciness seeped through every layer into her marrow.

Pain transformed into heat, and a heaviness engulfed her, like one of Mother's sleeping pills oozing through her bloodstream. She stopped flailing. *So easy, now I don't have to choose—I don't have to call off the wedding.*

Moonlight streamed through the water and strobed like empty frames of film. Images flickered through her mind. She saw her mother holding a swaddled baby. A vision of Dad kneeling in prayer flashed. *Funeral or wedding? I can't do this to Dad.*

Then, like the strike of a tuning fork, it came to her. *I am nothing like that woman.* Every cell in her body vibrated, screaming for oxygen, and buoyancy returned. She righted herself and kicked until her head broke the surface. Then, after coughing, gagging, and emptying her stomach, she kicked hard to raise her head above the peaked waves.

"Mom?" The screams tore at her raw throat as she doggy-paddled toward shore. Clouds plunged the glimmering chop into darkness. White spots swirled in front of her eyes. Disoriented, her heartbeat thundered.

The next wave started to lift her body, so she caught its momentum. Hands first, she rode it. When her fingers brushed the ocean bottom, she pushed onto her feet, and the water pulled off her robe as she stood. Like a flashlight snapping on, the moonlight shined and illuminated her silk sash as it cut through frothy foam toward Sylvia, who lay face down. Shuffling closer, she felt weightless, as if she were looking down from high above.

"Mom?" Tilly grabbed Sylvia's shoulders and flipped her without any reaction. She felt a weak pulse and saw the rise and fall of shallow breaths. "I've got you." Tilly scooped Sylvia up. Without sensation in her arms, Tilly's brain could hardly make sense of what she saw—her mother's head lolling around turned her stomach. "God, no."

She wanted to run, but the beach felt like air under her numb feet. Then gravity regained its power like a super magnet. She staggered from side to side and tripped. Tilly's elbows and forearms broke the worst of their fall, but hearing Sylvia groan on impact gave Tilly hope.

"Oomph," Tilly grunted to get them upright. Her senses rushed in with another kick of fresh adrenaline. She garnered the strength of all mothers who lift wrecked vehicles off their children. It took a million years—and only one breath—to get them back inside the house.

On autopilot, Tilly stripped a trembling Sylvia and wrapped her in the heavy quilt. After getting a blanket for herself, she pulled her bundled mother onto her lap. "Please, Mom." She leaned as far as she could. "I'll call

9-1-1." But the phone was too far. While rubbing all over the quilt, Tilly repeated, "You can't leave Dad alone."

Sylvia's tremors subsided, then she coughed and threw up. Her blue-tinged lips became a purple-ish pink. She opened bloodshot eyes and with a raspy voice said, "Oh Chantilly, thank God." She freed one arm from the quilt, sat up, and moved off Tilly's legs.

"Let me get an ambulance." Tilly reached for the bedside table.

Sylvia grabbed her arm. "Don't. I'm fine. I need to tell you something," she said between coughing jags.

"Just let me—"

"No." Sylvia tightened her grip as it slipped to Tilly's wrist with surprising firmness. "I'm such a coward." Wet sand dripped from Sylvia's long strands of hair.

"You came after me, Mom. You're not a coward."

"Not then. Before. I was too weak to choose. Even after you were born, I was too scared to reach out to you."

"Mom, you don't—"

Sylvia let go of Tilly's wrist and raised her hand. The fierceness in her eyes locked Tilly in place—there was nowhere to run. "Listen to me. Reminiscing is nice. Daydreams are fun. But our little family?" She pressed her fist to her chest. "I have never been more grateful for anything else in the whole world."

Tilly's body tingled with pins and needles. A pulse of electricity surged as Sylvia palmed her wet cheek.

"It just felt like you were never mine, like you were a gift for your father, like you were his and his alone. I just got in the way."

Tilly placed her hand over Sylvia's. "No, Mom."

"Yes, you are Leo Bastien's daughter. And you are so much stronger than I've ever been. You're a fighter—God knows we've had our brawls." Though Tilly couldn't argue the point, she pulled her mother's hand off her face.

Sylvia leaned closer. "You're a warrior, Chantilly, a lioness with the power of a thousand suns. Promise me you'll live a bold life. One I wasn't courageous enough to choose."

Tilly closed her eyes against the shock of her mother's emotional plea. Then, for a moment, she melted into its newfound warmth. "Okay, Mom." She broke away and moved toward the telephone.

Sylvia stood, wobbling. "I'll give you some privacy."

Tilly dialed her fiancé. "No, Mom." She motioned for Sylvia to sit. "Stay."

Dragging the quilt, Mother came around and sat beside her.

"Hi. It's me. Yeah, um." Tilly's throat clogged. The phone felt like a thirty-pound dumbbell as it dropped to the mattress. *I can't do this.*

Sylvia squeezed Tilly's free hand.

Tilly nodded and swallowed. She took a deep breath, clutched the phone and said, "We need to talk."

All very best! [signature]

THE HEART OF THE HOME

Hilary Hauck

The home is bristling the way it always does before a party. Smug and proud, it notices everyone's work. Everyone's except mine, that is.

I suppose this leaves me time to focus on my new hobby of blending in with patterns. It doesn't really matter what patterns—on bed covers, wallpaper, cushions—you name it, I can stretch, curl, or twist and camouflage anywhere. Silly really, going to such lengths to hide from everyone when nobody notices me on the best of days, but that's what my existence has become.

You might think I should be working on a new treasure hunt, and I would have agreed with you until recently. I'd even go so far as to say I used to think I had the most important job of all the home helpers, but one day Mr. C, normally one of the more observant people, found the playing card that I'd slid beneath his underwear drawer. He turned it over and over—it was exhilarating, any minute he was going to understand it was a clue. He even looked for more cards beneath his drawer but then the worst thing happened. He just blithely walked off, stuck the card back in the pack, and went about his day.

He had come so close and yet did he recognize it as a clue? Not in the least.

How is it that people can come across things in the most bizarrely wrong place and not wonder how they came to be there? Nobody—absolutely nobody–had ever once seen a clue for what it was... namely, a clue. People just don't seem to understand their abode contains all the answers, that it'll lead them straight to the heart of the home. That all they have to do is notice.

Then again, the home will only thrive if the person who finds its heart will treasure and nurture it. It takes a special kind of person. If the wrong person gets to it and moves or damages it, it won't be long before the unstoppable progression of a house doomed begins to appear.

So I suppose my work is to guide those who care to the heart, and keep away those not ready. But the lack of challenge exhausts me. I've even contemplated seeking a new job—aroma mixer, perhaps. Who doesn't notice when a strange smell appears? Even the task of coming up with themes has lost its appeal, though I suppose my latest hunt has a theme: so-easy-even-a-child-could-figure-it-out. Which is fine because no children have lived here for years.

Not that I want you to think I'm needy. I'm just saying that everybody else's efforts are noticed. The dust bunnies that Lana knits—the cleaning lady grumbles about them all the time. And Mrs. C responds to the odd sock crisis with regular shopping sprees. Even Mr. C creeps around in one of the said pairs of socks trying to sneak up on the source of the creaks and cracks.

But I must put my boredom on hold. The home is giving off that happy light, it's drawing in fresh air for a crisp, invigorating ambiance—the party must be drawing near. As if to confirm the pending festivities, the doorbell rings.

I almost fall into old habits and slip beneath the staircase, but after all the practice I've done and all the notice I've not attracted, I decide to take a chance and cartwheel and jump down the side of the staircase, blending in with the wallpaper patterns.

I hide behind an ornament and watch Mrs. C hug a man with exuberance, but when they pull back from the hug, I see it is not a man, but Louisa dressed in stylish jacket and pants. I must say, she carries the look quite dashingly.

Well, this explains the home's excitement and I should have guessed, because Louisa is here for all the best parties. And a party isn't the only thing to come with her— she has brought her daughter, too.

For a fleeting moment, I worry about my latest theme, so-easy-a-child-could-do-it, but the only time Sunny spends time indoors is when she's found an injured animal to nurse.

The exuberance of everyone greeting Louisa nearly drowns out the sound of a saucepan boiling over. Even if I am feeling sorry for myself, I can't help but giggle at the thought of Lara fanning the burner flames to make the water boil as soon as Cook turned her back.

Louise takes Sunny to the top bedroom. Of course, it's where my treasure hunt begins; it's a kids' room after all.

I vow to spend some time devising a new set of clues after the home has everyone cradled in slumber. But I settle into the flowery canopy around the top of the four-poster bed to listen to Sunny's bedtime story and I, too, am lulled to sleep.

In the morning, the home is standing taller—it must be party day. Sunny wakes up, pulls on some shorts and a shirt, takes a vase from the sideboard, and dashes out of the room. I do hope she stops in the kitchen for breakfast before heading outside, but I can't follow to make sure—I must change the clues. Or maybe I'll do a little stretching and pattern practice before I get stuck into it. I have all day, after all.

At some point, Lilliput, who always knows what the people are doing, stops by to announce that Sunny is decorating the shed to host a gathering of children at the party. Sunny appears twice more—both times I manage to perfectly camouflage, both times she takes an item with her, a lamp, a tray, presumably for her party shed.

It's not yet lunchtime when a storm rolls in. I am just about to slip a receipt for a flock of ceramic chickens into a book on the cedar chest when I hear footsteps in the hall. Mrs. C and a soggy and forlorn Sunny enter the room. I have just enough time to scramble under the bed.

As Mrs. C gets Sunny dried and dressed—a cotton dress this time—Sunny asks in a hundred different ways when she'll be allowed back outside.

"I'll have these ready for you before the rain stops." Mrs. C holds up Sunny's play clothes and leaves the room.

Sunny hops off the bed and moves two piles of books onto the floor. A dash of luck. All I have to do is slip the clue into one of the books for the whole hunt to be reset. Except no sooner do I have this thought than Sunny rips the cover from her bed. She spreads one end over the chest, the other over a chair, and she ducks beneath.

The so-easy-even-a-child-could-figure-it-out clue is in full view on the bedsheet.

But not to worry. I take two steps, hunched over to blend in with the flower pattern, when Sunny bursts from her hiding place and passes so close to me I feel the rush of air. She leans over and grabs the pillow from the bed. I'm a goner, I know it. Either she'll step on me or she'll see me. Either way I'll be found out, which is absolutely forbidden. The work we do is to be noticed. We, ourselves, are not.

As she twists, her heel is the width of a hair from my nose—I exaggerate not.

She disappears beneath her bedcover, and I sigh with relief. Then I hold my breath again. She's come back out. This time she steps short of me, leans on the bed and, even though I can't see her, I know she's come back for the dove.

The clue.

I am seconds from resetting the clues, and she has gone and found one. Even though the chance of her figuring out the dove is part of a treasure hunt is about as likely as the home up and swimming across the bay, the game is on. I can no longer change the course of things.

Fine, it was not my smartest move, making an easy trail, but let's face it, even the handful of times my clues have been found, nobody has ever, not once, realized they were part of a hunt. So is it really that terrible if the dove has been found? After all that effort to get it from the Christmas box in the attic? In a way, my work is being noticed.

I've not even climbed halfway up the bed skirt when Sunny suddenly darts up and out of the room. I drop to the floor and dash after her.

After my near miss with her foot, I slip down a gap in the baseboard and slide down the board beneath the staircase, following Sunny's thundering footsteps. I've forgotten how fun the chase can be, but my glee is dampened when she stops at the landing. I am positively alarmed when she falls to her knees in front of the doll-sized dove house—but then, what child wouldn't be drawn to it? It's a logical place to play if you find an ornament-sized dove in your bed. It doesn't mean she's figured out a clue. She has just come to play.

I can only hope I'm right as Sunny peers through each window of the dove house one by one until she gets to the very room where I wrestled with a pencil as tall as myself and drew a cow, very much like the cow on the rug in Louisa's bedroom.

Again, Sunny dashes off. Again, I follow the thunderous sound of her footsteps. Sure and alarmingly enough, she goes to Louisa's room. I shimmy through a floorboard and find her sitting on the rug, tracing one of the cows with her finger.

From dove to dove house was not much of a leap. Child's play. The way she's connected my dove house art to the rug means something else entirely. She has actively followed a clue. A child!

I'm a tad bit thrilled. It's a mighty accomplishment. I relish in this moment. It's never happened before. I'm also relieved that I made the next clue tricky. And yet minutes later, Sunny lifts a corner of the rug and pulls out a picture of a laughing pig, the one I pilfered from the butcher's ad in the paper.

This kid has got further than all the adults who have ever been here since the home was built. The home has noticed, too. It is no longer standing tall. It is hunched closer, paying attention to the girl.

I'm finding it hard not to root for Sunny as she dashes off again, me close on her heels. But when she stops at the front door to put the dove outside on the porch, the home positively shudders. It's thinking what I'm thinking. What will she do with the heart if she finds it?

There's nothing I can do except follow Sunny to the kitchen where Cook fetches her a cookie. Perhaps she's just hungry. Perhaps she did skip breakfast. After all, it would be astonishing if she had followed another clue. But, astonishing or not, what she does next almost knocks my tinker shoes off. She climbs up onto the counter near the bull's head, the one on the wall presiding over the wet bar and breakfast nook. The one with flowers in its garland. The one that's right next to the pig's head.

A chill runs through the kitchen. That comfortable kind of warmth that only the home can provide is fading. Cook feels it, too, because she holds her hands over the oven as she berates Sunny for climbing on the counter.

There is no doubt now, Sunny has recognized this as a hunt. And if she reaches the heart, there's a good chance it'll end up in the shed.

I know in my own heart it is time to call in the team. We have to protect the final clues. Once we've done that, I vow to go back to my dowdy, dull, nobody-will-ever-notice-them type of clues.

It might not be night, certainly not a full moon, but I have to use the quickest way to gather the helpers. I rush to the living room. Thankfully there are no people here. I wrestle to tip a brass monkey and allow it to fall back in place with a thud, then nestle myself into a corner beneath the sofa and wait for the others to answer my summons.

Am I to admit to what I have done in the name of boredom? My short-sightedness, risking everything just because nobody ever put two and two together?

Lizzy, Lilliput, Lara—in no time, all the helpers are gathered.

"Louisa's little girl, Sunny, she's two clues away from the heart." My statement is met with gasps from the helpers, a quiver from the home.

I will get my comeuppance at some point, for sure, but all that matters now is to work together. Avert the attention and stop Sunny before the home is doomed.

"We can lead her outside," Lana offers.

"The storm—Mrs. C won't allow it."

"I've had my eye on some hatchlings," Lizzy says. It's her job to keep the spider population thriving.

"A whole home onslaught," Laney says, a bit too enthusiastically if you ask me. "Mayhem!"

Before anyone can respond, someone turns the door handle. Sunny comes in and goes straight to the camel ornament. Yes, I nod to the others. She is at the clue.

Yes, they all nod in agreement. Mayhem it is.

Laney pulls one of the vials from a pouch tied to her waist, holds it up and pinches her nose to warn us what is coming. She pops open the lid and the smell of burning is immediately overwhelming. Yuck! Sure to get plenty of notice—and not of the right kind.

Sunny sniffs audibly and looks around the room. Satisfied she can see no source for the smell, she turns back to inspect the little houses. The home rumbles, no doubt in response to how close Sunny is to its heart.

The door opens again, this time thrust angrily. It's Mrs. C.

"Come, dear! Fire! Hurry down to the front door!"

Laney gives me a thumbs-up. I want to smile at her, I want to let her know all is well, but Sunny has tucked the camel beneath her arm.

Mrs. C hurries from the room, calling for her husband.

"Good start. Where's the next clue, Lila?" If I didn't know better, I'd think Laney was enjoying this.

Not me. My voice is barely more than a whisper. "The entryway."

We split up, as it's too risky traveling together, and regroup beneath the grandfather clock in the entryway.

Sunny has beaten us there and is sitting on the stair, turning the camel over in her hands just steps away from the heart of the home. The one part of the home that must be nurtured but never disturbed. As if hearing my thoughts, the walls squeak, becoming parched, a prelude to its downfall.

I have failed. I have doomed us all.

In the dining room next to the entryway, Lee and Leena, who often work together on hefty jobs like prying the stair treads until they creak, give me hand signals I take to mean they will set the window banging and funnel rainwater onto the plates already set out for the party, even if the wind is blowing the opposite way.

Lizzy imitates a spider scurrying with her hand, then disappears, no doubt to invite the new hatchlings in. I'm sure they'll be glad to get out of the rain.

Lilliput flaps her arms like wings and points to the fireplace. She'll wake the bats—perfect!

Laney is already waking the family of mice and whispering instructions to them.

The dining room window bangs repeatedly. Mr. C appears and tells Sunny no fire has been found. Mrs. C appears right behind him.

"Oh look, a spider," Sunny says, examining her shin.

Mr. C steps toward her, his palm ready to swat. "Where? I'll get it for you."

"No!" Sunny shrieks and opens the front door. The gust of air makes the dining room window bang even harder and Mr. C turns to shut it.

Sunny puts the spider on the porch and comes back inside. "Oh look, another one!" She sounds delighted.

"Spiders bite, Sunny. You must let me—" But Sunny nor any of us hear what Sunny must do because a mouse runs over Mrs. C's shoe, and then over her other shoe. Mrs. C screams the loudest scream Rehoboth has ever heard.

Sunny drops to her knees to try to catch the mouse so she doesn't see the arrival of the bat who flies in and out of the dining room before fixing its sights on circling Mrs. C, who has got up on a chair and is still screaming.

Sunny is herding the spiders, marching in a veritable trail up the wall, into an envelope. Mr. C is swatting the ones Sunny doesn't catch, apparently oblivious to the bat.

The dining room window bangs back open.

As if there were room for more in the chaos, Louisa appears and tries to stomp on the mice who are taking turns to run across the entryway.

"Leave them alone!" Sunny cries. At least she's let go of the clue, which sits perilously on the stair.

"The bat, Dad!" Louisa yells at Mr. C. He picks up a picture frame and uses it to swat at the bat. The bat flies into the dining room just as Cook shows up to see what's going on and walks right into Mr. C's picture frame. She falls on the floor.

Louisa mis-stomps, stumbles, and knocks the camel off the stair. It smashes. The clue is destroyed—the mayhem can end!

But it doesn't end. Louisa falls right next to Cook. Sunny shakes the spiders from the envelope outside then proceeds to crawl around the floor after the mice. Mrs. C carries on screaming.

"Stop! Stop!" I shout. I slap my hand over my mouth. There is a moment of pause. Mr. C looks over his shoulder to see who shouted. Cook and Louisa look up from where they are laying. Mrs. C carries on screaming. The bat flies out through the open doorway.

Except for Mrs. C, they have all noticed me. Am I, too, now doomed?

Even the home is holding its breath.

"Nana, the mouse has gone!" Sunny tugs at Mrs. C's skirt.

The home pulls itself back up and casts a calming glow over the stunned people, the shattered clue and picture frame, the rainwater dripping from the dining room tablecloth. Its heart must be safe.

Mr. C helps Louisa and Cook to their feet. Mrs. C sits on the side table, her feet on the chair, not yet ready for the floor.

"We should call off the party," Mr. C says.

"Not a chance." Louisa brushes herself down. "Everything's going to be okay." As the heart is safe and nobody has questioned who shouted stop, I'm inclined to believe her.

"Can I go outside now?" Sunny asks. It has indeed stopped raining. As she skips out, I notice one of the mice sticking its head out of her pocket.

The helpers head back to their work and the family begins to clean up the mayhem.

I suppose I got what I wished for—I was noticed. No doubt there will be stern words for me at supper tonight. I vow from now on to always do my work as though nobody is watching.

As for when I'm not working, well, there was a certain kind of thrill to the day. Just to keep things interesting, I sneak across the entryway, cartwheel and leap with the pattern up the stairway, watching the family who is not watching me.

LIFTING FOG

S. M. Kraftchak

Cora woke to a deep voice softly droning through a familiar passage from the Bible. Opening her eyes, she recognized she was in a hospital room but didn't know why. She turned her head to see the man who was reading. "Where am I?"

He snapped the book closed and moved closer. "Good Heavens, girl! You're awake! How are you feeling?"

A duty nurse appeared in the doorway looking at her watch. "Father Abrams, I have a few minutes free so you can step out to stretch your legs."

"Praise Heaven! She's awake!" His voice was jubilant.

"Let me get the doctor!"

Cora examined Father Abrams's deeply creased face. Her eyes locked with his penetrating green ones. "Why are you here and why am I in the hospital?"

"I've read to you every day since your accident, child. I knew you'd need help to find your way back." He placed something in her palm, and wrapped his cool gnarled hands around hers.

Cora frowned. "What accident? When? What's this?"

Before Father Abrams could answer, a man in a white doctor's coat, followed by the nurse, rushed into the room. "Welcome back, young lady," he said. "We're surprised, but quite pleased to see you're awake. I'm Dr. Block. I've been caring for you."

Cora watched the tall man with salt-and-pepper hair walk around her bed. "Why are you surprised? How long have I been asleep? What accident? Was anyone else hurt?"

"So many questions. I promise we'll get to them all. First let me have a look." He sat on the side of the bed and peered into her eyes with a scope before pressing gently on her collarbone. He took her nearest hand. "Squeeze tight."

Cora did.

He reached for her other hand.

"Oh, she has quite the grip." Father Abrams raised their embraced hands without letting go. "I assure you this one is strong."

Dr. Block pursed his lips momentarily before he moved on to finish checking Cora's reflexes. She giggled when he ran his finger up the bottom of her feet.

"Am I allowed to eat? I'm famished."

"I think we can arrange something small and soft to start. Let's find out how your melon is doing." Dr. Block tapped her head. "Can you tell me your name?"

"Cora Benner."

"How old are you?"

"Umm... I'm not sure. Is that bad?"

"Do you know what year it is?"

"2012."

The doctor's pleased expression flickered when he glanced at the nurse and Father Abrams. "That makes sense... the year of the accident." He looked back at Cora. "Do you know where you live?"

Cora thought for a minute. "I... I'm not sure. What happened to me? Why can't I remember where I live?"

"Do you have any pain? Are things blurry?" Dr. Block gently felt around her head before he sat back.

"A tiny bit of a headache but nothing is blurry. Why are you avoiding my questions?"

With a deep breath and a glance at Father Abrams, who still held her hand, Dr. Block began to explain. "You were in a serious accident. The car went over an embankment on an icy road. The police believe you were there for some time before anyone noticed the wreck. You were unconscious when they found you."

"Was anyone else hurt?"

Dr. Block's pleased expression faded when his eyes moved to Father Abrams. "The car you were in was the only one involved."

Cora stared at her doctor for a minute before turning to Father Abrams who had lowered his forehead onto their clasped hands. "What aren't you telling me?"

"Do you remember your father's name?" Dr. Block asked.

Cora turned back with a scowl, but didn't answer.

"Your mother's name? Do you have any siblings? A family pet?"

"No, no, I don't remember. Where are they? What's wrong with me?"

Dr. Block smiled sadly. "You appear to have dissociative amnesia. Not uncommon for someone who suffered severe head trauma and has been in a coma for fifteen months. We'll do a few more tests to be sure. Other than losing a little weight and strength, you appear healthy, but there's no way to know if your memory will ever return."

"Fifteen months!" Cora looked over at her hand still engulfed by Father Abrams and stared at him for a full minute. "You haven't said anything. He asked about my parents and siblings, so I assume I have them, but you never said where they are."

Father Abrams lifted his head, released only one of his hands, and reached into his jacket pocket. He presented her with a picture of a man and a woman with a teenaged girl holding a small birthday cake with sparkler candles.

Cora looked at the picture, turned it over and saw a date of May 4, 2010. "I don't know them, do I?"

"This is your family, on your birthday." Father Abrams pointed with a wrinkled finger.

"Where are they?"

He pressed his lips tightly before answering, "They are all with God."

Cora stared at the picture, then shook her head, unable to be sad about losing a family she didn't know she had. "I don't recognize them. Did they die in the accident I was in?"

Dr. Block spoke softly. "We assume you took the picture, and yes, they all died from the same accident."

Father Abrams continued. "Your father, who knew he was dying but lasted several days, arranged for the family assets to be put in a trust to pay for your care. Now that you are apparently recovered, the balance of that sizable trust is yours."

"Where did they live? Can I go there?"

"No, my dear. Apparently," Father Abrams glanced up at Dr. Block, "your family house burned to the ground three days before the accident. The insurance money is in your trust. As far as anyone knows, and I've researched extensively, you have no one else. You are welcome to stay at the clergy house until you can find somewhere suitable after you are discharged."

Cora stared at the photo. Still clutching the item he'd pressed into her palm, she pulled her hand from Father Abrams and whispered, "Thank you. I think I'd like to be alone now."

Four weeks after being discharged, Cora sat on the balcony of her extended-stay hotel room. The fog in her mind that hid her memories seemed as impenetrable as the fog clinging to the mountains.

She fiddled with the miniature conch shell, broken open to expose the spiral chamber, hanging on her necklace. The day after she'd left the hospital, the shell had triggered one memory—Shell House on Rehoboth Beach.

She'd done hundreds of searches on the internet, looking for something, anything that would further key her memory. She'd found the car accident report and visited the site. She wasn't sure where she belonged, but she knew it wasn't here in southern Virginia. Nothing revived more memories, not even weekly appointments with Dr. Block and Father Abrams. When the fog of isolation and despair coalesced into relentless waves that dragged her into an inky ocean of hopelessness, Cora bought a used car and began the 375-mile trip to Rehoboth Beach. There she'd find her answers or allow the ocean to drown her despair.

At 5:30 A.M., Cora arrived. Her headlights illuminated the concrete slab ending in a sand dune spiked with clusters of marram grass instead of a house—a driveway to another lost memory. With a sigh, she turned off the car and stood in the murky gray light of pre-dawn. A cool breeze blew a strand of hair into her mouth. She turned and breathed deeply. The salty air and distant crash of waves, a siren song of joy filled her heart. Tears streamed down her cheek as she first started walking then running toward the ocean.

Cora instinctively tossed her sandals aside at the end of the boardwalk and stepped onto the cool soft sand. It gave way underfoot until she reached the high tide sand, firm and still moist from the retreating tide. Shells and seaweed littered the beach in undulating lines where they'd been discarded by retreating waves.

She stepped into the fading remnants of the last wave, watching the swells crest and curl before crashing into tendrils racing up the sand. As foamy water engulfed her feet, snippets of memories slipped into her mind's eye. Afraid to move and interrupt these hard-fought prizes, she stood gazing at the horizon as it blushed pale crimson. She resisted the urge to examine the memories for fear they'd stop.

"You stand there much longer, you'll be knee deep in sand," a man said.

Cora turned to see who had spoken, but only saw the back of a man jogging away. She looked down and found she had sunk to her ankles in wet sand and the man's sneaker prints were already being washed away by a wave.

"Thank you," she shouted, and was rewarded with a thumbs-up as he kept jogging. She stepped back to the high tide line and waited for the sun to fully rise. The flow of new memories retreated with the tide. Suddenly exhausted from her all-night drive, she reluctantly left the beach with a last glance toward the distant jogger.

After two weeks of walking the beach at sunrise she'd added only a handful more memories; few of them made sense. The strangest was watching the sunrise from the front patio of the famous Shell House, an elegant seaside mansion built in 1920. Infuriated by her mind refusing to retrieve her past, Cora sat on the beach gazing at the photo Father Abrams had given her of the gray cedar-shake mansion nearly a hundred yards behind her. She examined it over and over and swore the family in her picture were perched on Shell House's front wall.

This morning she heard the rhythmic footfalls of the man who had jogged past her every day. He'd never said anything more, always passing behind her, and was moving away before she realized he was there. The couple of times she'd been bold enough to shout at his back, "Beautiful sunrise," she'd only gotten a retreating thumbs-up. This morning she was determined to meet him.

When she turned, he'd already stopped three feet away, his back to the ocean, hands on his hips. His breathing was barely labored from his jog.

"I see you're an early riser too," he said.

Cora shaded her eyes as she looked up at him. She couldn't see his face because of the deep shadows with the rising sun at his back. "Yeah. It's peaceful. It helps me think."

"I'm Josh. You live around here?"

Cora hesitated, waggling the photo back and forth. "I used to, I'm pretty sure."

Josh laughed and lowered one knee onto the hard sand. "Pretty sure?"

Cora looked at her toes and curled them deeper into the sand. Without looking up, she said, "Yeah, I was in a car accident a while back and I don't remember much before I woke up from a coma."

"That sucks!"

"Yeah, it feels really strange because I remember every moment since I've been awake, kind of like opening a book and finding the first hundred pages empty and the story starting in the middle."

"I bet that's frustrating. How'd the accident happen?"

"I was told the car skidded off an icy road. They said my father, mother, and sister all died that day."

"Oh, wow. I'm so sorry." Josh stood and gazed at the ocean.

"It's okay. I'm sure I loved them, but how can I grieve someone I don't remember?"

Josh brushed his cheek. "So, are you out here to celebrate your sister's birthday?"

"Huh?"

He pointed to the photo in Cora's hand. "I saw the cake in the photo and the date on the back. May 4th was my twin sister's birthday, too."

"Oh no, Father Abrams said it was my birth—"

"Wait. Father Abrams?" Josh suddenly stood, examining the dark figures of other early risers scattered along the beach.

"You know Father Abra—" Cora began until Josh grabbed the picture from her. "Hey, give that back!"

Josh evaded Cora's attempts to retrieve the photograph as he examined it in the first rays of morning. Finally grabbing it, Cora tucked the picture deep in her sweatshirt pocket. "Who are you and how do you know Father Abrams?"

"Does he know you're here?"

"I don't know, I guess. He gave me the shell that triggered my first memory—that house and this beach."

"What shell?"

Cora pulled out her necklace with the exposed miniature conch.

Josh reached for it, but Cora pulled away.

"Who are you? How do you know Father Abrams?"

Josh stared. Cora watched his face scrunch as his eyes filled with tears, with his lips tightly pressed.

"Fine, if you're not going to tell me, then get the hell away from me. I've enough problems without some perv accosting me," she shouted and started to walk away.

Josh grabbed her arm. "Don't go."

Cora yanked her arm free. "Leave me alone or I'll scream."

Josh leaned toward her and in a hushed voice said, "I'm your twin brother."

Rounding on him, she shouted, "Bullshit! You can't be. He's dead—drowned in the ocean. On... my... our... birth—" As the sunrise illuminated Josh's face, she froze, transfixed by those hazel eyes she knew so well.

Josh stepped close and laid a hand on her arm. "Listen, we don't have a lot of time. If Abrams gave you that shell and that photo, it's only a matter of time until someone tries to finish the job."

"What?" Cora's voice cracked.

"Cora, I am your brother."

"Tell me something only my brother would know."

Josh put his hands on his hips and exhaled loudly as he kept scanning up and down the beach. He pointed to Shell House. "Dad gave each of us a shell in the gardens behind that house." He dug his out, also on a necklace.

"He said, *'Always return to the ocean. It has all the answers.'*"

Cora stared, her mouth slowly falling open. "I remember." She abruptly punched him in the shoulder. "We thought you were dead! Where have you been? How could you?"

"Ow!" Josh rubbed his shoulder. He rolled his lips over his teeth before he finally blurted out, "Fine. I'm a deep cover agent. I was recruited in my senior year of high school. They made my death look like a riptide accident and my body was never recovered. Dad knew."

"What?"

"Abrams had Dad recruit me."

"He recruited you? So Dad was an undercover agent, too? No, that's crazy. Take your sicko prank somewhere else."

"Do we have to talk about this here?"

"If I'm supposed to believe you're a secret agent, how do I know you're not trying to get me off somewhere to finish what the car accident didn't? How do I know *you* didn't burn our house down?"

Josh raised his fingers to his mouth and gave an ear-piercing whistle.

Cora ducked behind him, peeking to see who responded. "Who are you calling?"

Suddenly, a long-legged brown and white hound leaped onto the low stone wall in front of the gray cedar-shake mansion, before bounding toward them. Cora stepped out from behind Josh and dropped to her knees as the dog raced toward them. "Pirate?" She hugged the wiggly dog tight as it kept licking her face.

"Now do you believe me? Dad never wanted you recruited, but Abrams did it behind his back."

"Now I know you're crazy. I'm no secret agent." Cora continued snuggling her dog.

"You've got important stuff up here." Josh tapped Cora's head. "Someone wants it before they finish eliminating the last of our family. Now can we get out of here?" Josh lifted Cora by the upper arm and started walking toward the dunes.

"Where are we going?" Cora asked, petting Pirate who needed no encouragement to follow.

"Somewhere they can't find us." Josh tipped his head to the right.

"Who?" Cora began to look.

"Don't look, just keep walking."

It didn't take long to reach the half-buried narrow boardwalk that led to the mansion's brick circle patio. "Josh, this is private property."

"Yes, it's very private. It will give us time to talk and maybe for you to remember." Pirate suddenly bolted away into the shrubs surrounding the house. "Only when that list is out of your brain..."

"What list?"

"A list of agents, handlers, and station chiefs, for both sides—a veritable goldmine in the intelligence community. It's a wonder there hasn't been more interest." Josh turned left on the patio and ducked behind several thick Norway spruce trees and headed to the southern end of the house.

"Are we sneaking in?" Cora peered in a set of French doors and gasped. "I remember those green and white Victorian chairs. We'd sit there in the evenings with the ocean breeze blowing through." She suddenly turned away from the window and pushed past Josh, as though she were sleepwalking. At the back of the house, she paused, gazing down the breezeway that ran the length of this wing of the house. Cora murmured, "I remember," before she stepped onto the circular brick patio dotted with terracotta potted plants and a central fountain. "You and Dad talked business out here. I hid over there to listen." She pointed to a sculpted shrub on the far side of the patio.

"He knew you were there. We discussed subjects that didn't matter, but we held our important conversation in sign language."

Cora stared at Josh for a moment, then signed, 'I remember,' before following a narrow brick path deeper into the formal gardens.

It didn't take long until they came upon a tiny cottage with its own raised miniature stone patio. Instead of going onto the patio, Cora walked halfway around the edge and sat on its low wall. "We'd sit here and talk for hours."

"Yeah," Josh said standing nearby, patiently allowing Cora's memories to flow as he kept watch.

"This is where Dad told me you had drowned. I cried so hard; I was sick for a week. He tried to convince me it wasn't my fault, but I knew it was."

"It wasn't your fault," Father Abrams said as he emerged from the back of the cottage. "I'd arranged his *accident.*"

Josh stepped to shield Cora, who continued to sit in her dream-like state.

"No, I knew it was my fault. Even Dad didn't know I'd been recruited when I accidentally intercepted a list of names with professions and all kinds of nasty deeds. I guessed at what it was and wanted it to go away, so I hid it where no one would find it."

Josh looked at his sister with wide eyes. "It exists?"

Cora looked up at her brother. "Yes. I remember every single name and detail. I wish I could wipe it out of my brain. And your name was on it. So was his," she said pointing to a different path.

"We can do that, after you hand over the actual list," Dr. Block said as he emerged from behind a sculpted boxwood with a pistol drawn. "You shouldn't have been a snoopy little sister. Now where's the list?"

"I burned it," Cora sing-songed then stared at Dr. Block.

"No, you'd have kept it as insurance on your own life. Now tell me where it is."

"Don't do it, Cora," Father Abrams said, easing up to the twins. "As soon as he has it, he has no use for you. Give it to me."

"If I'd wanted her dead for real, I've had plenty of opportunities over the last fifteen months, Robert, but we couldn't take the chance the original might fall into the wrong hands. Then she'd have the only list."

Cora reached down to the wall behind her knees, tapped a few stones, and pulled out one small one. Reaching into the hole, she extracted a sand-covered aluminum cigar tube. She held it up and looked at Dr. Block. "Thank you. I spent years verifying the names on this list. I knew them all, except one, until now—Trebor S. Marba, cover... a priest."

Father Abrams suddenly pulled a knife and lunged as he grabbed for the tube. Josh barely evaded and deflected the blade from his sister.

A gunshot shattered the early morning and Father Abrams fell to his knees, clutching his chest.

"Father Robert Abrams—that's Trebor S. Marba spelled backward. Who would have guessed you were a double agent, Section Chief, and recruiter?" Cora said. "My father's words were your damnation. *Always return to the ocean. It has all the answers.*"

Escape... the beach is waiting for you
Lorraine

A SHELL FOR A SHELL

Lorraine Donohue Bonzelet

Patsy hears their whispers. They're always whispering behind her back. When they decide to grace her with conversation, it's an inquisition. "What year is it? Did you eat? Do you remember our names?" *Fer'chrissake, who do they think gave them their names after hours of backbreaking pain, pushing them out into the world? Me, that's who!*

The question Patsy hates most, "What are your grandchildren's names?" She retaliates with a counter-question, "Do you really think I'd forget my adorable grandchildren?" *I might slip up on the ragamuffins' names once in a blue moon,* Patsy thinks, *but heaven have mercy on me, there're nine of them. Mixing up a few is nothing to be fussin' about!*

Her husband, Jonathan, reminds her that she's eighty-eight. She doesn't feel that old! *Or did he say seventy-eight?* He tells her to "do the math." *Typical engineer!* Then barrages her with more questions like, "What year were you born?"

Patsy shoo-shoos him. She doesn't care about the *math.* She's in great physical health, no need for a cane, walker, or wheelchair. All those years lugging half-the-house in her purse *(and listening to him complain about it)* wasn't for naught. It resulted in her strong physique. "Fit as a forty-year-old," the doctor said.

But no one, not even her doctors, know about Patsy's secret weapons. Her ears! They can hone in to the lowest whispers. That's how she knows that they, Jonathan and the kids, plan to take her car keys away. What they don't know is that Patsy has a plan, too!

Amidst the Sunday morning chaos of breakfast cleanup, clanking dishes, water splashes, and low murmurs, Patsy announces that she'll watch mass on the television later. She feigns exhaustion and a deep sleep on the recliner. Pulling the cotton-weave throw over her shoulders and tucking it under her chin, she releases a snarling, snorty-snore. The kitchen whisperers go silent. After some tiptoeing and scuttling about, the front door clicks shut and they are gone. Patsy hopes that they are off to mass, then the antique car show they've been obsessing over. *Or was it the boat show? Whatever!*

Scooting her butt back and forth on the recliner, she maneuvers to an upright position. Patsy shakes the pink plastic denture container that was hidden on the bookshelf. Breathing a sigh of relief, she releases a child-like Cheshire grin. Her car keys are still there!

In no time, with denture container and lunch cooler in hand, she's in the car. Patsy hates the "direction machine." They taught her how to use it. Over. And over. And over. Patsy does her best to enter the words "Rehoboth Beach." *If I could spell 'Rehoboth' it would make things much easier.*

Patsy's stomach somersaults as she pulls out of the driveway. It's been a while since she's driven. *They watch me like a hawk.* She's happy to be on the road early. Mornings are when her brain is freshest. Today, her brain feels super-fresh! Patsy concentrates on the nice lady's directions and before she knows it, she's seeing signs for the shore. Careful to hold the wheel steady and keep her foot on the pedal, Patsy gives a celebratory body wiggle.

I'm almost there, Richard!

Her stomach clenches. *Nerves? Hunger?* Patsy tries to remember if she ate breakfast. She spots the blue lunch cooler on the passenger seat, which is a pleasant surprise. *Glad I had enough wits to pack snacks!* She wonders what she brought, but supposes she should keep her eyes on the road. She remembers having one mishap. Her family dramatically claims she's had several "crashes" with the mailbox, trash can, and rosebushes. *Must've been mere 'oopsie-daisy' moments since there wasn't a scratch on me!*

As she rounds the bend, the panoramic view of Silver Lake melts Patsy's heart. Overcome with nostalgia, she slows to a crawl, glancing in quick spurts at the geometric sun-patterns shimmering on the water, the geese mindlessly bobbing, and her favorite spot near the bridge where she and Richard did what teenage lovers do. *Richard, I miss you!*

A sudden jolt of the car whips Patsy's head forward and locks her seat belt. *Phew, just the curb!* Patsy's hands tremble uncontrollably as she maneuvers the car. *Quick! Drive away!*

The sight of Lake Drive calms her nerves. It's narrow and looks more like a golf-cart path than a street. Patsy searches for Richard's house. Most of the structures have a modern, artsy feel. Metallic. Tall glass windows. Not at all like it used to be. She pulls into the sandy space in front of a beach-cottage-looking house that she hopes is

Richard's. She releases her tense grip off the steering wheel. *Yes, I think this is it!*

Pasty calls this "Richard's house" but it's been so very long since his family owned it. *So very long since we were supposed to own it.* Patsy hopes that the current owners don't think her absolutely crazy wanting to have a quick peek inside. *Maybe I should fake being an old lady with an urgent need for a restroom!*

Patsy barely takes a step from the car when she sees a weather-beaten For Sale sign on a dirty white post with the paint peeling off. The sign is sticking out from an overgrown bush. *Did Richard keep the house, waiting for me?*

The planks groan as Patsy steps up on the expanded, wrap-around front porch. It's not the porch she remembers by any stretch of the imagination. She rings. She knocks. She's greeted with silence.

Patsy strolls to the back, peeking through whatever windows permit peeking. The sound of the ocean signals the reflex to slip off her shoes. She places them next to her lunch cooler on the stone walkway. The trifecta—the sound of the seagulls, the smell of salt air, the cool ocean breeze—lures her. With each step, the warm sand sifts through her toes, taking her back to her childhood.

She follows the path over the dunes, weaving through beach grass. Memories of Richard flood her mind... tormenting her with those creepy horseshoe crabs, helping her build sandcastles only to demolish them, jumping the waves, tumbling in the surf, and waddling around like ducks with a load of sand in the bottom of their swimsuits. Eventually, sunburnt and half-starved, his grandma would rally them around to eat peanut butter and strawberry jam sandwiches. They'd wash it down with gulps of her sweet tea. Richard's grandma made the sweetest sweet tea!

I'll wait forever for you! The words flash in her brain as does the image of a male silhouette, dark, gray, and grainy. It's like a low-quality black-and-white film. Fuzzy. Jittery.

Patsy's tears well up. She shakes her head to rid the memories. Patsy draws her attention to a rising wave. She breathes in... and in... and in. Just as the wave can't take up any more water, Patsy can't take in any more air. They release in unison, swirling all their pent-up energy into a roaring rumble. Patsy is mesmerized watching the sand soak up the water. *He waited... Why didn't you?* She pushes her anxiety to her feet. She feels the sand welcoming it, soaking it in, and dissipating it! Her mind feels clearer. Lighter. *Whoa! Dizzy!*

Light-headedness and the burning sensation on Patsy's face indicate that it's time to return. Overworked knees and ankles make for a taxing trip back over the dunes. Patsy recalls Richard carrying her to the ocean and dunking her. *Oh, what I wouldn't give for him to carry me now!*

Relieved to be back at the cottage, she forcefully jiggles the handle to the French doors on the back patio. A frantic, frail, old face is in the glass panel looking out at her. The image sparks familiarity, yet it's strangely unfamiliar. The lady's eyes are sunken slivers, almost overtaken by layers of undereye wrinkles creasing on top of themselves. There's a sadness. A hollowness. *The image might represent the outer me—but the youthful, fun-loving, adventurous me is in there! It is! It is!* Patsy insists. She refuses to look at that old woman any longer.

She shuffles to the next door and gives the handle a twist. The door opens.

With nervous excitement, Patsy enters. Everything seems brand new, and it smells freshly painted, yet a layer of dust has settled on the furniture. The oversized wood end tables, adorned with lace doilies and Tiffany lamps, exude a charming hominess. It's gorgeous! *But not Richard's style.* Every detail is perfect, right down to the candelabra and dinnerware settings on the grand dining room table. *Definitely not Richard's style.*

Patsy is drawn to the Monopoly game set up on the coffee table. An eerie chill swarms her. *Monopoly. That was our game!* It brings back memories of Sundays with Richard's family. His grandma had strict church rules: no dungarees, not a smidge of knee peeking from skirt or dress, and it was sacrilegious to disgrace the chalice with lipstick. His grandma didn't have a cleavage rule. Maybe since the thought of showing cleavage was uncommon back then—or maybe because Patsy had no cleavage worth making rules about.

After Sunday service, as the homemade potato pancakes sizzled—and kielbasa and sauerkraut simmered, souring the air—Patsy and Richard played board games. Monopoly was their favorite. Patsy recalls the challenge of removing Richard's buildings, preferably without him noticing. Many games ended with the spewing of sentiments like "cheater" and "thief." *Richard, remember the time I 'accidentally' tipped the board over? Oh, you were angry! Tsk...tsk...* Patsy shakes her finger in the air. *Temper! Temper!* She lets out a full-blown belly laugh and loses her balance, lowering herself to the sofa.

Patsy examines the board. She grasps for memories and allows them to flow as they will, sporadic and disjointed. With her finger, she writes in the dust "Richard & Patsy." She encases it in a heart.

Patsy doesn't know how long she stared at her writing. *Did I doze off for a few?* She rallies her mind to focus, then mischievously grabs a wad of bills from the coffee table and stuffs them in her pocket. *That's for all the times you wouldn't allow me to pass 'GO' and I couldn't collect two-hundred! Take that, Richard!*

Her satisfaction is disrupted by a pang of hunger. Patsy scavenges through her lunch cooler. She pulls out a jar of pickles and bag of pistachios. She cracks open a pistachio shell, tosses it in the fireplace, and plops the salty seed in her mouth. Scanning the room, she's disappointed that nothing looks like it did when Richard lived here. Patsy searches for the coat closet. It isn't where she remembered it. *Who would move a coat closet? Richard, am I in the right house?*

Was I nine years old? Or was I ten? At his birthday party, she and Richard hid in the coat closet for a game of hide-and-seek. He refused to stay quiet, pretending the jacket arm-sleeves were an elephant's trunk. "Brrrrr..." he'd breathed, vibrating his lips and flipping the sleeve at her face. "Brrrr...." Patsy remembers cupping her hand tightly over her mouth to muffle her giggles. The more she muffled, the more Richard exaggerated his lip vibrations. Then Richard's golden, sundrenched arm touched hers. The warmth was electric. Shivers traveled to her toes. They both fell awkwardly silent.

A shiver runs down Patsy's arm. *Richard, did you feel that? Are you here with me?* Leaning back on the sofa, Patsy allows Richard's cathartic presence to soothe her. His stubble prickles her cheek, warm breath tickles her neck, his hands caress, and his lips kiss hers, softly and sensuously.

A devastating guilt—deep and shameful—engulfs Patsy.

Richard, I tried to wait! Do you know how many times I passed the house dreaming of your return? We were supposed to live here... happily... ever... after!

Patsy's knees buckle as she forces herself up from the couch. *I wish I had a cane!* Patsy shuffles to the dining room table and returns with two champagne flutes. *Real crystal? These would make nice souvenirs!* She fills the glasses with pickle juice. Cling-cling! *Cheers to you, Richard! Cheers to what could have been!* The overzealous gulp of pickle juice makes her pucker—and gag. *Blech!*

Patsy tours the living room, examining the exquisite collection of seashells placed about, unchipped, perfectly grooved, smooth as marble, like she's never seen before. Their perfection makes Patsy wonder if the shells were store-purchased from a shell manufacturing warehouse— or is it possible that such beauty was naturally birthed in the ocean? Patsy doesn't care. She wants them! *I wouldn't dare steal, Richard!*

Patsy gets a brilliant idea. For every seashell she takes, she'll replace it with a pistachio shell. *Doesn't get any fairer than that. A shell for a shell!*

Carefully swaddling her new haul, Patsy glances back at the living room, humored by the sight of the miniscule pistachio shells placed about. *I know you're humored too, Richard.*

After arranging the stash neatly on the passenger seat of the car, Patsy presses HOME on the machine. She is weary and her mind is losing its ability to concentrate—

normal for this time of day. She reminds herself to remain diligent, and repeat aloud the voice's directions so as not to get lost. *But first, remove the For Sale sign.* Patsy pulls at the post but it doesn't budge. She flips the leafy branches up and over the sign to hide it. *Good enough for now!*

Driving on the bridge over Silver Lake, Patsy wonders if they would've lived happily ever after. She wonders if Richard thought about her in his final days.

Lost in her tears, Patsy drives aimlessly, not listening to the machine lady's directions. Now, "the lady" is confused. "Recalculating!" is all she will say and Patsy thinks she's saying it in a rather nasty tone. It's pissing Patsy off! She pulls in to a gas station to let the direction machine regroup. Despite waiting for a while, the attendant doesn't leave his little booth. Patsy dreads getting out of the car. The sand dunes took their toll on her knees and ankles. She honks the horn.

"Fill 'er up! Regular!" Patsy yells out the car window.

The man yells back that it is a self-serve station.

"When in tarnation did that happen?" she growls as he approaches.

"Ummm... I dunno... like... decades ago!" the attendant snips back.

I'm in no mood to be messed with, Patsy thinks. "Fill 'er up! *Please!*" Patsy pulls out her wad of Monopoly bills and hands him a blue fifty.

I can't believe that snippety-snot has the nerve to walk back to the booth gabbing on his phone! Whatever happened to customer service? Patsy honks again.

Several minutes later, he returns to perform the most excruciatingly long fill-up she's ever experienced. Just as he is tightening the gas cap, a police cruiser stops in front of Patsy's car.

The young *(very young!)* officer introduces himself then politely asks what her name is. He requests to see her license, which she cannot find. She can't remember the last time she saw it. *Is it expired?* Patsy gains her composure long enough to emphatically tell the prepubescent officer that she's been driving since before he was a thought in his mama's mind!

"That well may be," he sweetly responds while adjusting his cap, "but ma'am, I can't permit you to drive without proof of a license."

Patsy is annoyed... much more than that, she's overly tired... downright exhausted. Being chauffeured around sounds good, without the drama of lights and sirens.

"No lights. No sirens," he assures her.

The officer makes sure her seat belt is securely fastened then promises she'll be home in no time. Patsy tries to keep her brain engaged as he tells a fascinating story of an elderly woman, a "Silver Alert," who had gone missing earlier that day. He says her husband and kids are worried sick about her.

Patsy gasps and tunes inward, *missing... her husband must...* Patsy's thoughts, words, and letters slam into each other. With trepidation, she tries to recall her husband's name.

The officer is still rambling, "nine grandchildren!"

"Richard and I don't have any." Patsy searches for the facts. Her mind tussles. "Jonathan, yes. Jonathan and I... nine..."

"Don't worry," the officer continues, smiling at her in his rearview mirror. "From the look of the beautiful seashells in the car, I think she had a wonderful day at the beach."

"She's blessed," Patsy nods. "Blessed!"

Patsy doesn't understand why she has a gnawing urge to ask this question, but she blurts it out anyway. "What year is it?"

"It's 2022," he responds.

Twenty. Twenty. Two. Twenty. Twenty. Two. That sounds weird.

She leans her head against the window and watches the streetlights blur past. She shakes the denture container cupped in her hands. As Patsy clutches it to her chest, she breathes a sigh of relief. *They didn't take my keys!*

From the soft rumbling of the police cruiser, Patsy's eyelids grow heavy. She feels sand grinding between her wiggling toes. *There's a beach cottage for sale, Jonathan... Rehoboth Beach. It's waiting for us.*

FRANNIE & ELI

Kathleen Shoop

Frannie laid on the beach, heaving for breath, arms and legs splayed. Her first plan—to run and swim herself to death—had failed. The second—to drink her weight in wine—would soon be underway. First though, she was waiting to see if the impromptu plot to get swept into the surf by a colossal wave would come to fruition.

When it didn't, her breath evened out and she sat up. Wave after wave rolled in, and one particularly gentle bit of surf deposited a green glass bottle into her lap. She grasped for it as the tide tried to take it back. She peeled seaweed away. The label was long gone. Champagne shaped. A gift from the sea. Perhaps this was an omen—a reason to look to the future. Ha. It wasn't as though the wave had dumped uncut diamonds. But something about the bottle, holding it, its hefty weight and mysterious origin felt special. As though the universe knew the frustrated historian needed something to reignite her interest in living.

Barefoot and without a towel, she ambled back to Shell House, wanting to get into the kitchen so she could look at the bottle without the incredible glare of the late June sun. Over the dune and onto the narrow boardwalk that led to the house, she felt a little lighter. Midway across the brick patio, a roaring sound filled the air and shook the ground, making her stop. Shoulders hunched, she turned to see a truckload of dirt being dumped. She leapt out of the way and lost her balance, falling, hands and knees skidding across the brick, bottle flying, crashing into the wall and splitting open.

"Hey!" She got to her feet and hobbled toward the back door to get away from the still pouring debris.

She picked up a handful of stones and threw them at the cab of the truck.

The engine shut off and a man jumped out, stalking toward Frannie. "Hey!" He removed his hat and swatted it against his leg. "What the hell?"

"What the hell is right!" She held up her scraped hands. After trying to exercise herself to death all day, she was surprised to find she still owned rights to survival instincts.

"You threw those stones?"

"You dumped a ton of dirt on me?"

He drew back, looking shaken, and replaced his hat. His voice went low. "I did? I mean, I did dump it, but I didn't know you were there, or that anyone was. I was told to... well, I thought the house was to be vacated this week."

She looked at her knees and dabbed at blood dripping down her shin.

"Oh, wow. You're really hurt." The man moved closer, reaching toward her legs.

She hopped back. "No, no. It's fine."

He grasped her hand, yanking her into him. She stiffened, trying to wiggle out of his grip.

"Broken glass," he loosened his grip. "I didn't want you to step on it with bare feet."

She exhaled. His peppery scent of fresh perspiration and mud smelled good. His strong embrace was shocking, but not bad.

Still.

He released her fully, but guided her by the elbow around the glass. "Let me get you inside at least."

She nodded and wiped her brow with the back of her hand. "Oh, the poor bottle. Thing just surfed in on a wave and now it's..."

He grabbed the door handle. "I'm sorry. Let me get it for you." He bent down. "The neck snapped off and shattered, but looks like the bottom's intact."

She nodded, wondering what she was going to do with a half-shattered bottle. He brushed the broken pieces into a pile with his boot and bent down to get the rest. "Wow."

She craned to see what had surprised him.

"There's a note."

"Did you say *note*?"

He met her gaze and nodded. His eyes lit and she felt as though his excitement matched hers. A note! She told herself not to get too thrilled, that it was probably nothing.

"Well, come in with me then." She jerked her head toward the house. "Let's take a gander."

"I was afraid you wouldn't ask after... well..." He gestured to her knees and to the pile of dirt on the terrace.

"I don't hold grudges."

"Lucky me," he said following behind her.

"Yes, lucky you... err..." She stopped and turned back to him as the storm door swung shut. "Who *are* you?"

He reached out. "Eli Jackson."

She glanced at her scraped palm then back at him.

"I'm so sorry, again. So very sorry."

She smiled.

"But having nearly buried you under a ton of dirt, please tell me your name."

"Frannie Clark."

And with the saying of their names, the excitement of a message in a bottle took over.

In the kitchen, they cleaned Frannie's scrapes and cuts then sat at the table near the windows, chattering about what the note might say, perched there rolled up tight, hiding its secrets. When they ran out of guesses, Frannie's heart raced. She reached for the curled paper. Her hands shook and she chuckled.

"I feel like I stumbled onto treasure even though I know this will end up being nothing and..."

"And what?" Eli asked.

She shook her head. It was one thing to share her message-in-a-bottle moment with a stranger, but she didn't have to share her failings and fears. So she drew a deep breath, held one end of the paper and unrolled the other, flattening it.

Eli slid his chair around the side to sit right next to Frannie. He helped her hold the top flat. They leaned in to decipher the handwriting.

"A recipe," Frannie said. "A recipe?"

"Pineapple upside down cake," Eli said.

They stared at the writing in silence, their fingertips butting against each other at the top of the paper.

"I love pineapple upside down cake," they said in unison, then drew back, the paper snapping to its rolled form. Frannie was suddenly acutely aware of their closeness but she didn't mind it a bit.

Eli looked back at the paper. "May I?" He gestured that he wanted to flip it over.

She nodded.

He turned it and flattened it. There was a drawing and some faded wording. They shifted so the light from the kitchen window hit the paper better.

"*Love is sharing a good cake,*" Frannie read aloud. "*Sometimes cake is more than cake.*"

Eli ran his finger under the next line. "Can you make that out?"

She attempted a couple times, but couldn't quite capture what it said. "I feel like it's on the tip of my tongue, but it's just not clear enough."

He sighed. "The sketch—it says pantry."

"The arrows point to a little door. A pie safe?"

They grew silent again, looking at each other. Frannie looked toward the hallway. "I just got here today, but something tells me this place must have a pantry so..."

They stood.

"I've been here many times. The pantry's down the hall," Eli said.

"You know the family who owns it?" she asked.

He nodded, waving for her to follow him. "Getting it ready for sale."

"Sale? Who would sell this place?"

"I sure wouldn't," Eli said.

They entered the pantry and turned on the light. There was a work table in the center and floor-to-ceiling shelves lined with flour, canned goods, detergents, and stacks of china.

"They used to have enormous parties here," Eli said. "Way back to the 1920s when the house was built."

Frannie crossed her arms. "I know. I'm here on assignment to write about one of the ten best historic vacation homes in the U.S."

"Who do you write for?"

She hated this question. She pressed her palm against her chest trying to keep her voice steady and nonchalant. "I'm between gigs. This is sort of my own foray into combining writing and history and..."

"Freelancer?"

She narrowed her gaze on him. Was he implying that wasn't a legitimate choice? Was he discounting the assignment because she gave it to herself? "Recently employed, but now, freelancing, yes."

"What was your job?"

She cleared her throat. Why be so shy? A job was a job. "List maker."

He drew back. "What now? Like *grocery* lists? Things to do?"

She bristled and fought off the embarrassment, telling her ego to calm itself down. "You know, lists. Ever heard of Babyface?" It felt like such a stupid job now that they were talking about it. But it had paid the bills. And coming up with fresh lists of names that are elegant but not pretentious, or masculine but debonair was harder than it sounded.

He scratched his chin. "Nope."

"It's for pregnant couples. Baby everything including name lists which was one of my domains."

He laughed. No... he guffawed. "I can see why you quit. That sounds..."

The sting of failure struck again and she nearly lashed out at him for mocking her former job. But his smile, his sweet gaze, the way he held hers with kindness emanating from him like a visible current, made her feel comfortable, safe to be vulnerable.

"Sounds like the most mundane job on the planet?" she asked.

He shrugged.

"And I got fired." It felt good to say it out loud. "Didn't quit." She hadn't even told her family yet.

"Why?"

"Babyface didn't appreciate the list I posted for names that portend future failure."

He chuckled, then broke into a full-bodied laugh. "You published that?"

"Hey, I included my own name, so they should have seen the humor."

"Extreme response from them. Surely they saw it was—"

"Then there was the list of names that will bring derision and should be avoided at all costs."

"Seems like a good list for parents to avoid."

"I put my boss's name on that one."

His eyes went wide.

"And then I did a list of strollers that only pretentious parents buy."

"Oh."

"Yes. The company owner's favorite pram was the headline item. I seem to have been sabotaging my job there."

"Why?"

She leaned against the work table. "I don't know. Bored? Afraid to make a change on my own? Maybe I'm a jerk? I can't even give you the exact reason because I don't know."

"Just wasn't the right job?"

She scoffed.

"What?"

"They fired me with a list. They titled it, *Top Ten Reasons Frannie Clark is Fired.* Number one was *Doesn't understand that any job in news is journalism (isn't really a writer).*"

He grimaced as though he could feel her pain. "Holeee shit, that's awful."

"Live by the list, die by the list."

"But here you are with a message in a bottle and a mysterious map and a handsome co-treasure hunter... so your first freelance gig is anything but boring."

She chuckled, stuck in his gaze, loving every second of it. "Why do I feel like I've known you forever?"

"I'm that kind of guy," he barely said above a whisper.

"Well, let's get busy then. Let's see where this leads." And she didn't know if she meant the map or the two of them.

Frannie and Eli worked their way around the pantry, first looking for the obvious sight of a vault. Nothing. At some point they began referring to the house as Old Girl, asking her to give up her secrets.

"Maybe it's not a big door," Frannie said. They studied the drawing again then surveyed the space. "Let's shift those supplies to the table to start."

When they'd cleared a couple shelves, Eli studied the canned goods, organizing them. "Look at that."

She didn't know what he meant.

He tapped several items. "The exact ingredients for the pineapple upside down cake recipe."

"That's weird."

"The note is old. No doubt. But would the owners just keep the ingredients on the off chance that a recipe might sweep up to shore and you could make a cake?"

She slipped the elastic band from her wrist and tied her hair back. "No. That's ridiculous. Coincidence. Though I am going to use this bottle to deepen the intrigue in my article. That's for sure."

"Good idea."

She watched him eyeing the ingredients, brow furrowed. "You're mighty interested in this."

He nodded. "Well, I'm a historian of sorts, too. Amateur in the traditional sense—I work at the historical society here. But I'm a landscape historian by trade—in practical and theoretical terms. And when the owners decided to sell this place they agreed that the historical society could have some of the heirloom plants—roses, hydrangeas..." His eyes lit up as he spoke.

"Wow. Now that's a job."

"I love it, yes. But the owners agreeing to let the historical society have such extensive plantings, replaced with mounds of dirt, made me question why they agreed so quickly."

"They're nice people?"

He shook his head. "Their buyers—the three of them who are bidding—are considering tearing the place down."

A chill worked through her. "No. A mansion? Like this? It's stunning and gorgeous and every bit of it holds a story." She spread her arms and turned. "I mean, look at this place."

He blew out a puff of air. "Well, maybe we've got the chance to capture one of those stories before it gets bulldozed into the sea."

She sighed. "I was feeling weird about doing this, but now that you said the house might be torn down..."

They worked for hours, moving china, feeling along the walls, gently lifting wallpaper that was curling up at its edges to see if it was like that on purpose. They moved the last tower of china and there it was.

A small door with a deadbolt.

Eli's eyes went wide.

"I can't believe this. It's like..." Frannie said.

"The story's writing itself?"

Frannie covered her mouth. She couldn't argue with that.

He jerked his head toward the door. "That's yours to open."

She reached for the knob on the bolt but didn't slide it.

"What?" Eli asked.

She looked at him. "This moment, before we know what's in the... whatever that is, this moment is probably more magnificent than anything will be in reality."

He cocked his head then put his hand over hers. "And sometimes, reality is as good—no, *better*—than what we could imagine."

The warmth of his hand on hers sent thrills spilling through her. "So you're one of those people."

He raised his eyebrows. "Exceptionally handsome and very, very insightful?"

Something in their closeness, his kindness, made her tumble through time without moving an inch. She'd only had these *I've known this person forever* experiences a couple times in life and not since freshman year of college. "Can't argue with that."

"Well then." He squeezed her hand.

And she slid the bolt and pulled the door open.

Darkness. Frannie looked over her shoulder as Eli retrieved his iPhone and turned on the flashlight, illuminating the space. Empty.

It couldn't be. A map to an empty vault? She leaned in, reaching back, back, back, patting the velvet space. Papers. She pulled them out along with a bottle that had a faded label.

"You know," she said, "I suspected there might be a giant diamond brooch or strand of rubies, but... *paper*? Even better." She trudged to the work table and sat down with her bounty.

He followed. "Paper? Really? You have a list you want to write?"

"Ha, ha. No. I'm kidding. I wanted diamonds more than I can say."

He sat beside her and they spread the papers out. A receipt. The name Flora Daniels was written at the top and underneath was a list of booze and beer and the number of each kind. At the bottom it said, "Paid in full, June 21, 1925."

Eli fell against the seat back and took off his hat. "It was supposed to be a myth."

"What?" Frannie grabbed his arm.

"All the articles indicated it was hysterical lore, spurred on by religious folk looking to scare people into good behavior."

She scrunched up her face in confusion.

"Bootleg bashes in Rehoboth. Huge soirees, they called them."

She nodded. "I read about bottles washing up on the beach over the years, yes."

"Well, there's loads of scuttlebutt about bootleggers along here down to Dewey and... well, a big party that got busted."

She paged through the rest of the papers. "More lists! Look at these names, these people, these jobs—Bevo man or Bevo bird—a delivery man bringing near beer bottles that could be swapped out for real beer if a bust was eminent!"

He leaned forward, running his finger down the sheet. Circus performers, wild animals, musicians... a governor, three senators, Rudolf Valentino, Lillian Gish...

"And here..." Frannie said. "A note." She read aloud. *"Sometimes the right thing to do is not the legal thing. Sometimes love comes like heat lightning, all scattered and soft. Other times, like tonight, it comes like a bolt. And so I resign from my work. And I from mine."*

The end of the word *work* and the beginning of *And* were intertwined as though connected on purpose. It was signed *George Wilk and Flora Daniels. Soon to be Mr. and Mrs. Wilk.*

"Oh, wow, wow, wow." Frannie spread the papers out. "Who *are* these two?"

"Look—the recipe, again. *Love no matter how it comes—the lovers must go with it. I like to think my cake had something to do with this pair finding their way to each other.* And it's signed by someone named Molly."

Eli rubbed his scruffy chin. "You know, 'cake-eater' in the '20s was slang for a ladies' man?"

"Well, this cake seems to have been made for love, not lust."

"Seems that way."

They paged through the rest of the papers, lists and lists of names of guests who'd come through the home to stay, to live, to revel. It was like a diary written just for her to discover.

They ran for their computers—Frannie upstairs to her rented room and Eli to his truck—to see what they could dig up about the people and things listed. Frannie opened the lid on hers to a black screen. "Battery's dead."

He opened his laptop. "Mine, too."

Before she could suggest putting off the data hunt portion of their quest, he was plugging his cord into her computer. Two Apple computers for two peas in a pod. She smiled at the thought. "Are you sure?" she asked.

He winked and grinned. "Anything for the soon to be famous writer in my midst."

She studied him, his words feeling sincere, not mocking. "Did you know her, this Molly? It looks like she lived here for..."

"A hundred years. Look at these dates. Wow. She must have been a child when she started at Shell House," Eli said.

They sat in silence staring at her laptop screen which remained black. She shut it. "Let's just deal with what's in front of us before we start digging on the internet."

He slid the cake ingredients into recipe order in front of them. Eli finally got up. "What's with the vault, though? Why have it here?"

Frannie searched her mind for the research she'd done before starting her tour of historic vacation homes. "If I remember correctly, some homes had these double-sided compartments for easy access to pay people—milkmen, coalmen, the grocer, anyone who might collect a debt from a homeowner."

"So it might open from outside?"

She stood, excited.

"And this *Flora* paid off bootleggers using the little compartment?" Eli asked. "Let's go see if there's another side."

They scampered out of the pantry, through the kitchen and onto the terrace. Deciding that the opening must be on the lake side of the house, they snaked around the perimeter, through the gardens, past the garage to the space they thought might line up to the pantry. It was surrounded by shrubs and bushes.

"Be gentle with these heirloom roses, but it's got to be behind them."

They crept along and found the panel, opened it and looked right into the pantry, light spilling in from outside, filling the space where they had just been.

They straightened and leaned against the house. His hand found hers, their fingers braiding together.

After a few minutes of silence, of Frannie trying to put together what had happened that day, a full-blown story came to life in her mind.

"I don't know exactly what we found, but I know there was a party, bootlegged booze, a cook and her cake, and Flora and George and a bust. And a list of names. *A list!* I've been making lists of names for a year now and this is the first time a list has sent me... literally sent me to another time and place and..."

He looked at her. She could feel his gaze like a hug.

"So you'll stay then? To research the story and write, I mean."

Eli's voice startled her. She released his hand and wormed back through the bushes to the pathway they'd taken.

She paced. "I don't know. I can't just write this part of the story because I stumbled on it. Who's going to answer my questions or... I can't just pretend I have a job and that I'm a real writer who—"

He came through the bush and shook a finger at her. "That's it, isn't it? What you didn't say earlier."

"What?"

"You started to think those Babyface.com lists were the extent of what you could do. You started to believe that you were just some name dropper and... those jerks who said you couldn't write... You can't possibly believe them."

She nodded, feeling again like she'd known Eli forever. That *was* it—the disabling source of her depression.

"Well, I haven't read your writing, but I'm quite sure the universe didn't drop this, this... whatever this is, right into your lap in the form of a message in a bottle, hidden compartment, bootlegged champagne bottle and a list of names of people who attended a party ninety-five years ago, just for you to turn away from it."

She crossed her arms. "You're sure, are you?"

"Quite sure."

She pressed her belly. He was right. Everything inside her agreed with him and the first ease she'd felt in ages fell over her. She knew exactly what she was meant to do, at least for as long as it took to piece together what happened at that party and the wondrous people who'd made their way through this home since it was built a hundred years before.

She nodded. "Will you stay for dinner? I want to know everything about the heirloom plantings, too, for the story. Stay so I can talk through this, make a plan..."

He shook his head.

She lifted one arm and then the other and sniffed. "A shower. I need a shower. I must stink, I mean after all..."

A wry grin pulled at his lips.

How stupid of her. She knew nothing of his life.

"Oh, a girlfriend?" Her eyes bugged and she covered her mouth. "A *wife*? Oh my god, I didn't even ask..."

"I don't want dinner."

"Oh."

"I'm sort of in the mood for... cake."

She smiled.

"You know," Eli said. "If we're going to sort through all of this, we might as well make the pineapple upside down cake. It must have meant something to Molly, to the guests..."

And before Frannie could finish agreeing, the two of them stepped into each other's arms, a gentle kiss and tight clasp connecting them. The world seemed to fall away as her insides melted. What on earth had just happened?

She couldn't grasp the ridiculousness of it all, but she didn't need to. For once in her life she was falling into something that inspired her, something that fit her interests and talents. She would ignore the list that came with her firing. She may not have been a good employee, but she knew she was a good writer. For that realization, she would be forever grateful. For the story—Shell House's and hers—she would stay. And she knew Eli would be part of it all. As much as she knew anything, she knew that.

Pineapple Upside Down Cake

Ingredients
Topping:
2 Tablespoons butter

1 cup dark brown sugar, lightly packed

1 (20-oz.) can sliced pineapples rings, drained

Maraschino cherries, about 12

Cake:
2 cups all-purpose flour

1 cup granulated sugar

2 tsp. baking powder

1/2 tsp. salt

1/2 cup whole milk, room temperature

1/2 cup butter, room temperature

2 eggs, separated

1 tsp. vanilla extract

Instructions:
1. Preheat oven to 350 degrees.

2. Place 2 Tablespoons butter in 9" or 10" cast iron skillet and put in oven for a few minutes just until butter is melted. Remove from oven and sprinkle brown sugar evenly over the melted butter.

3. Arrange pineapple rings and maraschino cherries in whatever pattern you like. Set aside while mixing cake portion.

4. Sift together flour, baking powder, and salt. Set aside.

5. In a small bowl, beat egg whites until frothy. In second small bowl, whisk egg yolks lightly. Set both aside.

6. In large mixing bowl, cream the 1/2 cup of butter and granulated sugar until light and fluffy, about 3 minutes, scraping bowl several times. Add egg yolks to the creamed mixture and mix well.

7. Add the flour and milk alternately in three additions, mixing well after each. Add vanilla and mix. Lastly, gently fold in the beaten egg whites.

8. Carefully pour batter over pineapple. Bake for 35 to 45 minutes until toothpick inserted near center comes out clean.

9. After removing cake from oven, immediately run a knife around the sides and then turn cake pan upside down on cake plate. Let pan sit for about a minute to allow all topping to release from pan. Carefully remove pan. There will be some steam! Serve slightly warm or at room temperature.

MOLLY'S MAGIC

Denise Weaver

The guests were due to arrive shortly, and Molly Macauley sensed this couple was different. She could feel it deep in her soul—tingling, twitching, with a sense of finality. Could her dominion have finally come to an end? How long had it been? Was her work and time about to end? She believed it was.

Molly bustled about, putting the finishing touches on the potato-crusted quiche, a sprinkle of fresh thyme and a drizzle of olive oil. How many couples had there been over the decades?

And had it really been decades? Well of course, she'd been there since the house was built in 1920. It was now 2019. Just amazing. And sad. But sweet, too, thinking of all the people she'd met over her 99 years of cooking and cajoling and conniving.

Some couples really stood out in Molly's memory. Her favorite was probably Nick and Josie. She recalled thinking of them as Nicholas and Josephine, wondering what history may have gone before them. The two were so deeply in love, it was obvious to anyone who had even an inkling of what love was or should be. But there were problems.

Over breakfast at the beach house's formal dining area, Molly listened in as Nick bore the bad news. "Josie, I don't think this is going to work. The company is sending me overseas, and to a not-nice place where I certainly can't take you."

Josie's breath catching was audible, even through the door to the gourmet kitchen. "Nick, what are you talking about? What do you mean, I can't go with you?"

"Just that, Josie, my dear. It's not safe for women there. We can't risk it. And I can't ask you to wait for me. I have no idea how long I'll be there—it could be years."

"But, Nick, how could you possibly take the job then? Isn't there some way around this?" Josie sobbed. "I mean, couldn't you ask? No, couldn't you *demand* that they give you another assignment? Surely they'd understand. We're about to be married, for heaven's sake. What are they thinking?"

Nick's voice faltered, then with a deep breath, he laid out the best- and worst-case scenarios, none of them good. "The only viable option is for us to call off the engagement."

Josie gasped. "Can't you find another job? That should be easy enough."

Shaking his head, Nick exhaled and stated quite firmly, "No."

Josie stared at him, shocked at the finality of his statement. She paused, caught her breath, then asked, "How can you be so certain?"

"Because I've exhausted every possible lead, every possible situation. There is nothing available and I'm completely out of luck. You know jobs are difficult to find, and with my skill set being so specific, it's just not possible. And I refuse to have you hanging on, waiting for me for who knows how long, and whether I'll even make it back, ever."

From her perch in the kitchen, Molly had sadly shaken her head. That one required her assistance, of that she'd had no doubt. She could not allow Nick and Josie to suffer that way. She knew with every fiber of her being that they belonged together.

In her inimitable style, she began plotting the magic meal. She entered the dining area and informed the young couple that lunch would be on the beach. "You know, Rehoboth is known as 'America's Summer Capital' for good reason. The sandy beach is divine, the ocean lapping onto shore is mesmerizing, and the salt air has a distinct healing scent. And I make a pretty darn good picnic lunch if I do say so myself."

After Molly's retreat into the kitchen, Nick and Josie agreed that they would have lunch on the beach, put the morning's conversation and issue on hold, just for the day. They'd revisit the problem the next morning but would allow themselves this little luxury.

As Molly sat back and recalled this couple and event, she smiled at the memory of crab salad in lettuce leaves, sliced red-ripe tomatoes and crispy cucumbers, fresh berries on clouds of meringue and whipped cream, and her signature home-baked bread, so soft and fluffy on the inside, crusty on the outside, yeasty flavor oozing with magic. *Molly's magic.*

Upon their return in late afternoon, Josie and Nick each beamed. Catching their breath, they bounded into the kitchen to return the basket. But what they really wanted was to share their excitement with Molly.

"We sat on the beach blanket, sipping the chilled white wine you gave us, enjoying every morsel of food. As we split the last piece of bread, a half-sheet of newspaper bounced along the sand, picked up and tossed about by the wind, and with a quick gust, landed right inside the open basket, on top of the empty containers we'd just put back in. Nick and I laughed at the absurdity of it. I pulled out the paper and began to read a comic strip, laughing, when he hushed me."

Nick jumped in, taking over the story. "I saw something on the back side of that paper as Josie read. I grasped it from her. Oh, Molly, my hands were trembling! I read the ad to myself, then aloud, then again even louder."

Josie couldn't contain herself. "It was a job ad, one ideal for Nick. And it's at home in Philadelphia. This company is opening a branch in Northern Liberties, and Nick is perfect for it."

The storytelling switched back to Nick. "If I can get this job, we can be married. We can stay in Philadelphia and remain near our parents." Nick swung Josie around the kitchen, nearly bumping into Molly. "And we can keep coming back here to this beautiful Shell House, several times a year. It will be wonderful."

Molly recalled the letter she later received from the couple along with a wedding invitation. Nick had been hired, Josie found her dream position working with kids in need, and it was all as if by magic. Molly smiled with a brief nod, bobbing her gray curls.

There were so many people she'd had the privilege of working her magic for through food, to great success and personal satisfaction. A few others really stood out, including the reconciliation of the Wagner sisters after a decade of not speaking to each other.

And from the early years in Shell House, she recalled Flora and George. She had been there when they met. They stood out in her memory for several reasons. It was during prohibition, and the exact day of a bootleg party that Flora called a Summer Soiree, to be held at Shell House. Molly recalled being thankful she was scheduled to be away, attending a rare family reunion. She was nervous about the reunion, hoping against hope that someone had news of her sons. But she was also jittery over the illegal party happening in her domain, even if she wasn't going to be present.

When she delivered coffee to Flora and her girlfriend on the beach that afternoon, George and another man seemed to appear out of nowhere, wrangling an invitation from the girls to that night's party. She could see the charge flowing between George and Flora, even before they were aware themselves, she was sure of it. And it was then that she knew the impetus for the urge she'd had to make a pineapple upside down cake that morning. A few years later she'd discovered notes from the two of them in a little hidey-hole in the pantry that explained their sudden disappearance from Shell House that night. She was certain things had worked out for them; she felt it in her bones.

Oh, and the Harrisons. They were on the precipice of parting as their daughter graduated from college and their son was entering West Point. But Molly's influence, initiated by a beach picnic that included late blooming lilacs, hoagies, and brownies along with a bottle of Prosecco, reminiscent of Mr. & Mrs. Harrison's first date decades before, started the couple on a journey of rediscovery.

Such great memories. Molly was going to miss this interaction, this calling, this gift. But most of all, she was sad and concerned that she didn't know what was going to happen to future guests in need. She fretted over who would fill the void.

The quiche Molly made that day sat in the warming oven. She hoped the potato crust wasn't getting soggy as she awaited the new arrivals. She'd heard the guests check in, rather she heard *a* guest. She knew from the reservation as well as the staff planning meeting that Shell House was expecting a couple that day.

With a tray of coffee, tea, and crumpets, Molly entered the courtyard. Seated near the fountain, Penelope Martin was gazing across the in-ground pool, and out over Silver Lake. Clearing her throat, Molly approached with the welcome tray.

"Excuse me, ma'am. May I serve you some light refreshments to help you settle in here at Shell House?"

Penelope looked at Molly, gave a tender smile, and sighed. "Thank you. Though I don't know if I'll ever be settled again."

Molly felt a nudge from within and sat across from the new arrival. "Ma'am, I don't mean to be forward, but would you like to talk?"

Penelope stared deeply into Molly's eyes, tilting her head left then right before responding. A flicker of emotion passed over her as she recognized something in Molly, something familiar perhaps. "Why yes, I think I do."

As Penelope spoke, Molly leaned forward, catching her breath. She was focusing on Penelope's dimple—the one dimple, not two—just like her older son had. Oh, that was so long ago, yet still vivid in her memory.

"As you are probably aware, my husband and I made our two-week reservations almost ten months ago and were thrilled. We'd heard such good things about Rehoboth with its beautiful beach, great restaurants, and entertainment, and even more complimentary sentiments about this lovely home. It sounded just like the holiday we both needed and seemed a great place to celebrate our tenth anniversary."

She paused, seeming to need a gathering of strength. Molly patiently waited, pouring tea, and setting a plate before her guest.

"Sean, that's my husband, was killed in a mining accident, just six months ago. He was an inspector, and while investigating some damage to an underground shaft, a support beam gave way and..."

Penelope stopped. With trembling hands, she wiped away tears, then took several deep breaths.

"You know," she continued. "I had a feeling, somehow I just knew this was going to happen to him."

There it is. Molly felt the connection. This woman must share her gift. Or at least part of the calling.

"Anyway, here I am. I had forgotten about the reservation until I received the reminder last month. With some deliberation, I decided to come on my own. I know that's what Sean would have wanted. I'm sure he wants me to be happy, to go on with life, to make the most of it. So, I came. Instead of celebrating our tenth I will celebrate the wonderful love and life we had together, even though it was cut short... much too short."

Molly reached out and grasped Penelope's hands. "Oh, my dear, I'm so sorry. Such a sad, sad thing to happen. I'm proud of you though for coming, for making your way, for going on."

Penelope felt oddly comforted by Molly, but her curiosity was piqued. Why would this woman feel pride for someone she didn't know? She thought for a moment, then shrugged it off as an older woman's manner of speech.

As the week progressed, Penelope found herself drawn to Molly's oversized kitchen, fascinated by the sub-zero refrigerators, multiple ovens, and lovely travertine flooring. Even more, however, Penelope was mesmerized by the woman herself.

The two had lively conversations about food choices, cooking and baking preferences, and a shared joy in expressing love through food. Penelope had studied to be a chemist, but after two years in the field, she discovered it was not her calling. She and Sean were already engaged when they decided together that Penelope should follow her heart and she enrolled in the CIA—the Culinary Institute of America.

Having completed the program, and loving every minute of it, Penelope worked as a private chef. She and Sean moved several times with his work, but Penelope was always able to find clients quickly, wherever they lived. Sean joked that with all their moving around, and Penelope's ease of immersing herself wherever they went, perhaps they could pass themselves off as working for the "other CIA."

With Monday approaching, typically Molly's slowest day of the week, she decided the time was right for a picnic basket for Penelope. The difference with this basket, however, was that Molly would accompany her guest on the beach picnic. She had things to say, things to ask, things to answer.

The urge to share her own story with Penelope was nearly overwhelming. Molly didn't understand this compulsion, yet she was sure Penelope would listen.

As always, Molly set about to administer to her guest. Monday at noon, she directed Penelope to the best spot on the beach for their conversation, with the best sightline and where fewer people tended to congregate. She did not want to be interrupted. They unpacked the basket, more a feast than a picnic, and a silence held them close.

While she poured the sangria she'd made with pineapple and strawberries sliced just right, Penelope seemed deep in thought. Molly set out the cheese board and pate, sliced the baguette, and poured dressing over their salads, meticulously arranging everything on the trays they would use as tables.

"My husband, Edgar, was a coal miner from Ireland, working in Wales," Molly began. "A mine collapsed on him, and I was left alone with two sons to provide for and raise. I took work cooking for others. One family offered to bring us with them to America to live in a cottage behind the main house they purchased."

Wide-eyed, Penelope leaned forward not wanting to miss a word. "Go on, please."

"Well, my employer had been duped. There was not a job for him, the house he purchased was dilapidated, and the cottage turned out to be a tiny shed used as a pigsty."

Penelope's hands flew to her mouth as she tried to quell a gasp, absorbing Molly's story.

"Our American dream fizzled. My sons were taken from me and sent to poor farms to earn their keep. I was devastated and desperate. After long months of tedious laundry and cleaning jobs here and there, through family contacts I found a position as a live-in cook for a moderately successful couple in Trenton, New Jersey, before I was later offered the position of head cook here at Shell House."

Her eyebrows furrowed, the younger woman couldn't contain her half sob, half sigh as she leaned in even closer.

"I sometimes had intuitions about the guests. Granny talked of the 'Second Sight,' but I'd never believed it before. There was just no other way to explain how I understood so deeply what others were feeling and experiencing."

Penelope nodded, her lips curving ever so slightly as a smile formed, her eyes brightening with recognition.

"I knew I had to use this gift for good. And I understood that food was the way I could help people."

Penelope started to speak, paused, began again, then stopped.

Molly smiled encouragingly. "Go ahead, dear. You have questions?"

"Well... Don't you think there's a strange similarity between our lives? I mean, being widowed early, and due to mining accidents? That we both love to cook and bake? That we feel that feeding people is our gift, our mission, our *raison d'etre*? And even more, were we meant to meet? To be here together, at this time? Molly, what do you think? Is there some meaning in this?"

Molly reached for Penelope's hand, held it gently between her own two callused palms and peered into her young friend's eyes. "Yes."

"Is that all? Just a simple yes?"

Molly nodded. "In the end, it does come down to a simple yes. We were meant to meet. We have some amazing similarities and common attributes. In short, yes to it all." She paused, gazing over their food. "Penelope, what do you plan to do with the rest of your life? Have you given it much thought during this grieving time?"

Penelope let out a deep sigh. "Unexpected as it may be, I have. I was devasted at the loss of my husband, but somehow, I knew it was coming. I don't know how, but... And there have been a few other instances, like coming here. Deep in my innermost being, I understood that I was meant to come here—that this place, and meeting you, was somehow my calling, my life. You have the same eyes as my mother, as my grandfather, and my great-grandfather. Perhaps we're even related. I have a sneaking suspicion that you're about to help me uncover my purpose and my dream."

Potato-Crusted Quiche

Ingredients:
 5-6 slices bacon
 1 small white or yellow onion, finely diced
 3-4 medium-sized Yukon Gold, sliced thinly
 6 eggs
 1 cup half-and-half

3/4 tsp. salt

1/2 tsp. black pepper, freshly ground

pinch of grated nutmeg

2 Tbsp. chopped fresh parsley

1 cup shredded Gruyere (or Swiss) cheese

Fresh thyme and olive oil to finish, if desired

Instructions:

1. Preheat oven to 400 degrees. Grease a 10-inch pie dish (or a 9-inch deep-dish pie plate).

2. Shingle the potato slices over the bottom and sides of dish. Brush or spray small amount of olive oil over the potatoes, then par-bake for 20 minutes. Set dish aside. Reduce oven temperature to 350 degrees.

3. While crust is baking, fry bacon in skillet until crisp. Drain on paper towels.

4. Reserve 1-2 Tbsp. bacon grease in skillet and cook diced onion over medium heat until soft, about 5 minutes.

5. In a large bowl, whisk together the eggs, half-and-half, and seasonings. Mix in cooked onions and parsley. Crumble bacon into mixture and stir in cheese.

6. Carefully pour mixture into the potato crust and bake at 350 until knife comes out clean when inserted near center of quiche, approximately 35 minutes for 10-inch dish or 45 minutes for 9-inch. Top of quiche should be golden brown.

7. Remove from oven and allow to cool slightly. Top with a sprinkling of fresh thyme leaves and a light drizzle of olive oil, if desired.

Notes:

* Diced ham can be substituted for the bacon. Use butter or olive oil to sauté onions if using ham.

* Adding an additional 1/2 cup shredded cheese over top of custard just before baking makes a richer dish.

* Quiche can be served hot or just slightly warm.

A SEASHELL OF LOVE

Carol Schoenig

Frank was walking sixty feet in the air inspecting newly installed beams when his boss waved him down.

"Aren't you from Rehoboth Beach?"

Frank frowned. He didn't want to think about the past. "Yeah, why?"

"The town hired our firm to restore an old structure. Since you're from the area, I thought you'd be a good fit for general contractor."

Frank's breathing slowed and his heart hurt, mentally replaying the past. "Restoration... what building?"

"Shell House."

A cacophony of emotions, happy and sad, engulfed him as he remembered Diana Sinclair. They'd grown up together. When they'd been in their teens, he thought they were in love. Part of him wanted to go back and see his hometown, but the memory of her rejection still stung.

"What do you think? Are you interested in the project?"

Frank rubbed the back of his neck; he hadn't been back since his mom died years ago. Too many painful reminders outweighed the good times. But then again, going back might help him finally exorcise the memories and move on, and the thought of restoring Shell House excited him. "Yeah, I'll do it. Might do me good to revisit my roots."

The first day on the project, Frank gazed at Shell House. His heart fluttered as he reflected on the last summer he and Diana spent together, the summer of her sixteenth birthday. They went for a walk as the sound of waves crashed with urgency. Their need for each other intensified, leading to their first sexual encounter.

It was then that he knew he wanted to spend his life with Diana. He wanted her to know how much she meant to him, but he didn't have a job yet and couldn't afford an engagement ring.

The end of summer was nearing, and he hadn't thought of a way to tell her he wanted them to be together forever. They'd been searching for shells, and he'd found a heart-shaped one. This he hoped she'd accept until he could buy her a ring.

He'd run to where she was kneeling and knelt beside her. "Close your eyes and open your hands."

When she complied, he put the heart-shaped item in her hands. "You can open your eyes."

She'd gasped. "It's lovely."

His words were rushed. "You hold my heart in your hands. Will you marry me after you graduate from high school? In the meantime, I'll work and save money."

Diana gazed into his eyes. "I love you so much," she'd told him.

The memories dissolved like their youthful plans. Instead of staying in touch, Diana had returned his letters and rejected his phone calls. That had been twelve years ago, but the wound still seeped.

Frank stepped on something hard and stooped to pick it up. A six-inch lion's paw shell had washed up on the shore. It reminded him of the heart-shaped seashell. On a whim, he withdrew a permanent marker from his pocket and wrote, "Diana, you still hold my heart in your hands. Love, Frank." He was about to throw the shell into the sea when a crewman called to him. He shoved it in his pocket and went to work. When he passed his truck, he tossed the shell into his toolbox.

It was an overcast day, but Diana wanted to go to the construction site. The crew had been working for three weeks. She'd waited to visit to give them time to get things started. She couldn't wait any longer.

The radio announcer was talking about pending tropical storms on the Atlantic side of Florida. Hurricane Igor was heading toward New Jersey. She hoped it would bypass Delaware.

Dark clouds hung low, and the air was hot and ominous. Early that morning, the weather forecaster tracking Igor had warned that a shift of cold air could change the path of the storm, sending it into the Delaware Bay and Rehoboth Beach.

As she drove through town, people were busy boarding up shop windows. Arriving at the construction site, she saw men hustling to get tarps on the roof. Several others carried plywood to board up the windows that remained.

As she passed the large garden fountain, a memory of eating an ice cream cone and rinsing her hands in the fountain brought a smile to her face. The wind picked up speed and the blowing sand stung her legs and arms. Debris was flying in the air and rolling around on the ground.

The sound of shingles being ripped from the roof prompted her to look up. She struggled to keep her balance against the powerful gusts of wind. Sand blew in her face and eyes. Reaching blindly for something to hold on to, she tripped and fell backward.

There was a grunt, and then a man whispered, "It can't be."

The voice sounded vaguely familiar, but she couldn't see. "There's sand in my eyes."

"Stay still," the voice said. "Someone get me an eyewash kit."

She heard men running and vehicle doors slamming. The man's voice made her think of her childhood friend Frank, but this voice was deeper and more confident. And what would Frank be doing here?

"Here you go, boss."

"Thanks, Jim, go on home to your family. We can't work until this passes."

It can't be my Frank. Diana's heart raced. *Not my Frank,* she corrected herself. He hadn't been hers in more than a decade.

Her eyes were stinging and watering, and she couldn't open them. She lifted her hand toward her face.

"Don't rub your eyes. I'm going to sit you up so I can flush them out. Stay still."

Diana wondered if he could feel the tension in her body. Along with the pain and discomfort in her eyes, a myriad of emotions churned, twisting and turning as crazily as the debris along the shore.

"Is it one or both eyes?" he asked.

"Both. Do you think it will cause permanent damage?"

"Trust me. I'm doing all I can to get the sand out. I know it's hard, but try to relax."

The way he said, "Trust me," confirmed that it was indeed her Frank. He had told her to trust him many times when they were kids. It had always been delivered with an air of authority that left her feeling she had no other option. Diana gulped.

When he rested her against his bent knee, his arm came around her head, and with his thumb, he opened her left eye and poured water into it. Diana hated feeling dependent and started to cry.

"Try to open your eyes slowly."

She blinked several times. They still burned and felt gritty. His face was a blur as she heard herself whisper, "Frank White."

"The one and only," he drawled.

Through the blur of sand-induced tears, she glimpsed his silvery-blue eyes and sun-streaked brown hair. With his face filled out, he had a rugged, masculine appearance. The last time she'd seen him, he'd been a skinny teenager with blond hair.

He had gone from cute to handsome and virile, and he took her breath away.

"Let me help you up," he said as a cold rain fell. He stood and helped her to her feet, putting his arm around her waist to anchor her against the driving wind. He led her to the porch. "Get in the house," he ordered. "I need to get a few things from my truck."

Diana gripped the railing to steady herself. She was about to open the door when she felt his fingers on the small of her back. Frank had reached around her to open it for her. The wind pushed them into the quaint entrance. Diana's breath caught at the differences in the house. Cracks in the walls had been patched, smoothed, and painted in the central area. One wall had been removed, providing a panoramic view of the sea.

She'd had a brief glimpse of the outside before she'd been blinded. In her mind, she imagined the trim on the outside, freshly painted and underscoring its Victorian charm. She turned in a slow circle, taking in all she could see.

Turning to talk to him, she smelled his coffee breath and musk cologne. "Thank you for helping me."

"Not a problem. I'd do the same for anyone."

His words stung, letting her know she wasn't special to him. The pain of rejection resurfaced and made her angry.

The thunk of debris hitting the house and something slamming startled her. It was nothing compared to the uneasiness of being stuck in the house with Frank while so much time and hurt hung between them.

He was fiddling around with a radio, adjusting the station dial. *"We urge people to..."* a crackle came. *"Winds are 90 mph, and heavy rain is expected through..."* More static and crackling. *"Stay tuned for updates as Igor progresses."*

Frank busied himself with the radio. Anything to keep himself from grabbing her and... and what? Damn, it was as if she hadn't disappeared from his life. And the intervening twelve years hadn't happened. He blinked and turned his back to her, remembering all the unopened and unread letters she'd returned. He shrugged. For one moment, he let himself think about what their life might be like if she had read his letters and believed in his promises of love and a future. For a fleeting moment, he wished they could rekindle their friendship.

"There's coffee in the thermos, and I think a few donuts left from the morning. It sounds like we'll be stuck here for a while." His voice held a matter-of-fact tone.

"I'm not staying here with you."

Her voice sounded like a squawking crow. He turned and stared at her for a moment, wondering what he had done to make her dislike him so much. She hadn't even bothered to send him a Dear John letter. He'd written her at least a dozen letters she hadn't bothered to open before returning.

"I don't know what has your drawers in a bunch, but I don't relish the idea either. However, it's too dangerous to go outside, so we're stuck with each other." He glared at her then Diana turned and walked to the settee at the end of the hall.

Frank watched her walk away. He rubbed the bridge of his nose. Several hours passed, and the rain worsened. He kept himself busy and avoided her by looking for signs of water leaks.

"What brings you back to Rehoboth after twelve years?" he asked finally.

"I'm working with the townspeople to preserve Shell House."

"I thought maybe you finally came looking for me," he said, wishing it was the truth.

"Don't flatter yourself. I came to bury the past."

The house creaked as gale-force winds hammered at it. The lights flickered... and then they went out. A small window in the kitchen was the only source of light.

Frank walked into the kitchen and pulled two flashlights out of his toolbox. He held a larger flashlight, which lit most of the room. He handed her the smaller one.

Timidly, she said, "I could use that coffee and donut now."

"Help yourself."

"Can I pour a cup for you?"

He gave her a nod.

They both took a seat at the small round table. Without air-conditioning, the house was hot and made him feel claustrophobic. The silence, like a ghostly slice of emptiness, was eerie.

"I take it you're the general contractor?"

"Correct. What about you? What are you doing these days?"

"I'm a real estate attorney." Her words had an uncertain edge.

He felt a surge of pride at her success and wondered if she'd have been this successful if they'd married.

"Too busy to write to me and tell me you wanted a career instead of marriage? Or did your parents finally convince you I wasn't good enough for you?" Just the mention of her parents caused an acidic taste in his mouth.

Diana glared at him. She wanted to defend her parents, but she couldn't. She had argued with her mother about falling in love with Frank. Diana shivered, remembering the argument.

"You cold?" he asked.

"No."

"I have some blankets if you're cold. I've been camping out here to keep looters away."

Diana giggled.

"What's so funny?"

"I was just remembering the time when we camped outside. I think we were ten years old. You couldn't get the tent to stay up."

Frank let out a laugh. He remembered it, too. He'd been trying to impress her and had failed miserably.

They were talking, and he didn't want it to end. "Let's go into the living room. It's more comfortable in there." A whiff of her floral perfume sent a message of wanting to his groin. "What prompted you to orchestrate the restoration of Shell House?"

"Sentimentality, I guess."

Her gaze was like a soft caress.

She swallowed. "You know my parents passed away."

"I'm sorry. I didn't know."

"How could you? You disappeared from the face of the earth." Sarcasm had seeped into her voice.

"What did you expect me to do when your mom told me you never wanted to talk to me again?" He paused. "She said you'd found someone at college and that you deserved a better life than I could give you."

"You broke my heart. One minute you're telling me we'll get married, and then the next you disappear. No explanation, no goodbye."

Frank gazed at her. The pain of betrayal was all too familiar. He needed to know why she'd rejected him... "Are you married?"

"No," she answered with an emphatic tone.

Her answer tugged on his heart.

"What about you?" she asked.

"Nope. I travel too much." Frank cleared his throat.

Diana sat down on the sofa, then pulled her knees into her chest, and hugged them.

Frank leaned against a wall. The brush of tree limbs hitting the house and rain pouring were the only sounds. The tension within the parlor wasn't from the storm outside; it was from the storm within.

"So, tell me, what's your life like now?" He pushed off the wall and sat down opposite her on the sofa.

"I work a lot. I travel."

Frank wondered if her travels included the places they had discussed seeing together. He shook his head. They had been dreamers and romantics as teens. Back then, they'd never considered they wouldn't be together. Maybe it had been puppy love. That's how his mom had described it. She'd said it would pass when he found someone new. It hadn't felt that way then, and he believed she'd loved him too.

He couldn't stand the not knowing. He had to ask. "So, what happened? Why did you return my letters?"

Diana raised her head. "I returned *your* letters? How dare you? You tell me you love me and want to marry me...." Her voice broke. "Then you return *my* letters."

"How could I return something I never received?"

They stared at each other, eyes flashing with skepticism.

Frank rubbed his chin. Nothing about this was making sense. If she'd sent letters to him, who had sent them back? His letters had come back, and someone had penned, "return to sender." The bigger question was, did it matter today, at this point in their lives?

Diana curled up on the sofa and fell asleep. He grabbed the blanket from the back of the couch and covered her.

Diana woke with a headache and a crick in her neck, still wondering why he claimed he hadn't received her letters. She felt like she needed to prove something to him.

As she crawled out from under the blanket, she lost her balance.

"What are you doing?" a deep, raspy voice asked.

"I'm sorry, I tripped. Go back to sleep." She stepped carefully. "I'll be back."

"Hmm." He laid his head back down.

As Diana walked away, he heard movement.

Why is she leaving when we have unfinished business? Losing her again with no answers would forever leave a hole in his heart. "Where the hell do you think you're going?" His long strides brought him within inches of her face.

"Out to my car. The letters I sent you are in the trunk."

When she opened the door, the sun was coming out. The air felt warm. She opened her trunk and grabbed an old shoebox.

When she returned, she saw Frank holding a pile of letters wrapped with a length of twine. "Here are the ones you returned to me." He sighed. "I hadn't gotten around to burying them yet."

A lump formed in her throat. With shaking hands, she held the box out to Frank. It slipped from her fingers, and the letters and heart-shaped shell landed on the floor.

Frank knelt and picked up the pink envelopes with hearts drawn on them... and the shell. "I remember when I gave this to you," he said, fingering the delicate ridges. "It was at the end of the summer, when I asked you to marry me." Inspecting one of the envelopes, he saw "return to sender," written next to the address.

"Why did you? I already gave you my virginity. You didn't need to ask me to marry you."

"Because I loved you."

Diana noticed Frank's brow crease and a puzzled expression take up residence on his face. "What's wrong?"

Frank was staring at the pink envelopes. He placed them side by side on the table next to his letters in plain white envelopes. "Yours have postmarks... but mine..." She could see a thousand thoughts wash through his mind, each one of them etched on his face. "Mine were apparently never mailed."

Diana grabbed one of the white envelopes. She didn't understand.

Frank stood in shock, comparing details of the pink and white letters. He pointed to the words "return to sender" on each stack. The handwriting was identical. "I think this is my mother's doing."

Everything had gone still, and an eerie silence settled around them. "But why?"

"She thought we were too young... that it was puppy love."

Diana's chin quivered as she thought of all the wasted years.

He tossed his letters on the table. "Diana, I'm sorry. I had no idea. Please forgive me."

Diana thought about the previous night when they had been reliving memories; it felt as if they'd never been apart. She wondered if they could bridge the gap after all these years of lies and distrust.

"I forgive you, but can you forgive me? We both should've trusted our feelings."

Diana stood staring at the letters.

Frank closed the space between them, not knowing what to say. All that time, he had thought Diana hadn't loved him. He blinked as he realized she had probably suffered beneath the same mistaken ideas.

Frank lightly caressed her back. She rested her head against his shoulder. "May I read this letter?"

Her head nodded against him.

It felt like Christmas. Frank eagerly opened the envelope and read aloud:

My dear Frank, I think about you every day. I can't wait for us to be together. I carry your heart with me everywhere I go. It's under my pillow at night when I sleep.

Frank tilted her face up. They gazed into the depths of each other's eyes.

Diana wrapped her arms around his waist, her slim body pressed tight against his. He lowered his head slightly, and she inched closer. When their lips touched, it was tentative and sweet. Excitement grew. The months and years fell away. When she opened her mouth, all the love inside his soul flowed into his kiss.

Frank grabbed his toolbox from the kitchen. He opened it and pulled out the tiger paw seashell. "I was going to throw it in the ocean. I'm glad I didn't. This is for you."

Diana read the inscription.

When she glanced up at him, she saw love in his eyes. Shell House had brought them together. Again.

LOVE DAWNS AT SHELL HOUSE

Cindy Moldovan

"They can't do that!" Lacey stared at her mother in disbelief.

"Oh honey, they can and will tear down that beautiful home. Huge machinery pulled up to the property yesterday. I think they're waiting for some permits."

"Who are *they*? And why is no one in town doing anything about it?" Lacey pulled out her cell phone and pressed the call button.

"Go away," said the voice on the other end, then promptly hung up.

"Does she ever get up before ten?" Lacey grumbled.

"Your dad and I just found out yesterday, and only because he's chief of police. The demolition company hired a police escort into town due to the size of the equipment." Mrs. Feeney shook her head, baffled at someone's decision to tear down the hundred-year-old historic Shell House.

Lacey's call connected again. "You need to drive to Rehoboth Beach, Sondra. Get up right now and do it. I'll tell you why as soon as you get on the road."

Lacey disconnected the call.

"I'm going to Dad's office. This is insanity. Just a year ago, the property was listed at an asking price of almost fifteen million dollars."

"Maybe the ladies at my bridge club know about it," her mother replied.

Lacey pushed off the barstool and raced upstairs. "I leave for one year, and all hell breaks loose."

"I don't know why you had to go away, Lacey. Beebe Healthcare needs nurses."

"I have to leave the nest at some point." Lacey ran back downstairs and sat to lace up her tennis shoes. "Plus, I like Pittsburgh."

"Where's the coffee, pooch?"

Snaps barked as the front door creaked open then slammed shut.

"Oh my god. She lives!" Lacey said as Sondra walked into the kitchen and pushed back her oversized sunglasses on her head.

"Barely." Sondra gave Mrs. Feeney a peck on her cheek. "You dropped a pin with directions in your text as if my parents' house is not right down the street from here."

"Here's a cuppa." Mrs. Feeney poured the hot liquid into a tumbler. "Have a good day, girls. Call me when you figure out what's going on."

Mrs. Feeney clipped the leash to Snaps's collar and took off for a walk on the beach.

"What's that all about?" Sondra's short Afro was flat on one side, her dark skin a contrast against the white T-shirt dress she wore.

"Your hair," Lacey giggled as she air-drew a halo around her head.

"Yeah. Have you seen yours? That ponytail is barely hanging on." Sondra copied the air-halo.

"Late night, huh?" Lacey walked to the kitchen sink and stared at the beach through the large kitchen window.

"So, what happened after I left The Spot last night?" Sondra asked.

"Not much at all," Lacey replied. "Quite forgettable. On the other hand, that guy took up your entire evening. He was so into you."

"Good try, but you're not going to deflect my inquisition. C'mon, the chemistry between you and that delicious man... Try again, but this time add all the gooey details." Sondra pinned her friend with a gaze.

"He was... good! Awesome! Great!" Lacey blushed as she washed out her cup and avoided eye contact with her friend.

"Oh my god. You did not..."

"No! No, goofy. Well, not yet. He is a kisser like none other. I honestly had to hang on to my teeny tiny panties."

Lacey laughed at Sondra's shocked expression.

"Trust me—he is definitely skilled," Lacey added.

"How come that never happens to me? And if it does happen, it's never by someone as blasted gorgeous as beach boy."

"Don't give me that BS. I could get drunk from all the free drinks we get when I go out with you. Men literally line up to send you a cocktail just for a chance to get a word in that might lead to a date."

Sondra snagged a donut from under the cake dome on the counter. "Your mysterious guy, oh dear god—he has a serious tan and perfect profile. Yes, I checked him out without him knowing. He does have the beach-bum vibe going on, but in a classy way."

"Hmm, well... I was too busy with the kiss to notice his tan." Lacey led the way through the front door and down the windy path to the street.

"Liar." Sondra's shoulder bumped into Lacey.

"Fine, I did notice, okay!" Lacey laughed as she skirted around the petunias growing in the front yard.

"Wait. I thought we were walking on the beach." Sondra paused.

"C'mon. Let's go to Shell House. Unfortunately, someone's tearing it down."

"What!" Sondra squealed. "Wait, that's a joke."

"Nope. A bad rumor, I hope. That's what Mom heard from Dad who heard it from the station where the demolition company got police-escorted into town with huge equipment to bash down Shell House," Lacey said all in one long breath.

"God-a-mighty!" Sondra's long legs ate up the last few blocks to the front door of the house.

"We grew up playing around the courtyard and swam in the pool." Lacey stared through the front door at the home that was now vacant.

"Molly was always so nice. She made the best homemade strawberry ice cream." Sondra stepped gingerly into the foyer.

Their voices echoed through the empty space. The girls walked through the living room, then the dining room—a pause here and there, each lost in their own thoughts.

"I remember this kitchen. I love the renovations." Lacey ran her hands across the cold, gray granite countertop. She stopped at the white industrial ceramic sink and pushed up the water faucet.

"The water must be turned off." Then, with a deep inhale, Lacey stepped back as the reality of the impending demolition gave her pause.

"Everything is still perfect inside. Like the home is waiting for new owners to arrive." Sondra fisted her hands on her hips.

"We're going to find out what's going on and fight like bloody hell to stop it! This house has life. It's survived for a hundred years." Lacey led the way out of the kitchen and up the wooden stairs. Her hands lovingly gripped the white handrails as she took the stairs two at a time.

She stopped at the primary bedroom. With a soft push, the door opened.

"This room is perfect. On one side, you can see Rehoboth Beach, and on the other side is Silver Lake." Lacey padded across the hardwood floor and stopped at the window that faced the beach.

"I'm taking photos," Sondra said. "Proof that this house is gorgeous and historic. It needs to be preserved." She snapped pictures from different angles in the vacant room.

"Good idea." Lacey pulled her phone from the pocket of her skinny jeans. At the door of the nursery, she said, "Look at this room—isn't it just perfect for babies?"

"Sure," Sondra smirked. "As long as they're not mine."

"Oh, my god. Look who's at the beach." Lacey snapped a photo of the man looking back at her.

Sondra joined her friend at the window. "Your mysterious beach bum."

The man ran up the rickety wooden steps that led from the beach to Shell House. He stopped to talk to the workers who were poring over paperwork. They spoke and glanced at the women peering through the nursery window.

"That man is the best damn kisser in the world. I can vouch for that," Lacey said. She touched her lips, a smile on her face.

"Probably works with the demolition crew," Sondra guessed.

"Hmm... agreed. Something laborious."

"Maybe like filling the dumpsters."

"Nah—I think more like driving one of the heavy machines." Lacey pivoted on her heels and snapped more photos.

"Well, he's gawking at the property as much as we are. It's hard not to be impressed at this house."

"I could give him a private tour," Lacey giggled. "And lay some sweet kisses along his neck."

"Oh yes," Sondra laughed. "You got it really bad, my friend."

Lacey rolled her eyes and rounded the corner in the hallway and slammed into a chiseled hard body. She came to a solid stop, the air momentarily knocked from her lungs.

"You're trespassing." His steely-blue eyes stared into Lacey's dark brown ones.

"So are you!" she replied.

"You need to leave now. This is private property." The man strode down the hallway and slammed the bedroom doors shut.

"Really?" Sondra shouted. "Who in the hell do you think you are?"

"I'm working, and you are trespassing," he replied.

"Don't be such an ass. You're just determined to smash this gorgeous property, but we won't have it." Lacey jutted her chin in defiance.

He didn't respond. His long legs took the stairs two at a time and headed outside again.

"You were a lot nicer last night," Lacey yelled after him.

He stopped mid-stride and swung back around. "Brice. The name is Brice."

"That's better. I'm La—"

"Lacey," he said and trotted back toward the group of men.

"Well, well—the first lover's quarrel," Sondra teased her friend as they walked down the stairs.

"With that nasty attitude, he's not getting lucky with this girl," Lacey fumed. "We're not leaving either. Let's take photos of the pool, garden, and tennis court."

There was a shuffle at the back door that led to the beach. "Ladies, I'm the foreman on this project. I'm afraid you'll need to leave."

"We're not going anywhere, and you can tell your little worker person that too. We are heading to the courthouse to get a cease-and-desist!" Lacey said.

"You'll need an injunction order if you want to stop the demolition, lady. And it's way too late for that," the foreman replied.

"It will only take a few minutes," Lacey said. "My father is the chief of police."

"And my dad is the judge," Sondra chimed in.

"The owner has all the necessary paperwork," the foreman responded. "It's a done deal."

"Coward. Who and where is the owner?" Lacey squinted, spoiling for a fight.

"That would be Brice." The foreman pointed at the beach bum.

"Come again? Is this a joke?" Sondra's eyes went wide. "That beach bum is the owner of Shell House?"

"Brice McDougal could buy half of your town without missing the money." The foreman hooked his thumbs in the pockets of his jeans.

"Okay, now we're more than curious." Lacey dangled her sunglasses between her fingers.

"You're kidding, right?" The foreman shifted his weight.

Sondra leaned in for the scoop. "Curious minds need to know."

"He's the son of one of the most successful commercial real estate developers in California."

"Hot damn! Brice McDougal!" Sondra googled the real estate mogul.

Lacey was staring at the back of Brice's head as he conversed with the other men. His tall form was easy to spot—light brown, wind-blown hair with wisps of blondish curls at the ends. She bit her lip as she thought about the previous night and how her head leaned back into his arms when he kissed her. She remembered how his muscles flexed at her touch, and the low growl he made as she nibbled at the corner of his lower lip.

"Thanks for the drink," he'd said as he ended the kiss.

"A welcome-to-town kind of drink. We do it for newcomers and really hot guys passing through." Her voice sounded breathy to her ears. She'd cautioned herself to keep the conversation easy as they had just met.

"Do they all get a welcome kiss?" He stared intently back at her face.

"No," she whispered.

"You are gorgeous." He pulled back as Lacey tried to step away.

"Thank you." She playfully patted her short red hair.

Lacey snapped back to the situation at hand as Sondra grasped her arm.

"Come on," her friend said. "We've no time to waste."

The girls walked across the backyard and around the swimming pool. Finally, they exited the property through the side gate.

"Lacey," Brice said from the front of the three-car garage.

"Back off, mister," Sondra said. "We're heading to the courthouse to stop this nonsense."

"Give me a minute," Lacey told her friend.

"See you downtown then." Sondra took off down the street.

"Do you have any idea what you are about to do to this gorgeous house? How much it means to the people of this town? The age of the property—care and cost it has taken over the many years to upkeep this house?" Lacey crossed her arms. She looked up at Brice with sincerity in her eyes.

"I suppose in my haste to acquire the property, I failed to realize its historical value or emotional attachment."

"Please don't do this. I know it sounds childish, and you probably won't consider my opinions, but this home has been here for generations."

"Why does it mean so much to you?"

"This house means a lot to many people, and for different reasons. For me, it is the perfect home—somewhere to walk by and gaze at its splendor, or the excitement when one is invited to attend a party, or as a child, to swim in the pool. News of the demolition has spread around the town. We're all in shock."

"Excuse me." Brice touched her forearm then stepped away. "Guys. Hold off. Take a break and come back in a couple of hours," she heard him instruct the demolition crew. Turning back to her, he asked, "Would you have lunch with me? And maybe we could drive around town. I'd like to see it from your perspective."

"Yes." She nodded, relieved to buy the house at least a few more hours of life. Reaching for her cell, she sent a quick text to Sondra.

Brice led her to a black Porsche SUV.

Lacey slid onto the leather seat.

"Allow me." He leaned around her and buckled her seat belt.

Lacey breathed in, deep and slow—sea mist and lemongrass with a touch of cinnamon.

He pulled away just as Lacey opened her eyes.

"Peaches with drops of honey." He smiled.

Lacey laughed. "We're both guilty. I did the same."

The vehicle pulled onto the street. Lacey was busy texting but pointed Brice in the direction of *Chez la Mer*.

"This is a nice place," Brice observed. "Quite a crowd, too." He opened her door, and Lacey exited the vehicle.

The noisy chatter quieted as they approached the front entry.

Sondra intercepted the two just under the red awning. "What took you so long? Everyone's headed this way."

"You invited the town to our lunch?" Brice asked, looking at Lacey.

"Not everyone—just those over the age of sixty-five. We want you to hear people's memories of Shell House," she explained.

Brice ogled the growing crowd. "Will I walk out of here alive?"

"That depends," Sondra smiled.

Brice looked worried, so Lacey hooked her arms through his and led him to the outdoor patio.

"Brice, meet Mrs. Morgan—she was the nanny for many years at Shell House."

"Hello, young man." Mrs. Morgan leaned onto her Rollator walker.

"How do you do, ma'am?" He extended his hand.

Mrs. Morgan graciously accepted.

He listened to her story of her thirty years of service at Shell House.

"Next is Mr. Jonas Bunting," Lacey introduced.

"My father insured the vehicles of Shell House for over forty years."

Brice listened intently to all the stories regarding Shell House.

"Mr. Connor owns antique stores all over the Northeast," Lacey said.

Mr. Connor sized up Brice then pulled himself up to his full height. "My father opened the first shop right here on Main Street over a hundred years ago." His voice was strong and clear. "He worked long and hard to find furnishings just perfect for that house. It took him many years."

"I appointed an antique dealer from New York to take special care of the furniture," Brice replied. "I can assure you that every piece was handled with care."

The introductions and stories went on until finally, Lacey and Sondra settled down with Brice at one of the tables to order a late lunch.

A month later, Lacey gazed toward the horizon, a smile touching her lips—soon, that smile turned to a cheeky grin, then a light giggle bubbled from deep within her soul and burst into laughter. Her laugh hung in the air and mingled with sea mist—the jubilant sound echoing around the small dunes, then settling between white grains of sand.

Lacey let the water lap against her ankles. The sun would be rising above the Atlantic Ocean soon.

"I am in love," she whispered. Her face turned to the inky sky. "For the first time—this feeling, it is total and complete."

Cool waters rippled gently onto shore as the horizon shifted from dark blue to creamy almond, then a delicate pink laced with light yellow streamers.

"This is my time," Lacey said louder. She splashed around the water and whistled out of tune to a small school of sandpipers as they scurried around the beach in search of crustaceans and mollusks.

Water splattered as she took off in an easy run toward Shell House.

Brice stood at the property's back gate as she ran up the wooden steps. "It's done."

Lacey stopped in front of him and cupped his face in her hands. "You won't regret this. I promise."

"You convinced me. The property is more valuable. This house belongs to the town and the people who love it most."

"You'll be our newest hero." Lacey squinted. "Don't let that go to your head."

"We'll turn Shell House into a meeting place—a space for everyone who loves her most," Brice said. He grasped Lacey's hands in his. "It will be opened for public tours, intimate parties, and special gatherings. Shell House will carry on for generations to come."

With fingers intertwined, Brice led Lacey to the front door then ushered her inside.

Lacey's breath caught. She stared at the teal brocade curtain draping the window below the staircase. A handsome Louis XVI two-drawer chest stood below.

Brice guided Lacey to the living room.

"How did you locate all the original furniture?" she whispered in amazement.

"I enlisted the help of Mr. Connor." He grinned, pleased with himself.

"That must've been a work of epic proportion."

Brice knelt in front of Lacey, grasping her hands firmly. "Will you do me the honor of becoming my wife?"

She nodded. "Yes, yes."

Brice slowly exhaled. "We haven't known each other long, but I know that I love you." He pulled her in for a soft kiss.

Lacey pulled back and eyed Brice. "But how did Mr. Connor—"

"He told me not to be a fool, twice." Brice laughed at Lacey's expression.

"What?" she giggled.

"I asked him to sell me back the furniture, and he made a hearty profit."

"Mr. Connor bought the furniture?" Lacey asked. "Why?"

"He couldn't stop the demolition, so he decided to put some of the furnishings in his own house. Oh, and he told me to propose to you before his son did."

Lacey threw her head back and laughed.

"What's so funny?"

"Mr. Connor's son is five years old."

"What? How can that be?"

"He may be seventy," Lacey explained, "but his wife is thirty-five."

"That son-of-a-gun."

"Hey, you did two brilliant things," Lacey said. "You saved Shell House and proposed to me. Win, win."

"I couldn't agree more." Brice pulled Lacey into his arms.

She reached into her pocket for her phone. "I want to share the news with Sondra."

"She already knows." Brice's smile grew wider. "She's planning your engagement party with all your friends—right here at Shell House."

Lacey stared at Brice.

"You wanted the house to become a meeting place. Our engagement party will be its first new event."

"You were that sure I would say yes?"

"I took a chance, held my breath—said at least a dozen Hail Mary's, spoke to your parents—I was just hoping that you'd at least give me the chance of a proper date."

"Fast work," Lacey said in amazement.

"I'm gifting the house to the town of Rehoboth Beach. You and Sondra will be executors of the estate and with full control of the property."

"Brice!" Lacey's eyes misted.

He lifted her easily against his body and swung her up in his arms. "Let's take a walk to celebrate," he suggested. "Then we can make our own memories at Shell House."

Thanks for saying "Hello" Tony Morley 8/20/22

SAY HELLO TO HENRY

Amy Morley & Michael Morley

I could smell my wife's *frutti di mare* permeating through the kitchen window of our beach rental, lingering above the sand path where I stood near the bluff overlooking the Atlantic Ocean. The aroma of shrimp, little-neck clams, and peppery *arrabiata* sauce mixed with the salty sea breeze and wafted at high tide this late July afternoon.

I turned and made my way back to one of Jack Lingo's notorious Rehoboth Beach rentals known by the tourists as "The Upside-Down House" which sat right-side up at 1 Penn Street. I picked up my pace and thanked the Lord Almighty that I not only married an Italian, but an Italian whose chosen occupation was that of a chef.

Standing on the edge of the bluff a warm breeze gently pillowed my face. I glanced back at the seagulls and stopped, taking in every moment of this vacation.

As my head turned toward the shore it wasn't a seagull that distracted me. Something else caught my eye, and for whatever reason I was drawn to it and couldn't move, as though the Delaware sand had suddenly turned to quicksand locking my feet. I could still smell the *frutti di mare*, and if one thing ignites my wife's pretty Italian temper it is when her food is not served hot. "Let's not

181

stand on ceremony, grab a plate and eat," was her signature phrase (though I secretly knew she stole it from one of those "*Real Housewives*").

As much as I wanted to keep walking toward our beach rental and my wife of nine years, I couldn't peel my eyes away from a different family. My own consisted of just my wife Angela, and it had been that way for nearly a decade.

Before she came into my life, my grandfather, "Pop" Murray Sr., also my namesake, was my only family. He passed away twelve years ago, a week shy of Christmas. My parents were, and still are, around and enjoying their retirement in West Palm Beach. They worked hard their entire lives in the airline industry to give me the best of everything. Yet privilege often comes with a price. I wanted for nothing throughout my childhood, except for maybe them. It was my pop who raised me, and he's the man I considered to be my dad. That's just a fact. His son is my biological father, but I don't harbor any negative feelings about how I grew up. Dad told me he often has regrets missing out on being my father. When Pop died, we bonded through grief. This brought us closer, but he feels more like a brother to me, or a close cousin. Pop gave me the best upbringing I could ever imagine. He showed me what it feels like to be home.

As a WWII veteran, Pop had traveled the world by plane, bus, and submarine all before the age of twenty-one. Yet he considered the simplicity which embodied the coastal town of Rehoboth Beach to be his favorite place in the entire world. Guilt forced my parents to take most of their vacation days in the summer months so they could get to know me. Even so, Pop would steal me away to Rehoboth for two whole weeks, just the two of us. The moment we cruised onto Coastal Highway, Pop would roll down the windows of his Cutlass Supreme, turn to me and say, "We are finally home."

Our vacations continued every summer throughout my childhood, and into my adulthood. But they came to an abrupt stop the summer before he passed when his doctor deemed him too sick to travel. Old age had taken a toll with the various ailments expected of living out the twilight years. But it was stage-four pancreatic cancer that took him quickly. He spent his final weeks in hospice at the VA Hospital in Aspinwall.

On his last day he told me what he believed was the secret to life. He said, "If you close your eyes and listen to the ocean, it will always have something to say." For years I tried to listen to the ocean. It never had anything to say to me.

With Pop gone and my parents in Florida, there was nothing left to keep me in Pittsburgh... until four months later when I met Angela. I reluctantly agreed to a blind date with my co-worker's cousin who was new in town. She and I were supposed to meet at the Istituto Mondo Italiano's community cooking class for a night of "*Pastina and Panna Cotta*." My date either had second thoughts, or got lost in the city, because she never showed up, but it all worked out in the end. Not only did I upgrade my cooking skills from microwavable mug meals and instant chocolate pudding to homemade, from scratch dinners, but that was also the night I met Angela, the chef who led the class. It was at that moment when my second life began.

Because I didn't grow up in a large family, I tend to notice them more than the average person. I thought Angela had a large (and loud) family, but the one vacationing next door now rivals hers. Multiple generations of lookalike cousins, aunts, uncles, brothers, and sisters were running around the top of the bluff and down the slope toward the toe, seemingly taunting the waves still at high tide. Plumes of smoke billowed from the patio grill. A man stacking chicken drumsticks onto a platter indicated that dinner would be served momentarily.

There was one specific individual from this family, presumably the patriarch, who stood out from the rest. It wasn't so much how he interacted, because he really didn't, but rather, it was how others acted and reacted around him. This man, who looked to be about ninety, was sitting alone on a wooden park bench on the edge of the bluff overlooking the Atlantic. Every so often a family member would say hello and wave to him, and he would respond by waving back. This exchange went on with various family members, and it seemed to put a smile on the older man's face. But I noticed a different emotion attached to his smile, which made me question what in the world was happening next door.

Curiosity got the best of me and I inched closer in hopes of getting a better look at his face until I heard my wife's voice call out behind me.

I turned and saw Angela standing on the second-floor balcony waving at me to come inside for dinner.

I took one final look at that family, our temporary neighbors on Penn Street, in the waterfront mansion known only as "Shell House." I sprang into a slight jog to my rental, over the cobblestone sand dollars, and around the front porch through the big red door.

"You can smell dinner the whole way down at the beach," I said, as I watched Angela ladle seafood and linguine into pasta bowls.

"Good," she replied and smiled. "And now everyone can smell what they are missing, and what you almost missed because of your *nebbing*."

"I wasn't nebbing," I said with a laugh as I grabbed two bottles of Pellegrino out of the fridge.

"Murray, you are the worst kind of nebshit because you don't even know you are nebbin' in everyone else's business."

"You can take the girl out of Pittsburgh, but you can't take the Pittsburghese out of the girl," I said as I handed her the bottle of Pellegrino.

I took my first bite of *frutti di mare* and it was the perfect way to start our second week here in Rehoboth. "This is so good," I said, with my mouth full.

"Thank you," she replied with a smile.

Looking at my wife sitting across from me at the table, I knew there was more she wanted to say. "Yes?" I prompted, wiping my mouth with the triangular point of the napkin.

"Seriously, why were you so interested in what they were doing next door? We could have had barbeque chicken if that's what you really wanted, but I spent half of my day down at Rippon's in Ocean City to get those little-neck clams you like."

"And you know how much I appreciate it. *Frutti di mare* is my favorite, and you, my darling, are my favorite chef."

Angela sighed as she placed her palm under her chin, leaning in closer. "Murray, I was watching you watch them, and you seemed lost in thought."

I paused for a moment and then took a sip of my water. "You know large families impress me."

"You mean intimidate you," she said with a wry smile.

"No, that's just your family." I laughed.

"They intimidate me as well, to be honest," she confessed. "But seriously, are you okay?"

I waved my hands to shrug it off. "I'm fine. There's an older man over there who sort of reminded me of Pop."

"How so?" she asked.

"I don't know. For some reason I felt drawn to this family, and to him. It's as though we're connected in some way, even though I've never met any of them. I can't really explain because I don't understand it." I spooned another serving of *frutti di mare* into my bowl.

"You know, when you go on vacation, sometimes you end up going on vacation with a family of complete strangers. You arrive when they arrive, you leave when they leave, you're camped out near each other on the beach, you spend the entire week running into each other at Thrasher's Fries or waiting in line for Dolle's caramel popcorn. By the end of the week, you seem to know their entire life story," Angela said.

"Maybe their story should remain a mystery," I said nodding in the direction of our neighbors.

"Or maybe you should just walk over there this evening and say hello."

After dinner, Angela and I took a stroll along the shore. Our neighbors seemed to be in after-dinner clean-up mode, clearing plates and wrapping leftovers. I looked up at the edge of the bluff and saw that same older man sitting alone on the wooden bench, waving to anyone who passed by.

Looking back at the patio I saw the other man from the grill gather a group of kids, waving at them and then motioning them in the direction of the older man. I couldn't make out what he was saying so I took a few steps closer. There were enough kids to block his sightline. Then all at once the youngsters ran toward the bluff.

The man from the grill was looking straight at me. I was certain my "deer in the headlights" reaction gave me away, and I knew there was no point trying to cover up my not-so-stellar sleuthing skills. I decided honesty should prevail.

"Hi, I'm Murray, your nebby neighbor," I said, waving.

"Nebby? You must be from Pittsburgh. Where's about?" he asked.

"East side, Edgewood area," I replied, "and you?"

"My wife and I live in Wexford but she's originally from Regent Square. That's where her father, Henry, still lives." He gave a nod toward the older man on the bench. "So, I'm real familiar with that area, blue slide park n'at. Small world, huh? You and my father-in-law are practically neighbors at home, and now you're neighbors at the beach."

"Well, neighbor, it's nice to meet you, and I'm sorry you caught me staring. Huge families fascinate me." I scanned the crowd. "You've got quite a crew here."

"Hey, don't worry about it. This family tends to draw an audience anywhere we go. My name's Gabriel, by the way. It's nice to meet you, neighbor."

"What's the story with the old man? You said his name was Henry?" I nodded in his direction. "Why does he sit on that bench all alone, away from everyone all day?"

"He owns this place, but given his age and declining health, my wife's family decided it would be best to put the house on the market. We wanted to get the entire family together for one last vacation before it's time to say goodbye."

"Sad to let go of such a beautiful property." I took a step back, tilting my head slightly up to admire the century-old architecture.

"The goodbye is for Henry," Gabriel said. "He's terminal. Only has a few months left until he leaves this world for good."

My jaw dropped, and I let out a slight gasp. I was surprised that this man, practically a stranger, had been so honest with me. The emotions of the situation must have been weighing heavy on his heart.

"I am so sorry. Wow. That's tough."

To which Gabriel replied, "That's life."

The next morning, I woke before sunrise. I liked to walk along the water's edge before the rest of Rehoboth Beach awakened. Wanting to be completely alone, I opted to walk along Silver Lake, only a block away from our rental. After years of trying to listen to the ocean, attempting to hear what it had to say, I'd come to the conclusion that it just wasn't interested in talking to me. Perhaps the lake would be more open to conversation.

Silver Lake was more serene and tranquil than I had remembered. It was still too early for cars to muffle the sound of waterfowl waking up, hissing at their flock. The gentle rustling grew into louder splashes as the birds glided along the water's surface. Stretched out to the middle of the water sat Victorian gazebos, which appeared to be floating. As I walked closer, I saw a person sitting inside one. Another block north I realized it was Gabriel.

He looked up from his newspaper as he sipped his coffee, but I must have been caught in his peripheral. Squinting in my direction, he waved me over. "I didn't think anyone would be up at this hour except for maybe the geese."

"It's hard not to get your day started before the sun when you're on vacation," I said. "There's never enough hours for everything you want to do."

"I can attest to that." He took another sip of his coffee. "Especially when you are in a house with twenty-seven other people. I need at least an hour of a vacation away from my vacation."

"I can only imagine. I don't think I could go on a trip with my wife's family. Don't get me wrong, they're great people, but Rehoboth Beach was my Pops' place. After he passed, this was the only place that truly felt like home to me."

"You sound like my wife. Growing up she spent summers working at Grotto's and living at Shell House. It was her idea to list the property because, according to her, when Henry dies, the Rehoboth Beach that she knows will die as well. I told her not to think of it that way, but what can you do?" Gabriel's voice trailed off and we sat together in silence.

That was until the sound of a goose honked nearby, catching us off guard. We both jumped and laughed at the same time. Looking out into the distance beyond the lake's horizon, the moon slowly began to disappear from the water's reflection, simultaneous to the sun's rising on the other side.

"Henry reminds me of Pop," I said. "I wasn't ready for my reaction when I first saw him. It made me sad to see him sitting all alone on that wooden bench."

"He may be terminal, but his mind is as sharp as ever. He knows his own fate. He also knows that we practically forced his entire family to spend one last summer with him. Against his own wishes, I might add. He wanted to be alone, but we needed this trip more than he did."

"So, sitting alone on the bench was Henry's compromise?" I asked.

"For as long as he sits alone on that bench, we still have a day to say hello and wave, to remind him that he's still here," Gabriel said. "But more importantly, to remind the family of how fortunate we were to be a part of his world, to be a part of his life. For my wife's family, Henry is everything that made Rehoboth Beach their home. Without him, it's just sand and saltwater. That's why we have to sell the place."

As I walked back to my beach rental, I could feel the temperature rising. Sweat beads formed along my brow. The summer sun was in full effect; there wasn't a single cloud in the sky, and the beachgoers of Rehoboth were gearing up for another beautiful day.

Standing near the sand path on the bluff, I saw the early risers getting a head start on water activities. Some were wading in and out near the water's crest while others were beachcombing for sea treasure. I noticed the waves sounded different in low tide. Closing my eyes, I heard the gentle swoosh of soft ripples rocking back and forth across the wet sand. I peeked out at the water's edge. How different it looked compared to just twelve hours earlier. The sand at the crest was draped in a blanket of sea glass, sand dollars, and opulent shells—"a mermaid's jewelry box," as Pop use to call it.

The ocean felt different today because it was different. In just twelve hours everything had changed. It fascinated me how the moon could be several hundred thousand miles away, yet still responsible for how the waves curl and crest, how they create currents and riptides. No matter what, nothing could be done to stop this powerful force.

I pondered this idea because it reminded me of how we move through life. Despite our efforts, there's very little we can control. Something bigger from the great beyond always call the shots.

"Rehoboth Beach feels like home, but the ocean feels like life," I heard a voice say. I was shocked to discover it was my own. And it was at this moment when I finally realized what Pop had been trying to tell me.

"You can find the answers to life's greatest questions only when you're ready to hear them," a voice said behind me.

I recognized that voice as Gabriel's, so I turned.

"At least that's what Henry always says." Gabriel looked up at the bluff. "And there he is, sitting alone again, gazing out into the sea, just like he's done for over eighty-seven years."

"Just like the ebb and flow of the ocean, Henry sees the ebb and flow of his life," I said. "He's now looking at the end."

Gabriel remained silent.

After a deep breath I continued, "Maybe he's just saying goodbye to his home."

"Or maybe he's just saying hello." Gabriel's smile was somber. He headed for Shell House, but then stopped and turned back. "Murray? Come with me, and say hello to Henry," he suggested, and we walked up the sand path toward the bluff's edge above Shell House.

AUTHORS' NOTE:

This fictional story was conceptualized, outlined, and drafted on the Delmarva Peninsula during the summer of 2020. Two newlywed authors were on their honeymoon, but soon found themselves captivated by the family vacationing in the beach rental below. What they witnessed that week served as the inspiration for both character and plot.

HOPE IN FLAMES

Gloria Bostic

Enjoy!

Gloria Bostic

Violet looked at the time and lit another cigarette. Frank's text said simply: "Don't hold dinner for me. I'll grab something in town." No explanation, but then he almost never bothered to give her a reason anymore. Was this really the man she'd married?

It had been only four years earlier that the rich, handsome high school senior had asked her to be his date for the prom. As a mere junior who'd had a crush on him since middle school, but was certain he'd never given her another look, she'd been shocked. All the girls fawned over him, yet he picked her.

Violet was instantly swept off her feet by his charm, his good looks and sophistication, and on top of all that he was stinking rich. In the year that followed they were nearly inseparable, and he introduced her to a life beyond her wildest imagination.

Growing up in a modest home in Lewes, Delaware, Violet Clover was close enough to Rehoboth Beach to have seen many of the big, beautiful homes, but the first time Frank Townsend picked her up from Cape Henlopen High and drove her to Shell House, she was stunned. Could this really be one family's home? Situated between the Atlantic Ocean and Silver Lake, the views were magnificent, and every time Violet spent time there, she felt like she was living in a fairy tale, and Frank was her Prince Charming.

Violet knew she was no Cinderella. When she was ten and her mother died of cancer, her father had never remarried, so there was no wicked stepmother in her life. Just a father who had slipped deeper and deeper into depression until she did more to take care of him than he was able to take care of her.

Frank and Violet married just days after her high school graduation, and following a whirlwind honeymoon where they traveled to Italy and spent a month in luxury hotels, she began to fathom how filthy rich Frank's family truly was.

Following the honeymoon, Violet settled in for the beginning of her happily ever after. Frank insisted there was no need for her to work, so after many futile attempts, Violet finally gave up her dream of becoming a nurse and settled into the lifestyle of the country club ladies.

She learned to play golf and bridge and spent the rest of her summers enjoying the beach and sipping pina coladas by their pool overlooking Silver Lake. She didn't even mind that they were living with her in-laws, Lynne and Jack. They were good, down-to-earth people who never put on airs. How could she complain about living in such luxury?

Frank was attentive back then, and it wasn't until eight months later when his parents were both tragically killed in a horrible accident on Route 1, coming back from Dover, that she began to see changes in him. He became moody with unexpected extreme highs and lows. Whenever Violet asked him about the business for which he was now solely responsible, he told her it was not her concern and not to "worry herself" over it. Violet resented his condescension, but accepted it along with his moodiness as part of his grief over losing his parents.

The massive mansion seemed so empty now. It was simply too big for two people, and Violet felt lost inside it. She longed for something smaller... something cozy and warm... something that was just theirs where they could begin to raise a family. But when she mentioned the possibility of a change, Frank flew into a rage and shut her down fast and hard.

Violet had watched her father's grief process, from which he never seemed to recover, but her dad never had these wild mood swings. He had only one mood... depressed. *We each grieve in our own way.* She hung onto that thought and tried to be understanding and patient.

Yet, as the weeks and months turned into years, Violet began to long for something more. She grew tired of doing nothing. Even her volunteer work at the nearby nursing home wasn't enough. Her marriage grew cold and lonely, and all their money could not seem to buy any kind of contentment, fulfillment, or warmth. She longed to be a mother, to hold a child she could love and who would love her back, but that didn't seem to be in the cards either. Frank said he wasn't ready to deal with a crying baby, and Violet began to wonder what kind of father he'd be anyway.

She looked at her husband's text again, didn't bother answering it, and put the steaks back in the fridge. There was no way she was going to cook a meal and eat alone again. Tonight, she would go where she wanted to go and eat what she wanted to eat.

After pulling a comb through her auburn hair and freshening her makeup, Violet grabbed the keys to her Lexus and headed for a place where she and her dad had eaten many times—J. D. Shuckers over on Route 24. Frank would never take her there. Apparently, it wasn't fancy enough. But Violet was suddenly drawn to it.

The parking lot was crowded as usual, but she managed to find a spot, and though there would be a bit of a wait for a table, there was immediate room in the bar area. She found a spot at a high-top and ordered a crab cake, stewed tomatoes, and green beans. It was what she'd almost always ordered growing up, but tonight she added a beer. No fancy wine tonight.

When she finished her meal, she ordered another drink and decided to linger, listening to the singer. It was live music night and he was pretty good.

"May I join you?"

Startled by the husky voice, Violet turned to look up at a tall muscular guy, with a grin accentuated by the cleft in his chin and hypnotic brown eyes.

"I'm sorry. I'm married," she said realizing in that moment she *was* sorry she was married.

"Well, I'm sorry to hear that, but would you mind if I just sit for a few while I finish my beer?"

Violet hesitated, unsure how to respond.

"My buddies just left for their shift at work, and I'd kind of like to stick around and listen to the singer. He's a friend, and I promise I won't be a bother."

"Okay, sure. I could use the company." As soon as the words were out of her mouth, she wondered if she'd lost her mind for saying them... yet they were true. And the way he smiled at her warmed her cheeks.

They didn't talk much at first—except for a comment or two between songs—but when he casually asked why she was dining alone, she found herself explaining what was going on with her husband. After sharing in way too much detail, Violet was embarrassed to have dumped her personal problems on a total stranger whose name she didn't even know, but then she reassured herself that it didn't matter since she would never see this man again. It was time to head home. Past time.

But at that moment the musician took a break and came directly to their table.

"Hey Sam, how's it going?" the country singer asked with a big grin spreading across his face. He looked her way and asked, "Aren't you going to introduce us?"

So, he wasn't lying about the guy being a friend... and now she knew his name. A good name. Sam. She liked it.

Sam now looked her way, and she could see the question in his eyes. Of course, how could he introduce her when she hadn't told him her name?

"Hi, my name's Violet, but my husband calls me Vi." *Why did I need to tell him that?*

"Nice to meet you, Vi. I'm Billy." The singer reached across the table and shook her hand warmly, but the warmth she was feeling came more from Sam's gaze.

"I don't think I'd call you Vi. Violet is a beautiful name. It suits you," he said.

Violet again felt the warmth growing in her cheeks. "Thank you, Sam. Now, if you'll excuse me, I've really got to get going."

She had paid her bill by then, so she checked the time and stood to leave.

"Don't go on my account," Billy said.

"No, I'm not, but it's getting late, and I really do have to get home." Pulling her handbag off the back of her chair, Violet smiled and said good night. She hurried to her car, suddenly nervous thinking of Frank's reaction.

Before she could get in, she heard that same husky voice that had startled her earlier in the night.

"Violet, wait."

What in the world? Fear crept up her spine as she saw Sam running toward her. She was about to slam the car door and lock it when she realized what he was waving over his head. It was her pack of Marlboros.

"You forgot these," he said breathlessly. He extended the cigarettes toward her, then just as quickly pulled it back and withdrew one. Handing her the rest he pleaded, "Do you have a pen I could borrow... just for a sec?"

Violet wordlessly handed him the one resting in her console and watched in fascination as he slowly, meticulously wrote tiny numbers on the cigarette, then slid it back into the pack she was still holding in her hand. When his fingers grazed her hand, Violet felt a shock... and an unfamiliar longing.

His smile faded, and his facial expression changed to one of concern. "Hang onto that, Miss Violet, okay? Just in case you ever need help, you can call me." Then his charming smile returned. "I'm kind of in the helping people business." He turned and headed back into Shuckers, and she carried the memory of his caring eyes all the way back to Shell House.

She needn't have worried about Frank's reaction. When she got home, she found the house as empty as she'd left it. No sign of Frank. No message either. *No loss.*

Life went on. The days passed slowly and dragged into weeks. Violet only smoked four cigarettes a day, determined to quit the disgusting habit completely, but it was hard. So as each pack got down to that last cigarette, she would open the next one, remove a new smoke to light, and slide the one with Sam's number in its place. Though she was sure she'd never call, she simply couldn't let it go.

It was early August when Frank struck her for the first time. He had raised his fist a couple of times, but had never before actually hit her... until that night. His temper erupted over little things these days, and when Violet made the mistake of saying he was acting like a crazy person, he spun around and hit the side of her face with the back of his hand so hard she fell against the stove. The shock and suddenness of the blow took them both by surprise.

"I'm sorry," Frank said. "I didn't mean it. I'm so sorry, okay?" His snarky tone said more than his words.

When he tried to take her in his arms, she pulled away. Infuriated, Frank stormed out of the room and out of the house. Violet finally saw her Prince Charming for the ugly frog he was.

By the time he finally came home the next afternoon, Violet had plenty of time to consider her future—and she decided she didn't have one with Frank. His reaction was not unexpected.

"I'm leaving, Frank."

"What do you mean, you're leaving?"

"I mean most of my bags are already in the car. I'm sorry, but I can't do this anymore. I'm filing for divorce."

"On what grounds?" It came out almost as a growl.

"Seriously?"

"C'mon, it was one time," he whined. Then, when Violet didn't react, he added, "Don't be ridiculous! You can't leave me."

"Watch me, Frank."

"Vi! Come back here!"

My name is Violet. She continued up the winding staircase to grab her last bag. Frank yelled after her, "Well, if you think you're getting anything out of this, you're the one who's crazy. You won't get a penny!"

Violet knew that was true, yet none of it mattered anymore. She felt sorry for Frank but knew she deserved a better life. She would stay with her dad until she figured things out... maybe follow her dream to finally go into nursing and find her true purpose in life. And then, all in good time, there was a phone number she knew she would call.

With her designer backpack on her shoulder, she grabbed her pocketbook and dashed down the steps hoping to get out the door without another confrontation.

But then she remembered. She'd left her pack of smokes on the coffee table. She'd have to risk one more clash. She wasn't leaving without Sam's number.

Charging into the living room, she searched the coffee table. Where were her cigarettes?

"Looking for these?" Frank tossed the pack across the floor in her direction, but as she reached down to get them, she heard the sound of his lighter.

No!

"What are you doing?"

"What do you mean, dear?" The smirk on his face showed he knew exactly what he was doing. Somehow, he'd known. And now she watched as the first number and her dream went up in smoke.

Without another word, she ran from the house and jumped into the car with her things, but she didn't start the engine. The tears she'd bottled up for so long came pouring out, and she struggled to get control.

She couldn't breathe. She got out of the car and ran. Throwing off her shoes, she raced toward the water then slowed and walked aimlessly up the beach swiping away tears as she went.

Unsure how long she'd been walking, Violet was surprised to discover she had reached the Rehoboth Boardwalk, nearly a mile from the house. Exhausted, she slowly turned back in the direction from which she'd come.

The dream of Sam may have gone up in smoke—she had no way of ever finding him—but she still had a future to pursue. She wasn't about to give it up this time.

The sound of sirens in the distance interrupted her thoughts, and she looked up to see flames and smoke shooting into the air from somewhere in the vicinity of her home.

Her steps quickened until she was running once more. She ran and ran through the sand until her heart pounded in her chest. She knew even before she got there, it was her gazebo. Her gazebo, where Frank brooded. The gorgeous Victorian structure that once stood proudly near Shell House was now in flames.

Frank...

An hour later, standing by one of the firetrucks as they wheeled away a body covered with a sheet, Violet felt nothing. The tears were all spent. Her throat was parched. Numb, she wondered if she was in shock.

"Ma'am? Can I help you?" a husky voice came from behind her.

Spinning around, she looked up at the fireman and saw the same surprise she was feeling mirrored on his face. The soot from the fire couldn't disguise his identity.

It was Sam.

*To Joyce,
I'm so honored to call you friend. Thank you for your support
Kim*

A Sunday Séance at the Sea

Kimberly Kurth Gray

My name is Lottie Gershwin. I'll say I'm over forty, but you'll never get an exact age out of me. Last weekend Mom and I visited our friend Leslie Talbot at her Rehoboth Beach cottage. I met Leslie eleven years ago at a conference in Chicago where she used to work as the personal secretary to horror novelist Winston Withers. Though he could only write about the supernatural, it was something I experienced often... I spend a lot of time talking to ghosts.

I was born with a caul—a membrane—over my face. The superstitious nurses wanted it burned, but Mom wouldn't hear of it. Instead she had it blessed and kept it stashed between the pages of her Bible, convinced this would keep me safe. Creepy, right?

It's believed that those born with a veil can see to the other side, to those who have passed over. Thrilled with this idea, Mom schlepped me to the most haunted areas of Baltimore hoping I would introduce her to the likes of Francis Scott Key and Edgar Allen Poe. I, on the other hand, refused to acknowledge those not made of flesh and blood. I realized at an early age that if I ignored the dead, they wouldn't bother me.

Eventually I had to come clean to Mom that I could indeed see the dearly departed when we had a ghostly encounter at The Lakeside Hotel one weekend in Rehoboth several years ago.

Once I decided to accept my calling, I agreed to help Leslie's boss Mr. Withers with a few novels, which pleased Mom to no end to see my name in the acknowledgments. My husband Carl, a homicide detective, was not as pleased. Mom considered my gift a blessing, but Carl saw it as a curse, especially when victims from his cases followed him home. But that's another story.

I picked Mom up early Friday evening. Daddy had been fed and watered and sat happily in his favorite chair with a bowl of Chubby Hubby ice cream watching *The Sopranos*. Again.

"Hey there, Lottie," Daddy said as I walked in the door. "I filled the thermos with coffee for you and Mom. Don't want you getting sleepy on the road. You gonna stop for the night or drive straight through?"

"Daddy, it's barely a three-hour drive. We'll be there before it's even dark."

"You don't say," Daddy said, never taking his eyes off the screen.

Mom clattered down the stairs in pink kitten heels and pedal pushers, her white-blonde hair still in rollers. "Hi, hon. Let me get a scarf and I'm ready. Now Ray, don't eat that entire carton of ice cream tonight. And don't think I won't know if you run out and buy another to replace this one."

"She's got spies everywhere," Daddy said, finally looking at me. "I think even the guys down at Scully's report to her when I've had more than one beer." Then he smiled and turned back to his show. Everyone knew he loved being pampered and enjoyed all Mom's fussing.

Two and a half hours later she and I pulled off Penn Street onto a pebbled drive toward Leslie's new house. The sun was low in the sky and an osprey flew overhead. I rolled the windows down to capture the ocean smell and let the sound of the tide roll in. Leslie waved from behind a weathered wooden gate. Mom and I sat stunned, peering through the windshield of the car.

What Leslie referred to as her beach cottage was an enormous faded-brown shake-shingle house that spread out in two directions from the main area. This was a cottage in the same way The Breakers in Newport was a cottage to the Vanderbilts.

Tired of waiting, Leslie made her way to the car and tapped on the hood. "You are coming in, aren't you?"

Leslie linked arms with Mom as they walked to the house. I followed carrying our overnight cases. We crossed the gray brick walkway and passed the three-car garage to the porch. The wide screen door slammed behind us as we entered the house. I wasn't surprised to see the dearly departed Mr. Withers waiting, but was simply horrified when Mom walked directly through him.

"Sorry about that," I said. "She can't see you."

"Not a problem, my dear." Mr. Withers winked at me.

"Hon, did you bring my sweater in? I feel a chill," Mom said. Then she realized she still had rollers in her hair under the scarf. "You girls excuse me a moment, won't you? I have to go put myself together. Leslie, where's your little girl's room?"

Leslie led Mom down the hallway and up a few steps to another hall that I hoped eventually led to a bathroom. Mr. Withers stood in front of the staircase.

I set the bags down and admired the house. Leslie told me the place had been built in the early 1920s with only two owners before her. I ventured into the living room where a long-ago party of young people still took place. The women wore long-waisted dresses with feathered headbands and the men were in cuffed trousers and wide-lapel jackets. No one appeared to notice that time had moved on without them. Another man in a Philadelphia Phillies uniform with the name O'Doul printed on the back roamed the stairs. A woman bearing a striking resemblance to Grace Kelly wandered past. All were oblivious to my presence.

"I'm so glad you've come," Mr. Withers said, moving next to me. "There's something I need to tell you, something I'm hoping you can do for me."

"Hon, wait until you see that bathroom," said Mom from behind me. "It's beautiful, done all up in a salmon pink with pretty gold palm trees on the wallpaper. I'm telling you, I was afraid to sit down."

Mom had pulled her hair into a chignon and the scarf was now tied jauntily around her neck. Leslie picked up one overnight case and we followed her up the stairs to the bedrooms. Mr. Withers was gone.

Leslie and I sat at the kitchen table with glasses of wine after dinner had been cleared and Mom called it a night. Though we spoke frequently on the phone and texted, it wasn't often we could get together.

"I must confess, I have an ulterior motive for asking you to visit," she said, pouring us another glass of Malbec.

"You want to know if Mr. Withers is with us," I said.

"Is he?" Leslie leaned back against the cushioned chair. She wore her dark brown hair shorter now and strands of gray had crept in. Her face was thinner with a hint of sadness.

"You were in love with him, weren't you?" I asked, feeling sure Mr. Withers was not around to overhear.

"Good heavens, no," Leslie said a little too loudly. She took a long sip from her glass. "I wasn't in love with him," she said after a few seconds. "The truth is Mr. Withers was my father. Well, at least he thought he might be."

I'd had it all wrong. When we worked together on the books, I'd seen the way he looked at Leslie, the way he admired her work ethic, and how he was always full of compliments for her. When he'd died of a heart attack the previous year and left money for Leslie in his will, I hadn't been surprised. I thought he was finally able to help her the way he'd wanted to in life.

"So, Mrs. Withers..."

"Is not my mother," Leslie finished. "It was no secret to me that I'd been adopted. Early on I noticed I didn't resemble my parents, or any of my siblings. There were no photographs of me as a baby either. When I was about eight I asked about it. Where had I come from? Mother told me that when she was a nurse she'd met my birth mother at the hospital. They struck up a friendship, and through that my adoption was arranged."

"Did she meet Mr. Withers?" I asked.

"No. Mother didn't know a thing about him. She suspected my biological father was young, probably a senior in high school or maybe a college freshman. My birth mother had wanted to go to college and be a writer. My adoptive mother thought she couldn't have any more children after her first. So, she and my father decided to adopt me because they wanted a big family. Little did they realize she would end up having two more children. She was pregnant with my sister at my adoption hearing."

"Did she stay in touch with your mother? I mean your birth mother."

"No. Unfortunately, the young woman died not long after I was born. She had an aneurism. Mother heard about it from another nurse who still worked at the hospital and knew of the connection."

"That's so sad." I didn't know what else to say, but found myself searching the kitchen for the face of a young woman. Only the man in the baseball uniform was still milling around.

"I wanted to ask you before if she was with me, you know, watching over me. Her name was Veronica."

"Veronica Huntington," said Mr. Withers who now stood behind Leslie's chair, his hands resting on her shoulders.

Leslie shivered. "He's here, isn't he?"

"Yes, he's standing behind you. I don't see anyone else."

"Veronica's not here. Can you find her?" Mr. Withers asked.

"What's happening? Is he saying something?" Leslie asked. "Ask him why he didn't tell me. Ask him why I had to read about it in a letter after he died. There's so much I want to know."

"He can hear you," I said.

"Tell Leslie I didn't know for a long time who she was," he said. "She looked so much like Veronica and she was the right age, but it wasn't until I hired a private detective that I found out for sure."

"He says he wasn't sure at first." I glanced up at Mr. Withers. "Anything else?"

"I want you to find Veronica. Can you do that? Can you bring her here so we might be reunited with our daughter?"

"It doesn't work that way. I'm unsure I can find Veronica," I said. "I don't call upon spirits or anything like that... I'm not sure I'd even know how. I can only communicate with those I see in front of me."

"Hon, you can do it. I know you can. You've got the gift," Mom said from the doorway. She never liked to miss a thing. "Don't worry. We are on the case."

"Case? What case?" I said to Mom from my canopy bed. "I have never, ever summoned a spirit and I'm pretty sure I don't want to."

"Come on now. How hard can it be? You don't want to disappoint Winston and Leslie, do you?"

"You weren't there when Leslie asked if Veronica was with her. You didn't see her face crumple when I said there was no one else around. Suppose I can't summon this woman? Or what if by some miracle I can but she doesn't want to see Leslie? What then? Did you consider that? She gave Leslie up for adoption... maybe that was the end of it for her."

"We won't know until we ask her. I've got an idea. We need to call in a medium."

"Oh, no you don't. Don't you dare call Aunt Rhett!"

"I already have. She'll be here on Sunday afternoon. Night-night, hon."

The Lincoln Town Car pulled up promptly at two in the afternoon on Sunday. Out stepped my grandmother Harriette, or Nana as I called her, from the driver's seat. She gave a slight wave before opening the rear door from which her sister Loretta emerged. Aunt Rhett was, as we say, a piece of work. She was nearly six feet tall with snow-white hair piled in a pyramid of curls. "The higher the hair, the closer to God," she always said. Her hair was so high, she must be closer to God than the Pope.

Both sisters wore purple, their signature color, and though they bickered constantly, they were never apart. Behind Aunt Rhett came her five dead husbands—they traveled in a pack. A man followed them who was unfamiliar to me.

"I seem to be lost," the new man said as he passed. "Is this Heaven?" He walked on without waiting for a reply.

"Hello, Charlotte," Aunt Rhett said and kissed me on my cheek. No one else, except my mother-in-law, ever called me Charlotte.

"Hello, Auntie," I said and led the way inside.

The main dining room had been selected for the séance. A dark blue cloth was draped over the table, six candles in a circle at the center, and in the middle lay a loaf of freshly baked bread and a tureen of vegetable soup Mom had made that morning. These were to entice the spirit who still hungered and sought light and warmth.

"Very good," Aunt Rhett said, nodding her approval. "Now, if someone could draw the blinds and close the curtains, we will begin."

I looked across the red brick patio, over the sands at the ocean. All seemed calm now, but I was not convinced this would end well. Drawing the heavy curtains shut, I turned to find an older blonde woman at my side. It was Mae West.

"I come up and see Rhett sometimes," she said, her hands on her hips. "She keeps me entertained. As long as she doesn't summon Rex Harrison, we'll get along fine." As she turned away, the scent of Joy filled the air. It'd been years since my mother had worn the same fragrance.

Aunt Rhett took a deep breath and smiled. "Good, Mae's here. She's wonderful at coaxing the spirits to me, especially the men."

Nana lit the candles and we gathered around the circular table. I sat between Leslie and Aunt Rhett. Mom, Nana, and Aja, a young woman I'd met several years ago while staying at The Lakeside Hotel, completed the circle. Like Mom, Aja was obsessed with ghosts and more than eager to participate in our séance. So were Viola and Harry, Lakeside's resident ghosts. They'd attached themselves to Aja and made their way here. Though she couldn't actually see them, she swore to me she could feel their presence.

Once we were settled, and Mae, Mr. Withers and the other ghosts found a place around the room, Auntie instructed us to join hands. Auntie's palm was cool, but poor Leslie's was sticky with sweat. "Sorry," she whispered and squeezed my hand lightly. "I'm a tad nervous."

"Me too," I assured her.

"Silence," Aunt Rhett said before closing her eyes. "You must be silent for me to concentrate." She then cleared her throat. "Our dearly departed Veronica, join us. Come to our gathering... share these gifts of life we offer... move among us."

The only movement came from my stomach which chose to growl loudly and set Leslie off in a fit of giggles. We were shushed by Nana and Mom.

Aunt Rhett glared at me through squinted eyes. "Quiet, girls. Now where was I?"

"Veronica, gifts, moment, yadda, yadda, yadda," Nana said.

"Right. Veronica. Dear Veronica, make your presence known to us. We await you."

A slight chill came over me. I'd had little faith in Auntie's abilities, but with Mae West lurking in the corner and now another tall apparition forming, it seemed maybe Auntie was gifted after all. This woman appeared with strands of long blonde hair falling over her right eye. She approached Mae.

"It's been years and years since I was invited to a pool party here," said the woman sliding a cigarette from a slim silver case. She lit it and the smell of smoke filled the room.

"I think you've mistakenly summoned Veronica Lake," I said quietly to Auntie.

Auntie huffed a bit but quickly regained her composure. "Veronica Lake, though your beauty is much appreciated and you are most welcome here, you are not the Veronica we seek."

"Once I was in demand and now bleach blondes are a dime a dozen." Veronica sighed then sized up the women, all of us blonde but Leslie. Then she sniffed over the offerings on the table before eyeing up Mr. Withers. "Not even a drop of champagne," she said to him and continued to smoke her cigarette.

"Veronica. Veronica," Auntie bellowed.

"Huntington. Veronica Huntington," Leslie said between clenched teeth.

"Veronica Huntington, we wait for you. You are much wanted and loved here. Come to us." Aunt Rhett's hands began to shake and she slowly rose from her chair. I kept my hand tightly clamped with hers. *"Don't break the circle,"* she had warned us. A humming began like a hundred bees and Veronica Lake disappeared. In her place came a small woman with dark hair and eyes, a younger version of Leslie.

"She's here," I said.

Auntie flopped back in her seat and Leslie began to cry.

"Winston? Where are we?" the new arrival asked.

Mr. Withers moved toward her and took her hands into his. "You are home, my darling, just like we always talked about. Now we can be together and with our daughter as well." They moved to Leslie.

"Leslie? She grew up and then I was unable to find her again, so I stayed in the nurse's house waiting for her to return." As Veronica spoke, her eyes never left Leslie. "No one says my name anymore. No one remembers me. Then I heard the voice calling and this blonde-haired woman showed me the way to you." Veronica pointed to Mae, who gave her a sly grin.

"What are they saying?" Leslie wanted to know.

"Your parents are happy to be reunited," I told her.

"Please ask them to stay," said Leslie.

"You must ask them yourself," I replied. "They can hear and see you."

Leslie turned her head in their direction, instinctively knowing where they stood. "You must stay, both of you. This house is too large for just me and I'd be so happy knowing you were close by."

"We wouldn't dream of leaving you again," said Veronica. She looked over at Mae. "Thank you for reuniting us."

"No thanks to me, kid," said Mae. "It's all Rhett there and her girl Lottie, they've got the power. I'm just along for the ride." With those words Mae drifted away.

"Things are settled then?" asked Auntie.

"I believe so," I said.

"Then, with the power vested in me, I declare this meeting adjourned." Auntie stood and we followed her lead. Together we blew out the candles then dropped hands.

"They're still here, right?" Leslie asked.

"Absolutely," I answered. "They're holding hands and Mr. Withers looks much younger. I suppose that's the way Veronica remembers him."

This was the second time I'd helped in reuniting a couple. Harry and Viola had been the first. They now gazed lovingly at each other and waited for Aja to take them back to the hotel.

Early Monday morning Aunt Rhett and Nana took off in the Lincoln, but Mom and I stayed for lunch. Leslie prepared a picnic that we carried to the beach. It was a warm, pleasant day. Most children had returned to school, but Rehoboth would remain busy on the weekends until Sea Witch at Halloween. I was happy to lay out on the blanket and watch the clouds blow by. I'd spent the evening writing down every word Veronica and Winston said for their daughter. Leslie was happy again.

It was always sad to leave the beach, but I knew I'd be back to visit Leslie soon. We waved goodbye to the reunited family and made our way down the drive.

"You know, hon, I've been thinking," said Mom as we drove up Route 1. "We need business cards, something real stylish. Gershwin and Porter." Mom spread her hands out along the dashboard as if I could see the words as she spoke. "Ghost Mediators."

"No, absolutely not," I insisted.

"We do the work so you and the dead can rest easy." Mom giggled.

"Mom!"

"Lottie, it will be fun."

LIFE IN THE MIRROR

Madhu Bazaz Wangu

A few turns through the meandering hallways and Jaya Bhagat finally found the sprawling master bedroom looking serene in sky blue and silver. But the eerie sensation with a touch of nausea that had overcome her at the imposing entrance still remained. The apartment where she had begun her married life with Jagat could fit inside this room. Would she be able to convert the huge space into a cozy home?

She walked over the honey-colored wood floor. The section on her left was decorated with two Victorian chairs flanking a round table with a ceramic vase, blue and white. The navy-blue canopy bed on her right shimmered from the sunlight filtering through the three floor-to-ceiling windows.

Against the distant side wall a full-length vanity mirror came into view. Flanked by a set of drawers, the vanity was built with mosaic glasswork and maroon lacquer. A knob-like crystal ring at the right edge of the mirror made it look like a door. She so admired its exquisite richness that she paced to open it. But when she tried, there was no ring. Just the mirror's edge.

"Jaya! Jaya!" she heard Jagat call.

"Coming," she said, then turned around and walked out of the room.

Located in Rehoboth, Delaware, the house faced the beach, with its back to Silver Lake. To a billionaire like Jagat, it was a steal at fourteen million. With a sweeping courtyard and fountain, seven spacious bedrooms, and six bathrooms, there was plenty of room for the children and more.

The whole family had come to see the house that could be their home soon. Two girls, ages fifteen and thirteen, immediately loved their rooms with pink canopy beds, but the twin boys, age seventeen, were more excited with the swimming pool and badminton court. They oohed and aahed, walking through the corridors with views of the water and manicured gardens. The sprawling trees must have been as old as the house. Oh, the stories they could tell! One could spend an hour walking under the cool shade. Jaya felt an affinity with them. But now her thoughts and sensations distracted her; she kept them to herself. Nausea overpowered the uncanny sensation she had felt earlier.

Dr. Jagat Bhagat, a business prodigy, had developed the world's largest cloud security trust model. Featured in *Forbes 400*, he could buy the whole neighborhood if he wanted. Though born in India to parents of modest means, he felt no qualms about buying Shell House—he was worth it.

Alone, nausea spread to Jaya's throat. She rubbed the back of her neck.

"Oh, there you are!" Jagat said. "So what do you think?"

She walked into the closest room and sat down on the pink-swathed bed. With her arms crossed she glanced at her husband. His cheerful mood didn't quell her queasiness.

"I think we should sign the papers," he announced.

"Isn't it too big?"

"Didn't you like the kitchen? Did you see the six-burner range and two large ovens? Which delectable dishes are you going to prepare?"

"How many appliances do I need to cook, to bake?"

"You won't know until you use them. What am I thinking! You'll have help. And what about the travertine tile floor in the kitchen cooling your feet, butler's pantry—impressive, what do you say?" To and fro he paced briskly in front of her.

"If you like it that much," she said, then got up abruptly and hurried to the bathroom.

In Jaya's maiden home the stream of guests never stopped arriving. Every month a new guest or more would arrive for the weekend or a long visit. And each evening someone would drop in for a cup of tea or to watch television. It was busy. During the day the guest room was used to chitchat. When the room was vacant she sat in the middle and practiced singing. She would see herself on the stage where the imaginary world of music lovers formed her audience. Her magnetic voice kept them entranced.

Then she got married. Jagat's investments started snowballing. He helped establish programs for cyber growth-based entrepreneurship at over 500 companies. His vision developed a network of branches where thousands of workers were hired. Subsequently, he was awarded an honorary doctorate by IIT Kanpur, winning a lifetime achievement award. Finally, he moved to Silicon Valley. Within a decade he was one of the leaders in the industry.

Jagat was proud that his children showed interest in electronics and business rather than literature, arts, music, or any other humanities. Jaya, on the other hand, had trained as a singer of Indian classical music. With her parents' support she graduated with a gold medal at age twenty-one. She knew how to play sitar and accompany other singers on tabla. Her teachers prophesied her to be a new sensation in the world of classical singers.

At her first solo performance, Jagat was in the audience with her brother and some of their friends. After the recital her brother had brought them backstage. Dressed in a blood-red sari and gold earrings, necklace and bangles, Jaya smiled sweetly as she greeted them. Her gentle demeanor, and humility—for she evaded their admiration and praise—charmed them. The next morning, critics in the local papers applauded her fresh voice and singing skills.

Jagat had fallen head over heels in love with Jaya—almond-eyed, demure, and biddable. To him, she was not just gold marriage material but an intricately molded ornament.

After a few days when he called to ask her out for tea, she consented. She entered the restaurant in a silk saffron sari. Jagat got up and happily showed her to the chair facing him. They chitchatted for a while about her future. Then he said, "On your musical night you won the hearts of the entire audience."

She simply lowered her long-lashed eyes and thanked him with a smile.

"...especially mine. The search for a woman of my dreams is over."

"How do you define your dream woman?" she asked.

"Beautiful and talented," he answered. "But once she marries, she ought to be compliant and dedicated to the children. A great cook, perfect hostess... everything one would expect of the wife of a highly successful man."

"Are you a 'highly successful man'?"

"Not yet. But one day."

"I admire your confidence," she said with affirmation.

"You are my perfect dream woman, Jaya. Will you marry me?"

Her face flushed. She had not expected him to be so serious. She scrutinized his gaze. He may be old-fashioned but he was honest.

"Will you marry me if your parents give permission?" he repeated.

"I'll think about it. Thank you for the tea," she said and asked him to drive her home.

In three months, they were married.

Jagat and the children had forgotten that it was her beautiful voice that had made him fall in love with her. Twenty-five years flew by as she dedicated time to her husband, and cared and nurtured their four children. But never had she given thought to what happened to the young woman who dreamed about becoming a professional musician. Now she hummed along with a record player or radio as she cooked or bathed. Not even once did she ask what happened to that potent seed of genius that had awakened at her first performance.

The first time Jagat mentioned moving from California to Delaware was when the deeply embedded bulb of her dream sprang through the brick repression. Perhaps things would be different. Perhaps the change of scenery would be creatively fertile. The children were independent and no longer needed as much attention. She would have more time to sing. As she thought thus, an emptiness creeped in. Wasn't it yet time for the bulb to grow through the crack?

"Should we sign the deed? What do you say?" Jagat asked again when she came out from the bathroom with her hand on her belly.

"If you don't mind, let me walk through the house once again."

"Go ahead! I've got to make a few calls anyway." He turned and walked to the family room.

The house was like a maze, easy to get lost in the spaces concealing mysteries and secrets. She meandered through the corridors, standing for many minutes at the two balconies to take in fresh air and look at the gently swaying tree branches.

As she passed by the two guest rooms, from the one painted yellow, filtered soft and soothing musical notes. She stopped and listened. The notes stirred tenderness inside her. She stepped inside to hear more and clearly. But she was greeted by silence. Confused, Jaya shook her head as if to clear her mind, then continued to saunter through the corridors until she finally reached the master bedroom. She made herself comfortable on one of the two Victorian chairs.

For a century, many families had lived in this mansion, each leaving memories behind. She wondered how many unrevealed secrets lingered, how many floated in spaces below the high ceilings. Sensitive souls would be able to detect them. She decided not to share her thoughts with Jagat or the children for fear of being labeled unhinged. Whether in 1920 or the present day, things hadn't changed much. Most people dreamed of bathing in the opulence and grandiosity of spectacular mansions.

Jagat walked into the bedroom, sat on the other chair, and looked at her expectantly for an answer.

Instead of saying what she was thinking she replied, "Let's sign the papers. You and the children love the house. I too am fine with it." This was her passive way to deal with a situation when she knew giving her opinion wouldn't matter, and she was not the argumentative type.

The teenagers, at first excited, slowly got used to the luxury. She took longer to adjust. Engagements, appointments, and business trips engulfed Jagat's iCalendar. One day he was in town and the next out of the country. Occasionally he was gone for days, even weeks.

Within a month of moving into the house, the Bhagats settled into regular routines. Jaya felt no need to leave. A long walk around the house through manicured gardens exhilarated her. Lost in her thoughts she would cross a row of mauve and magenta dogwood trees and enter the back woods of sprawling jacaranda, alms, and aspens. At times while humming a tune she mulled over her past as a singing prodigy and imagined what the future could have been, or still could be.

After all the unpacking, arranging, and decorating had been done, the mornings and afternoons were quiet before the children started returning home. One morning

Jaya was so tired that her body hurt. Exhaustion overcame her. A rejuvenating afternoon nap summoned. She left the kitchen and went to lie down in her bedroom.

By now, the unfamiliar surroundings had absorbed the feel and history of her personal stuff and family items. She had taken her time to help the kids arrange their rooms, had put away her and Jagat's possessions, seeing where to place each item and storing anything else for which she could not find a suitable place. Only when she felt comfortable and homey did she stop fussing.

Jaya walked by chairs and the round table and was about to plop onto the canopied bed when her gaze fell on the opulent vanity. She remembered the first time she had entered the room. That day she thought the mirror had a crystalline doorknob that made it look like a door. But she had not spotted that door ring since. She walked closer to the vanity and looked again. *Where exactly had that ring appeared?* Perhaps nausea had played tricks with her mind. Her friends did tease her for having a vivid imagination. She simpered then shifted her vision to look at her own reflection. For a long minute, she stared at herself. Had she turned younger?

Twenty-year old Jaya blinked back at her. From the corner of her eye she saw something glint. Jaya turned her gaze. A ring, in its crystalline brilliance, had appeared. It looked like a small door knocker. At first, she wanted to pull it out but then hesitated. Was she seeing things? A gentle touch assured her that it was real; its texture was cool to the touch. She inserted her index finger through the hole. And voila, it opened!

No sooner did the mirror door open than melodious music floated up. Was there an orchestra performing in her basement? Did they even have a basement? Taken by surprise, Jaya started to descend the circular staircase. As she stepped down, the music shifted to her favorite raga. A female singer was being accompanied by tabla and tanpura. She recognized it as her own voice.

She stepped on the floor. The white marble tiles cooled her soles. The light was dim. On the yellow walls were depicted scenes of singers and musicians from around the world. The sound turned clear and louder. The atmosphere was filled with the aroma of jasmine and marigolds mingling with melodies of the musicians from various races and ethnicities. The musicians were absorbed in harmonious singing and playing with gusto, and the audience relished the beauty of sound.

She breathed in the familiar floral smell that was an integral part of musical performances of her youth, taking in the joyful faces of the performers and listeners, some with their eyes closed. She too stood listening to the crescendo as her body animated. Jaya remained still until the music stopped. The audience applauded.

Slowly she walked to the stage at the center of the hall. The tanpura and tabla players tuned their instruments for the next piece. They stopped and looked at her as if expecting her to join them.

She greeted them with a smile and a nod but hesitated to step up. The players pointed her to the middle cushion, indicating that the prized seat was hers. They waited. Finally she positioned herself, sitting cross-legged, and made herself as comfortable as she could. The musicians went back to tuning their instruments.

Jaya took a few long and deep breaths and brought her attention to her body. She sensed her muscles tense. Realizing that she had not sung professionally for twenty-five years quickened her heartbeat. She feared if she sang she would be out of tune and her voice would be blunt or raspy. But was she going to miss this opportunity?

She inhaled and exhaled and cleared her throat. She began to hum. Humming felt good. But when she started to sing, her vocal cords were raw. She tried again. This time her voice cracked, eyes welling.

The tabla player handed her a glass of water. Jaya gently bowed to him and took a few sips. After three long and deep breaths, she started again. At first a broken voice, but within minutes she got into her groove. Her voice was like a nightingale singing a song of separation at dusk, after sunset but before the sky darkens. She felt as if no time had passed between the evening when Jagat and her brother had attended her performance to the present.

The first three songs were a warmup that prepared her for the main performance, a classical raga. She sang *alaap* slowly, softly, and tenderly. This was followed by a quickening of the pace with rhythm of the accompanying tabla and tanpura. By the time she was singing *jalap*, the crescendo and Jaya's immersion in the music was complete. She kept the beat with the tabla player on her right and tanpura player on the left as she gently hit her knee with the front and back of her hand. The other musicians too became one with their instruments as the rhythmic beats flowed.

When the raga ended people seated on the floor stood up and cheered. The sounds of "*vah, vah,* bravo, bravo" echoed. Fully spirited, she began to sing the same song she had sung when Bhagat was in the audience for the first time. She sang until exultation filled her body, until her music led to that euphoric zone where nothing else matters.

The song ended powerfully for Jaya. It seemed to have absorbed the tension of decades that she had been carrying. A sense of complete relief left her exhausted. The way she sang was as if she had been practicing her art, honing her craft for months. How she hoped none of her children were back from school or college and heard her sing or noticed her absence!

"Mom!" she heard the youngest one calling from the kitchen. "Mom, where are you? I'm back."

She got up, ran to the stairs, and climbed the spiral staircase. She found herself in front of the vanity with her head bent on her crossed arms. She was in the bedroom and realized she had never really left. Had she been right there, right in front of the mirror all along? Only a few minutes had passed. The crystalline ring seemed to wink at her

"Okay, sweetheart!" She turned toward her daughter's voice. "Have something to eat. I'll be there in a minute." When she looked at the mirror again the ring was gone.

The next day and every day from then on, after the children left home and she was alone, the ring appeared. The vanity had cast a spell on her. The mirror would turn into a portal through which she could pass without hurdle. One moment she was descending the spiral staircase to reach the magical spot at the central stage. The next, she would find herself seated in front of it. The pleasure and satisfaction of passing through the mirror-door was intense. Like an illicit love affair. Mustn't she avoid it? How long would she be able to hide it? Was she losing her mind? Why was she conjuring up a world that did not exist?

Jaya decided to avoid it. Instead, she used full-length mirrors in the master bathroom. She decorated the vanity with a sheer satin and lace cover. If Jagat asked the reason, she would say she wanted to make it look pretty and keep it from gathering dust.

Months passed. Jaya was able to avoid the mirror-door but it was constantly at the back of her mind. It had some hold on her. The illicit pleasure through her performances and its resultant contentment were over-whelming. The portal sucked her in during mornings after the family left for school and in evenings after they kissed her good night when Jagat was away on business.

After each session she would realize that she was under some sort of spell, an enchantment. But each time the ring appeared, the thought of singing with the beat of tabla and rhythm of the tanpura pulled her into the mirror. Oh, how ardor filled her with joy, and the subterranean place magnetized her like a lover's tryst! *Just one more time. Just one last time.* And the next day she would let it happen again. *What's the harm?*

As soon as she made herself comfortable on the stage, ready to sing, the audience welcomed with applause. During the performance she did not hear them cheer but at the end they would stand up and applaud and whistle.

The evening she sang the raga, "Malkauns," she maddened the crowd. When the singing ended, the hall echoed with thunderous applause. "Encore, Jaya! Encore." They wanted more from her. She'd sing one or two more songs. And the evening ended with heartful "*vah, vahs*" from the audience.

She could sing the whole night if they wanted! At her power spot the singing linked her mind, heart, and spirit into one. There she felt so empowered that nothing else mattered. There she experienced rapture.

One day when she was deep in the middle of the singing trance, she heard a distant but familiar voice. It came closer and closer until she felt a passionate kiss on the nape of her neck.

"I missed you, Jaya," Jagat said and continued to kiss her neck. "Separation from you for so long is unbearable."

She pressed her lips before the words, *how long has it been*, could escape her mouth.

She bolted up from her singing posture. "So glad you're back," she whispered.

"I do hear you sing occasionally. The day I left, I caught you singing the end part of the raga you sang the evening I met you. What was it, 'Malkauns'?"

She nodded.

"I must say, you haven't lost your touch! While driving to the airport and on the plane, I reminisced the evening we met."

He recalled and laughed about how he had fallen in love with her and how cleverly at first she had ignored him. But he had been persistent until she agreed. He sounded overtly excited that evening.

"Are you okay? Why are you so quiet?" But before she could think of an answer he added, "I have a surprise for you."

"What is it?" She was curious.

"Follow me." He turned and led her to the guest room with yellow walls. This was the room outside which once she had heard musical notes floating. The room had been neglected as no guests had yet visited. She wondered if anyone living overseas had come to stay for a few days, or perhaps an American friend who had been asking her how she liked living in the historic mansion was to spend the weekend with them. The most exciting thought that floated through her mind was perhaps it was her brother who had decided to surprise her.

The door to the room was closed. Jagat opened it slowly and let her enter. Her eyes widened and her jaw dropped at what she saw. The room was a smaller version of the subterranean hall she had been performing in! On a low platform, an ivory and gold inlaid tanpura and a twin set of tabalas thrilled her.

"Take a seat, please!" Jagat said.

She sat in the middle of the musical instruments in her usual singing posture.

"Do you like it?"

She didn't reply. She simply closed her eyes and began to hum. Jagat let her hum for a few minutes. There were sounds of tabla and tanpura being tuned. Was she imagining the sounds? She was too afraid to turn back and confirm if two musicians were playing the instruments. She took one long breath and began to sing, raga... "Mallkauns."

Jagat clapped and said, "Oh goodness, Jaya. You still sing beautifully!"

She did not open her eyes. *Go ahead, sing your heart out!* Her heart rejoiced. Her voice flowed as smoothly as a stream of fragrant freshwater. She sang to her heart's content. When the song ended she was physically drained but emotionally and spiritually fulfilled. She closed her welled eyes and let the tears drip.

The gentle beat of the tabla and rhythmic tanpura kept playing softly. She couldn't resist and turned to see if there were musicians seated behind her. But there was no one. Neither Jagat, nor the accompanists were there.

In a daze she rose from the platform and ran from the guest room to her bedroom and then straight to the vanity mirror. The crystalline ring was shining in its glory. She pulled the circle, stepped down the staircase, walked to her singing spot and sat down... this time to be one with her muse.

That was the last day Jaya was seen by anyone.

A year later when a demolition team came to gut the mansion with its back to Silver Lake, some of the workers heard musical sounds echoing from the ground. The unfamiliar gentle tunes were mixed with static. Those who heard nothing believed the ones who did hear to be "hearing voices." They said they were out of their minds.

MYSTERY AT SHELL HOUSE

Lisa Valli

After sitting on the market for over a year, a century-old beach mansion is being demolished just south of Rehoboth Beach. Originally built by Carson Dupree in the late 1800s, the property known as Shell House has 7 bedrooms, 6.5 baths and a pool, with views of the Atlantic Ocean and Silver Lake.

Sitting on two lots, the house was originally listed for $14.9M, and roughly a year later, reduced to $13.9M. However, the home is no longer listed. Instead, the two half-acre lots are now for sale at $6.99M each.

—John Olsen, Rehoboth Times

Sloan's eyes widened over the rim of her coffee cup. She slammed it down to re-read the newspaper article. This didn't make any sense. Always on the hunt for a good story, she grabbed her notebook and started scribbling, then reached for her cell phone and punched in a quick text to her editor.

> Story idea. I want to check it out. Heading to Rehoboth for the day.

She knew he trusted her knack for sniffing out a good story, so she wasn't at all surprised when he responded only a few seconds later.

Keep me posted.

Within thirty minutes, she was in her car, heading onto the beltway. When she turned on the radio, and heard the strains of her mother's favorite song, "The Long and Winding Road," she changed the station and cranked up the volume, rocking out to the sounds of REM.

At 2:00 P.M., she pulled up to the realtor's office. A curtain fluttered in one of the windows. As she opened the door, a little ding alerted her entrance. Probably a good thing, because as Sloan looked around, she saw no one sitting at any of the three desks. She craned her neck around the corner but only saw an empty hallway.

She glanced around the real estate office and noticed black-and-white photos lining the walls, depicting confederate soldiers standing next to a large pentagonal-shaped building, The small plaques underneath the photo referenced "Civil War re-enactors honor fallen confederate soldiers who died while imprisoned at Fort Delaware." Another photo showed a re-enactor pointing a saber at a monument that listed names of the fallen confederate soldiers.

Just as she wondered if she should call out, an elderly gentleman approached at a snail's pace. Stooped over and nearly bald, she suspected that even standing tall he couldn't have measured more than 5' 5". He stared at her blankly, his smudged eyeglasses teetering on his crooked nose. She recognized him as an older version of the man in Civil War garb from the photo.

"Can I help you, ma'am?" he coughed out the question.

She pulled out her notebook. "Yes. Can I speak with the listing agent for the Shell House property?"

"No, ma'am."

When he didn't go on, she lifted her eyes from her notes to stare at him. "My name is Sloan Parsons. I'm a reporter, and I wanted to ask him some questions. Is he here?"

"No, ma'am," he said ignoring her statement.

She studied him curiously. Had he just refused to put her in touch with the agent? If so, why?

She pulled out her business card and handed it to him. He looked at it absently before setting it aside.

Something was definitely off here. She tried again. "Can I set up a meeting with the realtor tomorrow, Mr...?"

"Mervis. The name is Mervis."

"Mr. Mervis, I'd like to meet with the listing agent or anyone else who could answer some questions about that property."

"Sam Reese, the listing agent, is out of the country. Unreachable. There's no one else familiar," he said. "Sorry to waste your time."

Quelling her impatience with the doddering old man, she replied, "Okay. Thank you, sir."

Frustrated, she walked out. On to Plan B.

Sloan slipped into the front seat of her car and checked the clock on the dash. There was enough time to stop by the *Rehoboth Times* before they closed. She hoped that John Olsen, a fellow reporter, might be more forthcoming.

The *Times* was a small neighborhood paper not too different from her own. They all struggled to stay in business while urging subscribers to go digital. The office, located on the main street, had a white and tan-striped awning atop a row of windows. Two planters flanked the front door and overflowed with red geraniums, purple and white petunias, and ivy cascading down the sides. It was a charming small-town office. Quite different from her antiseptic, gray, suburban office building.

Sloan opened the door and heard the familiar hubbub of a newsroom—computers clacking away and printers purring. The large front room had four desks spread across it. Two were occupied with reporters, intent on their work. Another woman swooshed past with a stack of file folders.

"Someone will be with you in a minute," she said.

Sloan nodded, feeling the energy and pace of the room. She needed this. It kept her mind off the pain about her mom. It had been far too long since she'd felt this comforting sense of belonging.

A deep voice behind her interrupted her thoughts and she turned to see a tall, dark-haired man with blue eyes and the kind of lashes any girl would kill for. "Can I help you?" he asked.

Struck speechless, she hesitated a beat too long before blurting out the words, "I'm here to see John Olsen. It's about Shell House."

The man smiled. She suspected he got a similar reaction from women all the time. "John isn't here. He's out of town. I'm Max Farrell. John and I often collaborate. Can I help?"

"Yes, I wondered if I could speak with you about his article on the demolition of Shell House? Did you work with him on it?"

"I did. What questions do you have?" he asked with an arched eyebrow.

"My name is Sloan Parsons. I'm with the *Gazette*." She flipped another business card out of her purse, handing it to him. "I'd like to work on a deeper story. Could we sit down and talk about it? Perhaps grab a cup of coffee?"

He reached up to scratch the back of his neck, almost wincing. "There's not much to tell. You read the story, right?"

"I think there is a lot missing, don't you? Why did they drop the price by a million dollars? And then six months later, tear it down?"

"It's very simple, Miss..." he glanced down at her card and finished, "Parsons. The house didn't sell. And then they got an offer to divide the property into two lots, so they accepted it and took action."

He continued to stare at her card, avoiding her eyes. Sloan's journalistic antennae spiked. *He's hiding something.*

"Max... I have a gut feeling. An instinct. You know those feelings, right? You must get them too." She stood her ground.

He looked up and met her eyes. She sensed he may have been waging some internal battle. "Okay, one cup of coffee. Let me grab a couple things and I'll be right back." He headed to one of the unoccupied desks, picked up his phone, and pulled out a folder from a drawer before coming back to her.

She felt victorious but did her best not to let him see it.

As she sipped her coffee, Sloan glanced around the quaint little café next door to the newspaper office. They sat at a table for two near a window graced with ruffly, white curtains. Ceiling fans spun above their heads and beachgoers sat at the counter ordering club sandwiches and burgers. She could get used to a town like this.

"Tell me about yourself, Sloan Parsons." Max eyed her as he took a sip of coffee.

Her cheeks heated, but she composed herself. "I grew up in Alexandria, not far from Mt. Vernon, and graduated from George Washington University with a journalism degree. I had dreams of working at the *Washington Post*, but that didn't materialize. Now I'm a feature writer at the *Gazette*. I'm hoping to move to the features editor position soon." She lifted her hands. "That's it. That's my story."

He raised that dark eyebrow again. "Sounds like a lot is missing from that story." He sat back in his seat with a smile, and she relished the challenge it offered. She returned the smile with one of her own.

"Tell you what. I'll fill in the gaps on my life story if you fill in the gaps about Shell House."

"I already told you." He leaned forward. "There isn't a story here. The owners made a profit when they divided it into two lots. The end."

"Did you have any involvement in the coverage, or was it just John?"

"It was primarily his article."

Now it was Sloan's turn to raise an arched eyebrow. "Then why are we having coffee?"

He smiled warmly, which made her blush again. A tingle went down her spine all the way to her toes. She felt instantly connected to him, and judging by his smile and the teasing note in his voice, it seemed he felt the same.

Still leaning forward, his forearms rested on the table. He turned the question back to her. "Why do you think I wanted to have coffee?"

She almost giggled. As far as she was concerned, they could do this all day. But that feeling evaporated when he asked her another question.

"And why didn't you end up with that dream job at the *Post*?"

The tingles stopped, like she'd been doused with cold water. All the air rushed out of Sloan's lungs. She looked down and stared into her coffee.

"Sloan, I'm sorry. I..." Perhaps he realized he had overstepped.

"No, it's okay," she said, still averting her eyes. "I'm going to have to start talking about it at some point, so I might as well start with you."

He covered her hand with his for a second, his grip warm and firm, but then, just as quickly, he pulled back. "Sorry."

"No, it's okay." She took a deep breath. "At the end of my senior year, my mom got sick. I skipped graduation. It turned out she had cancer, so I stayed home to take care of her. The *Gazette* allowed me a flexible schedule, so I worked from home most of the time." Her voice started to waver. "We lost her two months ago."

"I'm sorry," Max said. "I feel bad for pushing you."

"How could you have known?"

Perhaps to remedy the situation somehow, he said, "I did work with John on the story. At least on the research."

Sloan's eyes shot to his, eager to hear more. Anything to stop the gnawing pain in her stomach that seemed to be ever-present.

He caught the hopeful gaze. "I thought something about it was odd, too. After the Duprees sold it, the house changed hands almost every other year. No one stayed there very long." Max paused.

Sloan urged him to continue. "And...?"

He sighed. "How much do you know about the Dupree family?"

"Only that they're gazillionaires."

He laughed. "Unfortunately, they made their millions off the backs of their workers. They ignored all safety concerns, and even when some of their employees from the manufacturing plant were dying from lead poisoning, they refused to listen." Max leaned closer and lowered his voice. "And that's why the house didn't sell. People thought it was haunted. By the souls of all the people who died due to negligence."

Sloan started to laugh but then realized he was dead serious. "I realize that they did some shady and irresponsible things, but haunted? Really?"

"Really. Or at least that's what people think. Word started coming out that people heard strange sounds—wailing, moaning, even screeching. No one could ever find the source of the noises."

"Did anyone ever see anything?" Sloan shifted to the edge of her seat.

"As a matter of fact, there are many reports of unexplained sightings. But this is the only actual photo I could find." He opened the folder and right on top was a grainy photograph. "It was taken about five years ago."

He handed it to her.

Sloan squinted as she looked at an image of a dimly lit hallway with a shadowy figure in the middle. It appeared to be a man. She held it a little closer to her face and spied what seemed to be another cloudy figure behind him holding a long thin item by his side. "Where did you get this? It looks like an original."

"It is the original. Untouched and unedited. I got it from a former owner who lived there. He took it to the authorities, but they disregarded it. Before he sold the house and moved to California, he gave it to me. He said no one believed him. Not even the realtor. I started tracking down former owners and got a similar story from all of them."

Sloan continued staring at the shadow in the picture. "Did you get any other information about the images in the photo?"

Max sat back. "I had a photography expert look at it. He had special equipment that enhanced the photo. The first figure is wearing what appears to be a uniform."

"What kind of uniform?"

"It's very similar to the style worn by the workers in the Dupree manufacturing plant."

With widened eyes, she stared at him. "This gets more intriguing by the moment."

Studying the picture again, she said, "The other figure looks like he's holding something. A bat? A stick?"

"A sword," Max interjected.

"A sword? What the..." She squinted her eyes to focus better. "How can you—"

"The photo enhancement clearly showed some type of sword," he answered.

"Did you take the information to the local authorities?"

"Yes, but they weren't interested. Kind of shut me down."

"That's bizarre. Wasn't anyone bothered by this information?" she asked incredulously.

"Not really. Only one person has been interested in anything that's happened in that house. A guy named Frank Mervis."

Sloan's gaze shot to his and something clicked in her brain. "Frank Mervis? I met him today. He said that only someone named Sam Reese knew about the sale of the property. And Sam Reese is conveniently out of the country."

"Yeah, Frank's a strange old fellow. Keeps to himself. Doesn't live in town. Rumor is that he worked for the Duprees years ago."

This time her eyebrows nearly rose to her hairline, and when he nodded, she could tell they were thinking the same thing. "So, tell me, Max. Does this ghost have something to do with the Duprees? Or could it conveniently be appearing so that a certain real estate agent can get more commissions?"

He handed her the whole file folder. "You can read my notes from all the interviews. It appears the sightings didn't start until after the deaths at the Dupree plant."

"Why not share this information? None of it was in John's article."

"I reached out to the listing agent, but Sam basically said, 'no comment.' I later found out that he didn't actually conduct the sale."

"Don't tell me Frank Mervis sold it."

Max nodded.

"He just keeps showing up like a bad penny." She shook her head.

"Our editor told us to stand down. When it comes to bad press and the Duprees..." He left the implication hanging.

"And you're sharing this with me because?"

"Perhaps this could be your ticket into the *Washington Post*."

Thoughts started swirling in her brain. Max was handing her the means to her dream job. But why?

Sloan had an inkling this wouldn't be the last time she would see Max. The thought made her oddly happy.

"I hope so. One last thing. Can I use your copier?"

Fifteen minutes later she stood back at the door of the real estate agency. The familiar jingle of the bell greeted her, along with a still empty office. She waited, and a few moments later, Sloan heard Mervis come down the hall. It seemed he moved more quickly this time. And as he strode out to confront her, he stood a little straighter now and wasn't quite as frail as she'd first thought. His posture and stance struck her with a familiarity of something she'd noticed earlier.

"What can I help you with this time, Miss Parsons?"

Even his voice seemed stronger. There was no sign of the confused old man Sloan had met earlier.

"I want to talk with you about Shell House. I know that it was you, not Sam Reese, that conducted the sale." She pulled out the folder and slapped it down on the desk in front of him.

He glanced at it but made no motion to open it. "What is it you think you know, Miss Parsons?"

"Dozens of ghost sightings have been collected, unrecognizable inhuman sounds... even an original photograph of something paranormal."

"Really? You're here to talk about things that go bump in the night?"

"Do you mean to say that you know nothing about any of this?"

Mervis opened the file and flipped through the pages quickly with a bored expression. "I've seen and heard all of this before."

"But how does it connect to all the workers who died? Because my sources tell me that many of them died from lead poisoning, and it was all at the hands of the Dupree company. It's convenient the supposed haunting began right after that. Maybe too convenient."

Mervis yawned. "And?"

"The Duprees tried to suppress the story," she continued.

He laughed, but she heard a hint of irritation. "Be careful what you say. It sounds like you have no proof of any of this, and you don't want to go around accusing the wrong people. You may live to regret it."

Was that a threat? Sloan refused to back down. She met his gaze head-on. "I'll find out the truth. I'm not worried about that at all. Perhaps the dead workers from the Dupree plant are roaming the halls seeking justice for their untimely deaths? Or could it be something else entirely?"

Mervis slapped the folder down on the desk. "Do you hear yourself? You sound crazy!"

"Then how do you explain it? Apparently you participated in all those sales over the years. Every couple of years, it looks like. Did you think all those people were lying?"

"Do you think we were stupid enough not to have investigated this ourselves?" Mervis leaned across the desk. He was close now, his face only inches from hers. Sloan stepped back.

He ambled over to a file cabinet in the corner. Opening a drawer, he sifted through the various folders and pulled one out with a flourish—a plain manila file folder, just like the one Max had given her.

He handed it over. "Here you go. Knock yourself out."

She flipped through the slim contents and then looked at him with wide eyes. "You're blaming the sounds and ghost sightings on radio wave frequencies? You can't be serious." Sloan closed the file and pushed it away.

"The FCC and the Geological Society both signed off on it."

"It doesn't make sense—" she started.

He interrupted her, his tone flippant. "You're way out of your league, Miss Parsons. Go home to your little paper. I'm too busy to listen to your crazy ghost stories. And your wild accusations."

He picked up the folder and disappeared back down the hallway, just as she suspected he might.

Sloan stood there a long moment, giving him the chance to come back. When he didn't, it told her everything she needed to know. She glanced back at the Civil War re-enactment photo on the wall where she'd seen the "soldier" aiming his sword at the monument. A much younger Frank Mervis was smiling at the camera.

Grabbing the remaining file, she walked out the front door, but she knew she was not done with this town or this story. A small smile curved onto her lips. One way or another, she was onto something, and she looked forward to seeing how the story would unfold.

Turning her car onto Rehoboth Avenue, Sloan headed south.

Frank Mervis watched from behind the curtain of his dark office as the reporter drove away. Once her car was out of sight, he reached for the thick folder of interview notes in front of him. She hadn't even noticed when he'd grabbed her folder. He chuckled, opening it, looking at the grainy original photograph and flipping through the pages of Max's research.

"Oh dear. It begins again. But this time, no more evidence!" He fed the folder and all its contents into the shredder. And that's when he saw the hand-printed note stuck to the back of the file.

"Got you. I copied everything and kept the originals. I hope you like being in the news, because this story is going to blow up."

SEASHELLS AND COCKLE TALES
OF HIGH MAGIC

Michele Savaunah Zirkle

Liv woke over and over in the night, speaking words she didn't know. Sweat dripped down her chest. By morning she could only remember one word... "*Güç*." An online search revealed it was a Turkish word meaning "power." She realized her mom might be right. Maybe she had been chosen, but chosen to do what? Restoring peace to the world as she'd wanted to do since she was a teenager seemed a task too enormous for her alone.

Liv staggered out of bed and opened her balcony door to the fresh ocean breeze of Rehoboth Beach. It stirred her senses and blew her sweaty blonde hair dry. The ocean waves glistened like silver shells. The sea rolled with grace. There was an awesomeness to this three-dimensional world and she wanted nothing more than to save it.

"Liv!" her mom shouted from the sand below. "Come see what I found."

Liv slid into a loose jumper and sandals and joined her mom under the shade of a grove of palm trees near the fire pit. Apparently there was a species of palm, called *Trachycarpus fortunei*, hardy enough to grow in Rehoboth's coastal climate. The woman took Liv's hand

and touched it to a squiggly symbol carved into the bark of the tree.

Liv jerked away and inspected her palm. "Damn! Could've warned me. Feels like I got electrocuted."

Her mom shrugged. "You're tough," she said and burst out laughing. "Remember who wouldn't help me up when I fell on the sidewalk the other day? God broke the mold with you, Olivia Michele."

Liv punched her mom softly on the shoulder and smiled. "Okay, *Iris*, I knew you weren't hurt. You know I won't help you play the victim. If you tell yourself you are too weak to get up, you will—" She tipped her head toward her mother.

Iris finished for her. "...be too weak to get up." Iris snapped a picture of the symbol on the tree with her phone. "Sounds crazy, but that wasn't there until I got close. It just appeared as I walked by. Like it had been imprinted by an invisible hand." She reached out and touched the symbol. "Not zapping me."

"Interesting," Liv said, inspecting the symbol. "Looks like the images I've been seeing in my hands." She gazed at her palms. "They're all slightly different, but circular."

Liv squinted as the sun glared off the coast.

"We're obviously supposed to be here, Mom. I mean, winning this week vacation, and now this familiar symbol on the tree. It's like a scavenger hunt to discover my next step and with each clue it's like I part the veil between worlds."

"You've convinced me that there aren't coincidences," Iris said, "that we really do manifest our reality through our thoughts." Iris looking heavenward. "You've taught me how to create my world by being grateful for what I have and envisioning what I want."

They joined hands under the unique palm tree.

"You have such a gift for sharing what you've learned, Liv. The knowledge you've gained from all the shamanic trainings, but most of all, the real-life practice you've gotten could benefit so many people. You've mastered how to relate to people. To be honest. To be yourself. To stick up for yourself. To reinvent yourself. To face your fears and live fully in each moment. You live the example—the world needs your wisdom."

"World's full of wisdom," Liv said, pulling her shawl tight.

Iris braced Liv's shoulders and looked her square in the face. "Only you can teach it the way you do, Liv. Only you."

Liv placed her hand over her heart. "Of all the moms I've had in other lifetimes, you're my favorite. You'll keep getting my advice for free."

"Free! I pay dearly." Iris shook her fists in the air like she was shaking pom-poms. "I'm your lead cheerleader—a hungry one. Heck, I have to be in ketosis by now. You could run a diet boot camp. I'm so hungry I could even eat that dried out, grain-free coconut concoction you call a protein pancake."

"Lord." Liv rolled her eyes and strolled across the patio. "You must be delirious! We'll nab an omelet at the corner café."

Liv plopped onto a chair on the patio under the midday sun and massaged her forehead while Iris arranged peonies in a vase.

"I woke up speaking a foreign language again," Liv said, "and saw a woman in my dream who had a similar symbol in her hands as me. Mom, I have to find the woman who carries this symbol. I do know that. My last vision was clear. Finding her is critical to uncovering what I'm doing here. There are so many of these symbols. I can't draw them all. I don't even know what they mean."

Iris laughed and ducked as a crane swooped low and landed on the wooden pole at the edge of the patio.

"Whoa!" Liv exclaimed. She stared at the long-necked bird. "Yeah, I can only take so much power coursing through me at a time." She huffed. "Maybe I need to lighten up. Have a beer. Watch a soccer game. Keep myself from having a heart attack."

The crane squawked.

"That would bore you more than living an entire day in 3D."

"Even more than listening to the principal spout out school rules. Lord, I'm so glad I gave up teaching high school to follow my passion, even though I miss the students," Liv said. "No worries about kids skipping class." Liv's indigo eyes sparkled as she giggled over the squawking crane. "I cheered the absconders over the fence as the class watched."

Iris pointed to the bird, its sharp beak extending to the sky. "Seems it has a message for you."

Liv leaned forward and typed into her phone. "Crane totem meaning is the ability to complete a calling."

The bird lifted off and landed on a pamphlet on the sand, pecked at it, then flew toward the ocean.

Liv snatched the paper and skimmed. "Message received," she said, saluting in the direction the bird had flown. "Mom, I'm going on a trip in two days."

The red rocks of Sedona, Arizona, served a decadent view to the venue of lightworkers from around the world who'd gathered to learn the mystical ways of shamanism.

Liv felt out of place, but many of the people seemed familiar. This whole scenario was like she'd lived it before. She was scoping the lobby when a lady with piercing eyes glided toward her. The woman seemed to glow from within.

"You've seen the sigils, haven't you?" she asked.

Liv shook her head. "Sigils?"

The lady wrinkled her nose. "Can I see your hands?"

Liv couldn't tell if this woman was thirty or seventy, but her beauty surpassed that of the most prominent runway models. Tiny painted toes were barely visible beneath a long skirt. She was a mixture of Mother Mary and a Celtic goddess.

Liv pushed up her long sleeves and extended her hands.

The lady cupped them and turned them palm-side up. "Do you see them move?"

Liv felt like the building was swaying. She widened her stance and studied the lady.

"You mean the symbols I keep seeing?" Liv gazed into her left palm like it was a crystal ball. "Yeah, they pulse, but don't vibrate as much as I feel like I am right now. My head is spinning."

"Here, dear," she said, leading Liv to a nearby set of chairs.

The lady settled beside Liv, keeping a hand on her arm. "I didn't mean to overwhelm you. My energy sometimes needs to be tamed. My name is Gloria and I see them too." Gloria's eyes scoped the eighty or so men and women chatting in the lobby. "We all do."

Liv took a deep breath and closed her eyes. She could sense this lady was an Ascended Master in human form. "So, what are sigils, and what do I do with them?" She scanned the lobby and adjoining conference room where folks from all races and creeds were whispering in small groups and inspecting each other's hands.

"Sigils are different than symbols," Gloria explained. "A sigil is alive with the frequency of a specific power itself, unlike a symbol that is representative of a concept or place, or in healing, a healer can access energy by drawing certain symbols. Some of the sigils we are receiving are angel names and some are healing frequencies for body systems, organs and emotions. We've come to heal people with them and therefore, save this planet."

Liv was nodding slowly, her eyes so wide that she seemed to be in a trance.

"Relax. We've done it before and can do it again."

Liv motioned for a glass of wine from a passing waitress while Gloria opted for water. "I slip through dimensions easily after breaking my luminous cocoon years ago so I only sip a bit when I'm home."

Liv pulled the glass from her lips. "You broke your energy field? How'd you do that?"

"I didn't mean to. Had a near-death experience and it shattered. Felt like my essence was pulled through a straw. Wouldn't recommend it." Gloria giggled and Liv joined her.

"I could be more chill about all this mystical, metaphysical stuff," Liv said, smiling. "Humor help?"

"You mean like walking into your home office and seeing Archangel Michael who's so big his head is busting through your roof, and just asking him what he's there for, like he's the next door neighbor knocking?"

Liv held the wine glass midair, her eyes like a bullfrog's.

"Just a normal day for me." Gloria waved her hand through the air.

"I want to see Michael!" Liv said, slapping her leg. "I did drive through a tree once that must have existed in a different dimension, but wow, an angel. How fabulous!" She chuckled. "I will say hearing everyone's thoughts in a restaurant makes it hard to enjoy the meal, especially if they're arguing."

"Many ways to block that. Have you tried blasting colors? Each one has a different frequency which blocks different energies."

Liv hung her head. "When I remember. I need to get better at protecting myself."

Gloria smiled. "Let's focus on the bigger picture now—the reason we are here in this moment in history. We have all gathered to elevate the masses to higher dimensions. Without our group utilizing these sigils we are getting downloaded with, humans will self-destruct."

"Does that mean I'm not human?" Liv tucked her chin.

"We're from a planet outside Earth's solar system," Gloria offered. "Your awakening started ten years ago. I've been at it for thirty. The sigils you're seeing now are the newest batch and their purpose is to heal the Earth body herself. It is critical you answer the calling. The ones to whom the sigils are given are granted immense power."

Liv set her wine on the table and nodded. "I talk in Turkish in my sleep. The one word I remember is *güç*, and it means—"

"Power. And power comes at a price," Gloria added, winking. "My grandmother was from Turkey." Gloria continued while Liv sat as still as a statue. "Others won't understand you. Loneliness will be your companion, but you'll find comfort in this light family that extends around the world. I know you're building your healing and life-coaching business now, but much of your gift to the world is through your writing. You will inspire others through your words. After this weekend's training, many more will gravitate to you, even if they don't know what draws them. Your words will have great impact."

"I do have a small client base, but I've tried for years to support myself financially from it and it hasn't prospered. How—"

"Don't worry about the how," Gloria advised. "You just need to do you. Your presence is enough. You'll be an even stronger walking, talking vessel of inspiration when you finish here."

"You sound like my mom," Liv said. "She stayed back at the beach where we were vacationing and… a pamphlet there is how I found you."

"You've learned to follow signs from the Divine. Some call them God winks or laws of attraction. They lead you where you need to go. Now, you must teach others to do the same."

The Master smiled and they shuffled into the meeting room where a wall-sized screen displayed a picture of a group of cranes.

Liv returned to Shell House on a Sunday flight and over dinner excitedly told her mom that she'd met people from all over the globe who also saw the sigils. She explained she could incorporate them into her holistic healing practice when they returned home to Ohio and that they work in distant healing as well.

Liv knew too much now. She couldn't ever unknow what she knew. And she wouldn't even try. It would endanger the entire human race and set her soul plunging into an underworld she'd fought to avoid.

Liv cracked open another lobster shell. "The most amazing thing about this healing isn't that these living sigils, as they are called, show up in the hands of those who are supposed to use them," Liv said. "It's that we healers have sigils to heal the Earth and when we empower others by helping them heal, we, by proxy, heal the entire world."

Iris slid Liv a folded paper with a sigil at the bottom. "Found this tucked into a cookbook here in the kitchen while you were gone. Not your usual recipe."

Liv smiled a buttery smile and read it aloud:

Make a circle of shells in the sand.
Sit in the middle, draw with your hand.
The sigils you learned will come alive.
Buzzing your hands like a beehive.

Spiral hope deep within.
The earth and the sea
And in you and me.

Give thanks for the lessons
Both easy and hard
That led you to me in the cupboard.
Replace this recipe you must do
For those who will come behind you.

Find the shell that calls your name.
This is the most fun part of the game.
String it on a necklace around your neck.
Polish it with hope and give it a peck.
Strength will be yours to heal the world each day
That you heal yourself and remember to play.

Liv smoothed her left hand over the sigil on the paper and felt a pulse emanating from it.

"I didn't notice before," Iris said from across the table. "Upside down, it looks like your initials, *OM*. Olivia Michele."

Liv let out a deep "Ommm," sound like in yoga class. "Yep, you knew I was a yogi before I could talk."

"Om means Source, right?" Iris asked. "Must've known that, too."

Monday morning Liv woke early to an earthquake. Every cell in her body vibrated. When she stood and braced herself against the nightstand, the feeling stopped.

She knocked on her mother's door. "Mom, you okay?"

"Come in." Iris was propped on one arm in bed.

Liv strode to the wall-length window where the sun darted through partially parted curtains. "How in the hell did you sleep through that?" she asked.

"Through what?"

Liv pushed the curtains wide. "Seriously, Mom. That earthquake."

Iris scooted out of bed and blinked hard. "Earthquake? I didn't feel any earthquake."

Liv pointed to her mom's phone. "See how strong it was."

Iris searched the news app. "Honey, I don't see anything."

Liv flipped her hand to the sky. "What's happening to me?"

All day and into the evening Liv practiced drawing the opening sigils for love, praise, gratitude, trust and hope that she'd learned in Arizona. She recited the spell on the recipe paper. She fasted and prayed. She strolled the beach and released old beliefs about herself and about others—about right and wrong, Heaven and Hell, and the stigma that came with her abilities.

Liv cried and prayed for strength. She wished she could give up having to know the answers for "why" that her mind so desperately craved.

She had visions of aliens descending from the clouds, some hostile and others coming to aid humanity. She saw floods; throngs of homeless folks; hungry, abused children; and meteors hitting the Earth.

Liv referred to her sigil notebook and drew the appropriate healing ones on a map with gridlines of the planet where she witnessed catastrophic events happening. She sketched them above pictures of religious leaders and political figures, both the honest and corrupt. She placed them on children's heads and wounded hearts of all sorts.

She knew deep within her soul that she had been born to do this. Overanalyzing would only destroy the very faith required for her to be effective. She accepted she would be walking a balance beam between worlds. Sharing too much would get her committed to the nut house. Some things she could share with others and some secrets would go with her to the grave. She'd be unpopular in certain groups and shunned by others. It was a price she was willing to pay.

As for her current boyfriend, she only hoped he would remain supportive and accepting of her unusual line of work.

By sunset, Liv sat motionless on the sand, the tide licking her toes.

Iris sauntered up and sat beside her. "Olivia Michele, my bell, my little seashell," she sang. "Done saving the world?"

"I may never know the outcome of what I do," Liv said, briefly laying her head on her mom's shoulder. "I must live by proxy the principles of high magic for the humans whose eyes are shut."

"What principles?" Iris asked.

"There's a ton of them. Like living with integrity and wholesomeness, finding joy in the moment, and trusting God—or the universal life force—to lead the way. Allowing myself to explore how to live my life rather than mimic society or image-driven media."

Liv scooped sand into her hand and let it dribble through her fingers. "Our lives are short. We're all just falling out windows and waiting to hit the ground. If I change, everything around me changes. I want to create a good change... but all the disasters I see?"

Iris pursed her lips and rubbed Liv's knee.

"I'm scared I'm not resilient enough or powerful enough to make a difference."

"The results of your work might be more immediate than you think," Iris said as they meandered back to Shell House. "It's been all over the news. A solar flare almost knocked us back to the stone age. If it would've hit the outer ring of the Earth's atmosphere, the electric grid would've been demolished."

Liv slid her arm around her mom's waist. "I'm relieved I don't have to do this work alone. I'm part of an enormous light family spread throughout the globe, and Mom, you may not get shocked when you touch the sigils, but you're a healer and important to mankind's collective healing. There are many types of healers. You're a prayer warrior with wings of steel."

As soon as they reached the patio, Liv heard her phone ringing inside. It was Gloria. Liv settled into the hammock to talk while Iris munched from a fruit tray and relaxed into an Adirondack chair with a book.

"Hi, love," Liv said. "It's so good to hear your voice. I felt you with me all day while I worked my magic."

Gloria replied, "Yes, we were lightning rods, deflecting that solar flare. Think my eyebrows are even singed!" Her laugh echoed off the stone patio. "Which beach are you at? I used to own a house along the Delaware coast. Actually, saw my first sigil in a tree there."

Liv blinked fast. "A tree? I'm in Rehoboth at a place called Sh—"

"Shell House! Of course you are!" Gloria exclaimed. "That's where I lived decades ago. The tree stands to the right of the patio as you look at the ocean."

"The spell Mom found in the cookbook was yours then," Liv said. "Do you have a magic tree where you live now?"

"The magic is in you, dear. The tree was just a willing participant to the cacophony of an ever-changing universe. Our journeys are unique though we have a similar calling. Just remember—people need your words, written or spoken. You are inspiration. Keep writing. Words are power."

Liv's whole body shook, and goosebumps percolated up her back and neck. She recognized the truth when she heard it. She had the magic cocktail, and it wasn't found in a bottle of liquor. It was her soul's language speaking from deep within her belly. It was her native tongue and needed no transcription.

A long-necked crane squawked above Liv's laughter as tales of high magic soared across the phone waves and Shell House shimmered with hope.

SEE YOU AROUND THE COSMOS, SWEET CHEEKS!

Phil Giunta

Dewey Beach, Delaware
November 1983

In the chill of late autumn, Jenna wriggled her toes in the wet sand while gelid waves soaked the rolled cuffs of her jeans. She had driven to her family's beach house in Delaware from the University of Maryland and arrived a few hours after sunset. No sooner had she parked her Fiero in the garage than she kicked off her Keds and rushed to the edge of the surf.

"Knew I'd find you out here, *garotinha*," a voice called. "Only you would stand barefoot in freezing water to stare at the sky. Just like when you were little."

Jenna grinned at the familiar Portuguese diminutive for *little girl*, but her gaze remained fixed on the heavens as her family's housekeeper, Rosa, trudged toward her with flashlight in hand. "It feels wonderful. You should try it."

"No, thanks. This old gal can see the stars just fine from back here."

"I might bring my telescope out to the patio tonight."

"You'll have plenty of time for it. Your mother called a few minutes ago. There was some legal problem with that big merger. Your father had to go into the office to help with negotiations."

Jenna kicked a clump of wet sand into the water. "Always business before family."

"Your parents and brother won't get here until after midnight. Want me to stay until they arrive?"

Jenna sauntered up the beach and wrapped her arms around Rosa. "As much as I would love your company, I don't want to keep you from your family the night before Thanksgiving."

Rosa shrugged. "I'm only going to Dover to stay with my sister and her husband for the weekend. They're doing all the cooking. A traditional Portuguese feast."

"Sounds wonderful, but don't worry about me. I'll be fine tonight. I'm a big girl now, you know."

"You'll always be *garotinha* to me. Can I make you something to eat before I leave?"

"I grabbed pizza on the way."

"I don't know how you college kids survive on junk food. Look, a shooting star!" Rosa thrust a finger toward the sky where a small white orb streaked through the constellation Pegasus. "Make a wish."

"I'm not a kid anymore, Rosa."

"You were a lot more agreeable when you were."

"That's moving too slow for a meteor."

"Maybe it's a jet or a satel—" The orb turned forty-five degrees west and shot across the sky until it disappeared behind the trees. "*Meu Deus!*" Rosa gaped at Jenna. "Tell me that was a UFO."

"Well, it was no jet or satellite and sure as hell wasn't debris."

"You can tell your family you saw an alien ship."

Jenna snickered. "I'm an astronomy major and a sci-fi nerd. They'd never believe me."

"I'll back you up."

"I doubt that'll help. You've been my partner in crime since I was five."

"True, but what else could it have been?"

"I guess we'll never know."

"I can't wait to tell my sister about it. Anyway, the turkeys are in the fridge and the dining room table is set."

"And I'm sure the place is immaculate as always. We'll make sure it stays that way." The women embraced once more. "Thank you for getting the house ready for us, Rosa. Safe drive to Dover and have a fabulous holiday."

"You, too. Hose the sand off your feet before you go inside and no wild parties tonight, *garotinha*."

"Just me, my telescope, and the stars. I'm sure that UFO was the craziest thing that'll happen this evening."

On the patio an hour later, Jenna peered through her telescope's eyepiece at the Pleiades in the northwestern quadrant of Taurus. "Lovely to see you again, my friends."

No sooner had she spoken than the star cluster vanished. Jenna yanked a flashlight from her coat pocket and examined the telescope's lens. There were no obstructions.

She lifted her gaze skyward and gasped. A ring of pulsing red lights, easily fifty feet across, glided toward the beach where she and Rosa had stood earlier. Its crimson glow illuminated the bottom of an enormous craft. It was too dark to discern its exact shape, but the

UFO—for what else could it be?—obscured most of the stars.

My God! You were right, Rosa.

Jenna's flashlight winked out. After sliding the button back and forth to no avail, she tossed it onto a nearby table and raced to the edge of the property. She threw open the gate and tore her gaze away from the spaceship to glance along the short path ahead of her. In the distance, a man in dark clothes stood with his hands clasped behind him, head tilted up. One of the neighbors? There weren't many homes in this part of town, but it was possible someone else had decided to spend Thanksgiving by the sea. *How did he get out there so quickly?*

The craft hovered directly above him. Its pulsing red lights brightened to a steady white halo. The man backed away and raised a hand to his temple. His lips moved, but his words were drowned by the crashing surf.

If he's not afraid, then maybe he's an—

Jenna's thought died with a scream as a column of blinding white light shot straight down and burrowed into the beach with a thunderous roar, propelling sand and seashells in all directions. The ground shuddered under the force of the assault. Jenna shielded her eyes and scanned the area, but the man was nowhere to be found. Had he been obliterated by the blast or was he merely concealed by the dust plume?

Fearing the worst, Jenna crept toward the scene until a second temblor knocked her off her feet. Undaunted, she picked herself up but failed to notice the massive whelk shell until it slammed into the side of her head.

Jenna's knees buckled and the wondrous spectacle faded into the night.

Three beeps. Two beeps. One beep.

Three beeps. Two beeps. One beep.

"Perfect. You should be just fine in a moment."

Jenna winced at the throbbing in her skull. Something was clamped around her forehead. She opened her eyes to the warm glow of a nearby lamp. A hand reached down. The beeping stopped. The pressure on her head subsided.

Jenna peered up at the tall, lean young man standing over her. He met her gaze with wide gray eyes that were only a few shades lighter than his perfectly coiffed hair.

He cocked his head and flashed a disarming grin. "And she's back. No sudden moves now. You took a nasty hit from flying debris. I apologize for that. The drill can be dangerous, but..." He held up a narrow, jointed apparatus laden with solid and flashing lights. "After healing your wound, I ran a scan and I'm pleased to say there's no permanent damage."

Jenna raised her head from the pillow and sat up on the sofa. "Thank you." *Ran a scan?* Her eyes shot open. *Shit, it's the guy from the beach!* She scrambled to her feet and snatched a cast iron seahorse statue from the end table. "Who are you?"

The man clasped his hands behind him. "Sometimes I'm a treasure hunter, other times an archaeologist. On this expedition, I am but a humble scavenger."

"With a spaceship. Are you an alien?"

"Only when I'm on someone else's planet, sweet cheeks."

Jenna raised an eyebrow. "Excuse me?"

"Is that not a term of endearment?"

"I think you meant sweet*heart*."

"My apologies. English is my two hundred and sixty-fourth language." He glanced around the room. "Do you live in this enormous house all by yourself?"

"No. My family will be here any minute. You should leave."

"Can't. Looking for something."

"Did you find it?"

"Maybe. How are you feeling, by the way?"

Jenna's hazy, frantic thoughts filled with lurid accounts of alien abductions, something she'd never believed—until now. "What are you planning to do with me?"

All humor fled the man's expression as he held up a small silver tube about the size of a cigar. "I'm afraid I'm going to have to paralyze you and take you back to my ship. There, you will be stripped naked and probed."

Jenna raised the iron seahorse.

The man held up his hands. "I'm being facetious. Probe you? I don't even know you. This is just an airbrush. I use it to blast dirt off artifacts." He pressed a button atop the tube, releasing a loud hiss. "It pulls in ambient air through the back and blasts it out through the nozzle using a built-in microcompressor."

After a moment, Jenna lowered the statue. "Jerk."

"My name is Deverin." He extended a hand. It certainly appeared human—five fingers, opposable thumb, even manicured nails. "I believe this is still the customary greeting in this region of your world? I promise it won't transform into a mouth and bite your arm off."

She tightened her grip on the iron seahorse as she sidestepped the coffee table and leaned toward him.

"Jenna." She gave his fingers a perfunctory squeeze and backed away. "You're hot."

"You ain't so bad yourself, sweet cheeks."

She rolled her eyes. "No, I mean your hand is hot to the touch."

"My body temperature is approximately nine degrees higher than the average human."

"You look like one of us."

"I'm a shapeshifter."

"Really? Where are you from?"

"My homeworld is called Crelsaria. It's over two hundred light years away. We don't often venture out this far. In fact, this is only my third visit to your lovely planet."

"Can I see the inside of your ship?"

Deverin smiled. "That wouldn't be my first choice."

Without turning her back on him, Jenna crossed the room and gazed through the window into complete darkness. Once again, the stars were visible above the beach. "Where is it?"

"Still up there, waiting for my next command."

"What were you digging for out there?"

"You ask a lot of questions."

"As a student of astronomy and planetary science, I have an interest in all things related to space."

"Is that so?" Deverin lifted a hand to his temple. For a moment, his eyes seemed to focus on something directly in front of his face. "Then this is your lucky day. You can't see it from here, but there's now a gaping hole in the beach and at the bottom lies a probe, crude by today's standards. Well, by the standards of any species with interstellar capability. It crashed here about three thousand years ago. Probably collided with an asteroid or was pulled into the gravity well of one of your outer planets and thrown off course. It's still transmitting a low subspace signal."

"After all this time?"

"Their purpose was to explore the galaxy, sweet cheeks. They were built to last."

"Stop calling me that! My name is Jenna. If I can't go aboard your ship, can I at least see this probe?"

Deverin pondered it for a moment. "I suppose it couldn't hurt. Least I could do after all I've put you through tonight. How's your head?"

"I'll live. Any chance you can stick around until my family gets here? They'll never believe me otherwise."

"I'm on a tight schedule, sweet cheeks."

"For an alien, you certainly have a smart mouth."

"In my true form, I have three of them."

"I don't want to know."

On the beach, Jenna peered down into an enormous pit surrounded by mounds of sand, stone, and seashell fragments. "I don't know how I'm going to explain this."

"Don't worry about the hole. When we're done, it'll be as if I was never here." Deverin lifted his gaze to the ring of pulsing red lights. "And no more screeching death rays, I promise."

Nevertheless, Jenna backed away when a narrow beam of crimson light fired into the pit. "How are you controlling the ship?"

Deverin pressed two fingers against his right temple. "Implant. It generates a holographic image in front of me that only I can see and manipulate purely by thought."

"Totally rad. How does it interface with your brain?"

"As I said, I am but a simple archaeologist and cannot explain the intricacies of biotechnology. It works and that's enough for me."

"Does your ship have a name?"

"Yes, the *Arquanla*. She was a goddess from Crelsarian mythology. Ah, here we are." Deverin held up a hand. "Wait for it... wait for it."

An immense clump of wet sand and dirt emerged, levitating at the end of what Jenna realized was a tractor beam. The ancient probe was as large as a refrigerator but roughly triangular in shape, like an enormous cone.

Deverin stood beside Jenna as the mass lifted above their heads. "That's high enough, thank you." Ghost crabs tumbled onto the beach and scurried off toward the surf as the column of light carried its burden away from the edge of the pit. "Perfect." And abruptly it shut off.

The probe crashed to the beach with a muffled thud.

"Yaakit! Oh, pardon my language." He raised a hand to his temple. "They just upgraded my interface before I left. Rearranged all the icons. Pain in the eulbees."

"Icons... right. What are eulbees?"

"Male genitalia."

"Huh. I'm learning so much tonight."

The impact had knocked just enough sand off the probe to reveal what appeared to be a six-foot arrowhead covered in black tiles of various sizes. Deverin disappeared around its aft section.

"What kind of propulsion does it have?" As Jenna approached, her foot rolled over something smooth and round. She crouched down and wiped sand off the object's surface to reveal a bluish glow.

"Plasma engines," Deverin replied. "But this craft should have a small device that uses exotic matter to create what your scientists call a wormhole. It's what allows our vessels to cross thousands of light-years in a short time."

"What's it look like?"

"A glowing blue spheroid. Using your measurements, it's about seventeen centimeters long and ten around."

"Is it dangerous?"

"It isn't radioactive, if that's what you mean."

While Deverin was distracted, Jenna shoved the device deeper into the sand until it was completely concealed. Perfect evidence of her close encounter. She would return for it once Deverin had left. For now, she strolled around the front of the probe, running a hand over its surface.

"It isn't here, but I found a hull breach." Deverin backed away from an open hatch. "If this probe did collide with an asteroid or was struck by a meteoroid, the device might have been ejected into space. Disappointing. They're becoming scarce."

"I'm sorry you didn't find what you were looking for. So, now what?"

"I'll take this relic back to my ship. Some of its other parts might be salvageable." He turned to her with a smile. "So, I guess this is where you and I part ways. When your family gets here, you can tell them you met an alien from outer space. By then, I'll be long gone."

Jenna waved toward the pit. "What about this mess?"

"I believe in leaving a place as clean as I found it. No one will ever know I was here."

"Can I watch?"

"I think you've seen enough for one night, sweet cheeks."

"We've come this far, what's the harm—" Jenna shielded her eyes against a blast of blue light that enveloped her from above. Overcome by fatigue, she stumbled backward. The light tracked her every move. She recovered her footing and dashed toward the house, but the beam locked onto her within seconds.

She never made it to the gate.

"Asleep in front of the TV as usual, and watching *Cosmos* no less."

"What's with all the sand in here? There's no way Rosa would have left the place like this."

"Looks like Jenna tracked it in."

"For all I know, we may be visited by a different extraterrestrial civilization every second Tuesday—"

"Wake up, sweetie."

Extraterrestrial? Jenna's eyes shot open, heart pounding. With a yelp, she swatted away the hand shaking her shoulder and kicked at the blanket, tangling it around her feet in the process. She tumbled to the floor. Laughter erupted from across the room.

"Jenna, it's okay. Calm down."

Extricating herself from the blanket, she snatched the iron seahorse from the end table.

Her gaze swept across four familiar faces—her bemused father, concerned mother, smirking little brother, and Carl Sagan. The latter was, of course, speaking from the TV.

"—but the extraordinary claims are not supported by extraordinary evidence."

"Evidence," she muttered. "I have evidence. I buried it out there."

"Jenna, sweetie." Her father lowered his hands. "You okay?"

"Did you see him? Is he still out there?"

"Who?"

"The alien!" Jenna's arms flailed as her words tumbled out. "He was on the beach. He had a massive spaceship. It blasted a hole in the sand with a beam of light and hauled out this ancient probe that crashed here three thousand years ago."

"Breathe, Jenna." Her father pointed to the seahorse. "And please put that down."

"I'll have what she's having." Her brother headed for the stairs. "On second thought, I don't want to become a nerd. I'm going to bed. Wake me if the alien comes back."

"It was a dream, honey." Her mother shook her head before turning off the TV. "You have too much space stuff on the brain."

"Her head's been in the stars ever since we took her to that planetarium when she was what... eight?"

"Nine," Jenna muttered.

"Your mother and I walked out to the beach when we got here." Her father picked up the blanket from the floor, shook the sand out of it, and tossed it onto the sofa. "I assure you, it's completely intact. No gaping holes, no spaceships, no little green men, but you're more than welcome to see for yourself."

"I can prove it." Jenna marched to the front door. "Something fell out of that probe he excavated. I buried it on the beach until I could go back for it. Wait here."

"Remember to hose the sand off your feet this time!"

Handfuls of sand flew in all directions, yet Jenna came up empty again. She rocked back on her haunches. "It was here, damn it!"

"A little to your left."

"Oh, thanks." She whirled, scanning the beach in every direction, but there was no one in sight. "Deverin?"

"Down here."

Jenna leaned to her left and resumed digging until she unearthed a palm-sized device that resembled a hockey puck topped with a flashing red light.

"It's a holo-emitter," the voice said. "Press the button."

She tapped it with her thumb. The red light turned solid green and the undulating hologram of a gray-skinned spindly creature appeared less than two meters away complete with four arms, four legs—and three mouths. Despite all of that, it had only two eyes.

It took a moment for Jenna's voice to catch up with her brain. "Deverin?"

"Nice try, sweet cheeks, but that device you tried to steal emits a unique particle wave that's detectable on my scanners. Believe me when I say that your species isn't ready for that kind of technology."

"You could have just said so. I ought to kick you in your eulbees for knocking me out."

He bowed his head. "My apologies. I admit that was uncivil of me, but as I said, I'm on a tight schedule. I'll leave you with this. Your race shows great promise and many eyes are watching from out here. We admire your insatiable curiosity and indomitable spirit, but you still lack wisdom. If you survive your adolescence, and overcome your destructive tendencies, we hope you'll join us someday."

Jenna's tone softened. "I hope so, too. Thank you for showing me what's possible. Maybe we'll meet again... out there."

Deverin cocked his head. "See you around the cosmos, sweet cheeks!"

With that, the hologram vanished. Far above, a chasing loop of red lights glided into view and was joined by a wider halo of white. The *Arquanla* ascended into the sky until it faded to a small orb sailing toward the horizon.

Jenna's father ambled onto the beach and slipped an arm around her shoulder. "Find what you were looking for?"

She tightened her grip on the holo-emitter. "More than I ever imagined."

"Hey, a shooting star!" He pointed to the orb. "Make a wish, kiddo."

Wriggling her toes in the sand, Jenna smiled. "I already did."

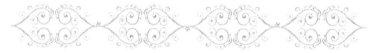

VACATION
IT'S A FAMILY AFFAIR

James Robinson, Jr.

For as long as I can remember, vacations have been a family affair. The participants may have changed, the venues may have improved—the locations higher class and more costly throughout the years—but basically, the spirit of the getaways remained the same.

I began vacationing at about eight years old in Wildwood, New Jersey. My companions on those initial weekly forays included my parents and paternal grandparents, who lived in Connellsville about fifty miles from Pittsburgh. During these early beach years, I spent most of my time in the sun, playing in the sand and floundering about in the ocean waiting for a rogue wave to knock me off my feet.

One of my fondest, yet devilish, recollections was of sneaking up behind Grandfather Robinson in the ocean and pulling down his swim trunks to expose his light-brown derriere. As you might imagine, it was quite a shock to Pop Pop. Just a bit of tomfoolery.

I've never been to the beach with my own grandchildren, but I suspect they would have more maturity than to yank down Pap's trunks. But now that I've broached the subject, I can envision the little suckers ganging up on me, getting my swimwear off, throwing them about, and playing "keep the swim trunks from Pap." The thought of it gives me a chill.

No wonder I've never been to the shore with the little cretins.

But it's a moot point; I don't go near the water anyway. I sit under the umbrella wearing a hat, a T-shirt and swim trunks. I still get a tan.

Anyhow, my father wasn't upset about the trunks episode. In fact, he got a big kick out of it. He'll often chuckle and say, "Remember the time you pulled my old man's pants down?"

Bit of the devil in my father. Now you see where I got it.

My next vacation memories center around a whole new wave (no pun intended) of beach goers: my mother and father, my aunt Marva and uncle Gene, and my grandmother and grandfather on my mother's side, Rema and Earl. This group provided a very different beach-going experience.

During 1964-67, I was in my pubescent years. We rented a house from a woman I knew only as "Miss Jackson." We paid her about $125 for a week. Damn you, inflation! She was a very enterprising black woman, owning the home we rented and other properties in Wildwood.

For the purpose of this piece let's call Miss Jackson, "Ms. Jackson." It suits her better in modern times. I never knew her first name. I wonder if anyone in the group did. Perhaps my grandmother who wrote the check.

I didn't know the term *lesbian*, and never heard Ms. Jackson described in that manner by my family, but the picture of her I am dredging up in my mind as I write is "lesbianesque"—a solidly built woman in manly attire with a rough demeanor and brusque attitude... the type of woman who might have a female companion—a woman that people would speak of in hushed whispers back then.

Perhaps my family spoke of her in similar whispers when I was out of earshot. Or maybe we were all just too innocent to know.

Ms. Jackson's rentals were not to be compared with a Ramada Inn. We weren't welcome in the large-chain hotels and beach motels anyway.

I remember driving down the beachfront road. The Jolly Roger Motel always caught my eye. And little wonder. The Jolly Roger had a huge pirate—eyepatch, bandana, and tri-cornered hat—standing over the roof, ratcheted down by long taut cables.

To me the whole extravaganza always said: "Don't bother trying to stay here, mate. Don't even get out of your car. Try Ms. Jackson."

"Oh, and by the way, *shiver me timbers.*"

I also recall busloads of blacks coming in on Saturdays from Philadelphia and parking in the local ballfield for a day of cheap beach fun. Caught between a rock and a hard place, they did the best they could. I always felt bad when I saw seagulls fighting over the scraps of food on the empty ballfield on Sunday—remnants of a one-day stay by the group. They were even more unwelcome at the Jolly Roger than we were. I'm betting very few members of the group could even have afforded a week at a Ms. Jackson home. Yes, Ms. Jackson rented homes, warm inviting houses with antiques, and cooking-friendly kitchens, wooden staircases and banisters, and three full bedrooms.

But no pirate.

Unfortunately, only one bathroom with one bathtub. And no shower. But we made do. More about this later.

Although warm and inviting, Ms. Jackson's homes were definitely not beachfront. Actually, I don't remember any beachfront homes being able to compete with the boardwalk. The Jolly Roger and friends had that all sewed up.

Every day when beach time rolled around, we slipped into our suits; packed up our blankets, cooler, towels, umbrella, and snacks; and trudged the five blocks through the city streets to sun and fun.

Sunblock? HA! The sun was our friend back then. We wanted to get a tan so we could go back home and be the envy of friends and family.

"O-o-o-o-h," they would say, "you got a suntan."

Suntan was synonymous with a warm, relaxing, sunny vacation. And you didn't *get* a suntan; you *earned* a suntan.

Now we realize that the sun is, in fact, not our friend but rather, a huge, necessary, evil yellow orb from which we protect our eyes. For some reason, however, we allow it to make toast out of our skin. When we thought we were being tanned by the sun we were actually being fried like an egg. Such shoddy treatment by a so-called friend causes premature skin aging. Still, I see young adults— mainly ladies—lying on towels in direct sunlight, seemingly oblivious to the evil rays, flipping themselves every thirty minutes like breakfast flapjacks on a hot griddle.

Little wonder most of us no longer pay homage to the sun god. As Graham Chapman of Monty Python might be heard to say, "We spit in the sun's general direction."

These days, we trek to the beach or pool armed with sunblock SPF 35 or higher.

But, despite our ignorance, my family certainly had fun lying around on our beach towels and frolicking in the ocean. When we were done late that afternoon, we packed up our belongings and our sand-covered physiques for the five-block trip home across cement tundra.

On the pilgrimage to Ms. Jackson's Eden began one of my all-time favorite beach rituals. Covered with sand and soil and with only one tub to accommodate our grime, we would sing a little jingle to mark our spot in the wash line.

"First in the bathtub..." someone would carol the familiar refrain.

Funny thing. It usually took a couple of blocks for a member of the group to remember to sing the little ditty and stake their claim. You would think it would be on everyone's mind.

Then, one-by-one, the tune went down the line: *second in the bathtub, third, fourth...* Number five didn't bother to join in; it was a humiliating spot to be in.

I recall being in that five-spot quite often. Once I heard the initial *first in the bathtub,* I just couldn't pull the trigger. I stood flatfooted, tongue tied until all of the numbers were rattled off.

Sitting in beach soot for four bathings, listening to the splashing of bath water running, wasn't a terrible thing. But it was an ignominious way to spend the end of a delightful shore encounter.

Each bather was required to clean the tub for the tubber behind them. But if you've ever cleaned beach sand and scruff from a tub (I'm going to say you probably haven't), you know it's difficult. Sand is a tricky thug—a stubborn, little granular bugger without a conscience.

Well, one time when I was in the fourth spot, my uncle took offense that I hadn't put enough elbow grease into cleaning the tub prior to his use. I got a ten-minute lecture on how to clean a cast-iron water bucket... including directions on how to find the sponge and cleanser. And we're not talking about eighty-year-old, crotchety Uncle Joe here. I was twelve and he was twenty-four.

As far as I was concerned, the last person who used the tub should clean it. It was all part of the shame and disgrace of being number five.

Those were the unwritten rules.

And besides, why scrub the porcelain enclosure with claw feet like some Merry Maid service when someone else was coming behind you to wipe off their grit?

I'm sure he saw me as a spoiled kid who didn't clean his room. I saw him as a bozo who had pulled me aside to pass along his tough love and expertise in Tubbery—a little known major with a minor in Tubology.

Okay, I'm done now. Sorry, just venting. Thank God for showers.

I got married in 1976 and started a family soon after ending my Wildwood vacation tradition. In 1987, I was a benefits analyst at the University of Pittsburgh. I related my family's interest in Hilton Head Island and my assistant—a Hilton Head veteran—gave us directions.

My children were ages four, five, and seven and we decided they were ready for our first beach trip. I would start my own family beach tradition.

At first, Hilton Head trips were all about piling in the car and driving to the destination. We drove separately from my parents. It was a 600-mile trip, one day for many Pittsburgh-to-Paradise travelers, but we made it a two-day effort. As we got more familiar with the jaunt, we found more suitable places to make the overnight stop.

While others travel to exotic parts of the world, I reached the pinnacle of my vacation experience in Hilton Head Island. Why? Well, for as much of what Hilton Head didn't have as what it did.

For the most part, Hilton Head was a golf mecca. When we told friends and acquaintances that we vacationed there, the first thing they asked was, "Do you golf?" We told them, "No, we don't golf. We just relax."

My mother and father pretty much did exactly what they did at home on 1400 Pennsylvania Avenue. They just did it while lounging on a balcony or sitting on the beach. My father stayed inside and watched TV. My mother went to the beach and read a book.

We stayed in homes and condos but after a couple of years, we discovered the almighty timeshare. You could buy a week and use it anytime of the year. Since we traveled the same time every year, it worked out pretty well.

Representatives of timeshare companies often accosted vacationers outside of popular restaurants. "Do you come here every year?" they asked. Then they suggested you attend a seminar. If you survived said seminar without buying a week in wonderful Hilton Head, you were given a great gift. But they were persistent.

We have good friends who had no problem turning down the timeshare bombardment and came away with gift luggage which they used to carry back all of the things they bought during vacation.

Our first timeshare was called The Cottages. These tidy little beach homes were as the name implied, cute little bungalows each with their own private swimming pool. The kids, getting older by then, loved the pool. I even spent some time in what the *Beverly Hillbillies'* Clampetts used to call "the c-e-e-ment pond" but quickly learned that the evil sun's rays were worse on the skin in a pool because they reflect off the water.

Apparently, I had spent most of my time in indoor pools. I got sunburned in places that I didn't know one could sunburn—underneath the arms, between the legs, and behind my knees... Those UVA and UVB rays found my weak spots. It was as if the sun sent them on a search and destroy mission.

Unfortunately, there was one problem with The Cottages—the distance to fun and sun. We had to drive half a mile to get to the beach. But that just wasn't good enough. We had a hankering to get to the mountaintop, the promised land.

We wanted beachfront.

Yes, we set our sights high, but there was one problem. Hilton Head, with its hot (I feel like the humidity has got me by the throat) beautiful weather, well-manicured shrubbery and lawns, and top-rated beaches, limited our sight landscapes to parking lot views and golf courses.

We didn't play golf; why would we want to spend a week looking out the window at overweight Caucasians hitting golf balls? Wildwood may have been just a speck in our rearview mirrors, but we were spoiled as the devil.

We kept moving up in the timeshare world—they were popular and easy to sell back then—but the best we could do was "beach view." Beach view was nothing more than beachfront's ugly sister. Beach view meant: *you can see the ocean if you squint at just the right angle...*

But as our kids reached their teen years, the lure of Hilton Head began to wane. They grew bored. After all, there was no boardwalk like Ms. Jackson's Wildwood.

In my teen years, we walked the boardwalk practically every night. I bought this little trashy miniature camera from a Ringo Starr lookalike. I forget what I paid for it but it was absolutely worthless. I guess that's the lure of the boardwalk.

Somewhere, lookalike Ringo was singing *I Took That Black Boy's Money and He'll Never Get No Pictures.*

Hilton Head offered only movie theaters, lunch at Fuddruckers, cable TV, and the occasional excitement of an alligator running roughshod on Route 278. The sheriffs weren't havin' that. But the gators walked with impunity on the golf courses.

And the white golfers just played on through.

In truth, Hilton Head was a bit on the ritzy, exclusive side—laid back, nothing to get excited about. But they want to keep it that way. One might even call it "bougie," if that's the way you want to look at it. Vacationers go there for rest, relaxation, golf, bike riding (lots of bike riding), some good restaurant food, and lots of beach time.

There's a camp for motor homes, a public beach and a Red Roof Inn but there won't be any busloads of overnight guests coming from Beaufort (the only area near Hilton Head that had a city-like atmosphere), and the Jolly Roger is way too unseemly. Oh, there are plenty of down-home food stores... like Piggly Wiggly and Harris Teeters.

Visitors stock up on groceries and snacks upon arrival. In the early days, I couldn't believe that there was one entire aisle of liquor and spirits. More alcohol than I'd ever seen in a State Store.

Someone was doing a lot of relaxing.

But there were no lights on the main-drag Route 278 at night. Everything closed like a quaint, small town. No boardwalks or roller coasters or arcades. Lookalike Ringo need not apply.

Eventually, we allowed the kids to stay home. Then there were just four of us. We discovered that one week wasn't enough for four boring adults. We began booking houses for two-week stays and paid a deposit over the winter, renting homes through agencies as close as possible to the beach.

Reality struck.

We got a face full of what beachfront living costs. What would Ms. Jackson say? Oh, if she could see us now. We had to walk maybe the equivalent of two blocks before our feet touched sand. Big, beautiful homes lined the beaches costing upward of five figures a week. I spit in the general direction of people who could afford such rarified air, although three or four families could stay and split the tariff.

Times changed in our favorite South Carolina hotspot, too. In 1988, my youngest daughter wrote an essay about what she did over the summer as a newbie second grader. "We went to Hilton Head Island, South Carolina. It cost a thousand dollars."

Short and sweet.

Our last vacation was in 2013. I managed to book an eighth-floor condo with a magnificent ocean view—an elevator down, a short walk through the complex, and we were there.

We all flew that year because my parents were getting too old to fly alone. We also discovered that if we put my eighty-six-year-old father in a wheelchair it was easier to get through security.

Hey! He had a hard time walking, too.

We got to the Savannah airport late on the way back and missed our flight to Pittsburgh. We waited for eight hours for the next flight. Some might say a sad ending to almost ten decades of vacationing. But I did write a book about our airport escapade (*Book of Samuel*) and two books after that. My parents, now ninety-two and ninety-four, won't be taking anymore vacations and my wife and I—now their caretakers—wonder if we'll ever again smell the Hilton Head breeze. Debbie will soon be sixty-five and I'll be seventy in the next vacation cycle.

My oldest daughter is now forty-two; the others forty and thirty-nine. Thirty-nine-year-old Kimberly was the one who once wrote about Hilton Island costing an exorbitant $1,000.

Thankfully, everyone had a shower.

To all who made my vacations possible:

> Thanks, Mable and Franklin
> Thanks, Earl and Rema
> Thanks, James Sr. and Betty Robinson
> Thanks, Gene and Marva
> Thanks, Ms. Jackson
> Thanks, Jaime, Erin and Kimberly Robinson
> Thanks, Debbie Robinson
> Thanks for nothin', Lookalike Ringo
> Kiss my behind, Jolly Roger

First in the bathtub, second, third, fourth... see the sponge, see the cleanser?

SLAUGHTER BEACH

Deborah Hetrick Catanese

Deidre and John had arrived with the perfect announcement of a screeching seagull. The road trip with their small infant from Western Pennsylvania to Rehoboth Beach via Cape May had gone far easier than the new parents expected.

Once their car reached the end of the secluded sandy driveway, the front door of the inviting cedar-shake beach house flew open. As Deidre unbuckled the straps of the rear-facing car seat, her friend Nancy ran outside in her usual barefooted state, wavy hair and long floral skirt blowing in the salty ocean breeze. Their hilarious self-effacing friend Tad, Nancy's latest obsession, followed close behind, along with dear friends Laura and Craig, just arrived from acting gigs in New York City for the Rehoboth Beach gathering.

"Oh darling child, your auntie Nan needs to smell your sweet baby scent!" coocd Nancy, as she received ten-week-old Tina from Deidre's arms, the transfer as effortless as one would expect from an experienced mother of four. "Look at these dark almond eyes staring straight into mine, oh my heart!"

Smiling over at Deidre, Laura chimed in, "She is so alert, isn't she?"

Deidre nodded. And beamed. This reunion at the beach in Rehoboth came about solely because of the happy arrival of baby Tina. The child had already caused so much joy and excitement in every aspect of Deidre's new life as a mother.

She was a bit older mother than most people expected, she realized. But she felt so prepared to be a mom at age thirty-eight and so ready to commit to this sacred endeavor that, in her heart, she knew everything evolved the way it was meant to.

As excited as she and John were to be parents, their past few days in Cape May convinced her of a wee baby's power to please many people, even total strangers. Everywhere Deidre and John walked, or tried to sit and relax while taking in the colorfully painted Victorian mansions, or stopped for free samples at the Fudge House, people paused in their tracks to fawn over their new baby. Deidre imagined that Robert Redford himself could hardly stir up more fuss on the boardwalk than this little one.

"What a sweetie you have there! A true living doll!"

"This bambina has the face of a Bocelli!"

"Oh my, Charlie, quick! Come have a look at this adorable little baby!"

This traffic-stopping adulation persisted throughout their ferry ride from Cape May Point south to Lewes, Delaware.

From there it was only a short drive to join the waiting friends at the lovely summer home owned by Nancy's parents, finely situated between the Atlantic Ocean and a freshwater pond, radiant with the soft sheen of inter-coastal waters. Deidre took in the breathtaking beauty of cirrus cloud-filtered sun lighting up the edges of every ripple on the dark blue-green water, and her heart swelled.

As Nancy showed them to their well-appointed room and its oceanside view of the rolling waves, Deidre had to laugh at the contrast to Nancy's home in the woods near Deep Creek, Maryland. Nancy's natural style permeated her mountain cabin—vintage doilies, colorful beaded curtains, faded hand-sewn quilts covering cushy sofas, and fresh wildflowers in antique glass vases adorning every surface in sight. Her hippie chic living area transitioned into the cozy kitchen, with numerous copper and cast iron pans hanging in front of wide open unscreened windows... and flies everywhere. Nancy never minded the flies—part of nature, she said—nor did she concern herself with such lowly matters as obsessive handling of housekeeping chores.

Tad saw Nancy as his dream goddess, a free spirited bohemian with a Newport mansion sophistication and a Parisian *savor faire*. And Nancy was quite taken with Tad. A downhome guy with a blazing intellect and a history of moody struggles, he charmed everyone with wry jokes about his several stays in the "loony bin," as he dubbed it, where he became fast pals with John and Deidre's equally troubled friend Meyer, and was quickly welcomed into the group.

"So, my dear friend, make yourself at home. Take whatever space you need for the half a trailer worth of supplies you brought to care for a ten-pound human! There's certainly room to spread out here," gestured Nancy grandly as they took in the rich comfort of the deceivingly spacious house.

"I do need to nurse her. She is starting to fuss a bit..."

"Fuss?" Nancy smiled. "Teensy is even dainty about being hungry."

After eagerly nursing with barnyard animal sound effects, Tina pulled off her mama's second breast with a slurp and a flourish, then rolled her head back limply as if in a stupor in Deidre's cradling arms, a bit of milk still dribbling on her satisfied little face. "Drunk with milk," Deidre and John called this pose, finding delight in all her antics.

Deidre tiptoed over to the Port-a-Crib John had set up, careful not to wake her baby as she set her down.

"How long will she nap, do you think?" asked Laura. "Is she on a schedule?"

"Well, she stayed awake while charming her admirers on the ferry, so I suspect she will sleep two or three hours. Especially since she has a full tummy now."

"Hey, D! I think you and John should come with me and Tad to the beach. Let Laura and Craig take care of your Sleeping Beauty!" Nancy urged. "You have been at this steadily for two and a half months. You could use some of our patented seaside rejuvenation!"

Laura chimed in immediately. "Craig and I would be most happy to watch our goddaughter. Go, you two! Take an afternoon for an ocean swim."

"Oh, how I could use a dose of the Atlantic! I'll be back in two hours, I promise! I'll scurry and change into my suit."

"Our Teensy will be fine!" they all reassured her.

"I'll be back soon, sweetheart..." Deidre whispered before running out the door, as Tina's funny little face made sucking movements in her sleep.

The ocean waves were perfect, reminding Deidre of summers with her family at Myrtle Beach, with breakers crashing close to shore and pleasing rolling waves awaiting once you worked your way past. There seemed little threat of a renegade wave catching them off guard.

Ah, riding the waves! Deidre thought back on floating in the ocean with her father many years before, their inflated canvas raft their special happy place.

The four friends shared one raft, now out beyond the breakers, catching up with one another. Nancy and Deidre relaxed on the raft, with the two guys casually hanging on or floating around them. The ease of swimming in the slow rise and fall of the waves lent to meandering conversation and blissful sighs.

"Wow, look at that glorious house hiding in the sea grass dunes near your parents' place!" exclaimed Deidre.

"They call it Shell House," explained Nancy. "It has stories associated with it, like many old houses near the sea. It's so beautiful though—I'd almost give up my cabin in the woods if I could live there..."

"Stories?" asked Tad, feigning trepidation.

Nancy laughed and brushed him off. "Oh, I know an unhinged guy who believes all that nonsense..."

"Well, what do you expect in a place with a spot called Slaughter Beach?" parleyed Ted.

"We could float right by Slaughter, if this current keeps pulling us downward," Nancy noted, with a less teasing tone.

"It feels so gentle though, doesn't it?" said Deidre, clearly benefitting from the ocean cure-all for motherly exhaustion. Water was her relaxing place. She always felt comfortable there.

Nancy shook her head. "There was a couple here recently, who floated easily for several hours, near Slaughter Beach, and then realized how far out they were. They were found on the beach, drowned from their effort to fight the undertow."

Deidre stared out at the swells that seemed quite benign... "Oh my, the famous Undertoad..."

"That sounds so familiar! Where is that from?" asked John.

"*The World According to Garp*. Remember? The little boy thought his parents were saying Undertoad when they said undertow, and he searched for this purported sea monster in the waters with great concern. Garp used Undertoad to describe his persistent anxiety," Deidre answered, while continuing to roll on the waves, looking quite serene.

"Well, anyone know how Slaughter Beach got that name?" Tad asked.

Nancy sighed. "What a beautiful place... it's where Cedar Creek flows through marshland and into Delaware Bay. Slaughter Neck is upland from the boundary areas there. But what an ugly history Slaughter Beach is rumored to have, even before this recent drowning."

"Do tell," said Tad.

"Well, in the early days settlers came to that area because it was fish and mollusk heaven, but they purportedly suffered attacks from tribal peoples. The leader of the settlers then requested a meeting with the chief, promising that the god of the White people would be there to give his almighty approval to their peace treaty if everyone in the tribe showed up. He totally betrayed them. The White man's 'god' was a loaded cannon, and once the tribe had gathered in front of it as they were instructed, the ruthless bastard set off the cannon, killing all of the Indians."

"*Real* nice..." said John. "History banging us in the head once again. Let's say we skip Slaughter Beach."

"Well, if you don't like that version of the story, there is the one that says Slaughter was named after the myriad of horseshoe crabs that converge all at once on the beach to lay their eggs... and then afterward, they die, *en masse*!" Nancy responded with feigned horror.

"Oh, you guys!" laughed Deidre. "This is awesome, but we should head back to the baby. I feel my milk coming in, right on schedule." Relaxed and happy to have had the diversion, she was ready to go back.

It wasn't that simple, though. The undetected undertow had indeed pulled them out. They gasped when they saw how far they had drifted.

"I can't believe how stupid we are!" cried Deidre. "We were just talking about people who died this way, and then we go and do the same thing!"

"We'll be okay," said the ever-reassuring John. "You ladies get on the raft and kick, while Tad and I get in front and pull you with the ropes."

They kicked and pulled, not yet concerned. Ten, fifteen minutes went by...

"Are we making any progress?" asked Tad.

"Um, it doesn't look like it," answered Nancy. "*Come on*, guys. Try harder!"

With each kick, Deidre got more frightened. The shore was no closer than a wish.

"We aren't getting anywhere like this," admitted John. "I think we have to separate. I'm going to swim in to shore and get us some help..."

Again, this seemed overly optimistic to Deidre. The beach looked deserted, no help in sight.

Tad reluctantly agreed with John. "I think you will do better without us. You'll be more free to kick, as well as use your arms!"

Deidre and Nancy exchanged one long look, and called out with every bit of determination they could muster, "Okay, let's *GO!*"

It was harder than Deidre ever imagined. It seemed they would never succeed. Her muscles ached and screamed and felt like they would give out, and her mind reeled even worse. Their progress felt scant, at best.

But how could she give up? She was a mother now! She had a baby waiting for her. Why hadn't they paid attention after hearing about that other doomed couple? If she survived this, she needed to be a lot smarter from here on out!

Long tortuous units of fearful time later, the four lay panting, bedraggled, and sand-covered on the beach. Deidre's last bit of energy was spent on soaring gratitude. She remained prostrate on the foamy wet shore, as limp as baby Tina had been just hours ago in her arms.

Tad and John had exerted all their strength to make it back, and then fought hip deep in the thrashing waves to grab the girls as they struggled in the last seemingly impossible stretch to shore after their raft had capsized when they hit the heavy surf.

"Wow. Who started with all those scary stories?" Tad finally uttered, his breath beginning to normalize. "Isn't that what you Pittsburghers call a jinx?"

It felt perfect to laugh.

They grabbed the raft that had crashed into shore just down-current from them and headed back.

Laura was waiting at the door with a warm welcome, holding Tina.

"Teensy started looking around for her mommy just minutes ago!' Laura smiled, with not a clue how uncertain their return had been.

Deidre took her hungry baby into her arms. "I told you I'd be back soon," she spoke as lullaby soft as the whisper of the bay breeze on a calm day, her eyes brimming with good tears that tasted even saltier than the sea.

Author's Note:

This work of creative nonfiction is dedicated to the July 2022 anticipated arrival of Teensy/Christina's first baby and the author's first grandchild.

—Deborah Hetrick Catanese (aka Deidre)

SUMMER MEMORIES AT
AUNT MABEL'S PLACE
Judy England-McCarthy

My footsteps on the stair treads seemed hollow. The only sound was his steady, rasping breath. A reminder of what I was leaving behind. Words once said could not be unspoken. It was too late to go back, to change my mind.

The weathered, olive-green suitcase rubbing against my shin had seen me through many choices. It would see me through this one. Opening the front door, the breath of a spring touch caressed my face, releasing me from my tomb of a lifetime. I headed down the front steps and out into the new morning and its promise. I was moving on to a new place, new adventures, and letting go of this chapter of my life.

It is happening tonight, I thought, as I stood in front of my old but reliable '72 Dodge Plymouth with one battered green suitcase in hand. It was the total of my meager possessions until the movers arrived next week with all the rest of my stuff. The realtor assured me the house was up and running, but I knew I'd have no food until I went shopping for basics like peanut butter, tea, milk, and fresh bakery bread. Taking a stretch and gulp of air I let the quiet night noises encircle me. The air was clear and crisp like biting into a McIntosh apple after hours in a car and leaving an overcrowded city behind.

Reaching the landing of the porch outside the entrance, I set down the luggage, and with my right hand, I searched my outer coat pocket. From there, I produced an old-fashioned skeleton key with a weathered tag attached by a thick cotton string. Written on the paper tag, in faded pencil, were the words "Mabel's Front Door Key," and typed neatly on the back, "Beach House." Utilizing the light of the half-moon, and with some maneuvering, I located the key opening and managed to unlock it. Standing at the doorway brought back memories of summers spent in this rambling house with my siblings. In the twilight, I could almost imagine my aunt and mother sitting in the two rocking chairs that still resided on the long front porch.

The door creaked open a couple of inches before it jammed stuck like a peanut butter sandwich to the roof of your mouth. The humidity so close to the beach always played havoc with the doors and windows. The heavy oak door gave way like a freed rusty release valve when I exerted all my slender 124 pounds. I tumbled into a large empty foyer like a person who had one drink too many. Righting myself, I stood and looked around at my new residence. As of today, I was officially the new owner of 217 Bayard Avenue in Rehoboth Beach, Delaware.

This Atlantic Coast town was the home of many childhood memories and near the famous "Shell House." My recently departed well-to-do aunt Mabel had given money to all of us, but to me alone, she had bestowed her lifelong dwelling. It was located within walking distance of the Atlantic Ocean and was one of the most desirable locations along the Delaware coast. No one was surprised, as she always said, "You will get this place when I'm dead and gone, because I know you will see the life and stories within its walls."

I went back to the porch and retrieved my suitcase. Shoving the door shut with a little less muscle, I headed for the lights. After several minutes of searching, I located the downstairs light switches, a row of six that controlled the front section of the house. The first activated a chandelier and lit up the foyer like a birthday cake with too many candles. From where I stood, the chandelier was perhaps fifteen feet above me. *Damn, that's going to be a pain in the butt to clean... Well, that's another problem for another day.*

I flicked on the other five switches, and other parts of the house began to light up along with thoughts and childhood memories of days spent at the ocean or nearby Silver Lake. Odd as it may seem, both were only a couple of blocks away. This strange anomaly of having a lake and the ocean within mere feet of each other, as children we took for granted. Sometimes we were able to head out, on our own, with provisions of peanut butter sandwiches and water. Depending on our daily aspirations or the "adults' will" we could go for fresh or saltwater fun and even sometimes both on the same day. In all cases, we would come back hungry, sandy, and full of stories.

To the right of me was a large formal dining room. A brief recollection of a time when Sunday dinners and manners were obligatory crossed my mind. Mostly, meals were taken in the sit-down kitchen in the back, where conversation and behavior had more of a Wild West feel.

The living room lay to the left and had a large stone fireplace with enough wood and kindling to torch the place if I were so inclined. The living room directly connected the study to the rest of the house by a well-worn carved maple door. Like a lot of the remainder of the house, it spoke of a time when wealth meant high quality and workmanship. The study was more like a library with wall-to-wall books lining its shelves. It held volumes of all sorts and supplied ample reading material on rain-soaked days. I enjoyed the stories that had a magical twist because anything was possible in them.

On such days my aunt would announce in her best military voice, "Outside is fit for neither man nor beast. So, my little beasties, you must stay inside."

Sighs, groans, and the occasional rebuttal would follow this proclamation. Ultimately arguments were futile. Many a foul day would find us all over the house in its various nooks and crannies reading our newest plunder from the study. At the end of the foyer, on the left, was a staircase now lit and revealing an upstairs landing. Carrying my travel-everywhere green suitcase, acquired in my college days, I headed up the flight of wooden stairs to the rooms beyond, still cloaked in shadows.

Though I had my choice of any space in the house, I headed for the room with the bay window of my youth. Many a soulful night of hushed conversations with my sister had been held in its walls.

As I entered, light poured in from the outside; the autumn moon lit the room with constantly changing light and shadows. The single-panes I remembered from my youth had finally been replaced by my aunt in the late '60s with more cost-efficient windows. Though they kept the cold out and the heat in, it signaled that all things inevitably change. To me, the newer windows lacked character and no longer seemed like the eyes of the place.

With their loss, some timeless aspect of my youth had been given a facelift and a favored feature stripped away.

Yet, some things remained as I remembered. I walked toward the two side-by-side bunk beds, with a writing desk and chair in between. On each bed was one pillow at the top and a hand-quilted comforter neatly folded at the end of the bed for those unexpected cold nights. "Always be prepared" was definitely one of my aunt's mottos.

Putting my suitcase on the long dresser, which still held some trinkets, shells, rocks and even a piece of blue weathered glass, I picked up the shell and could still smell the ocean in its crevices. It brought back running, laughing and so much fun from my childhood forays along the sandy beaches.

I grabbed my toothbrush, toothpaste, and a long flannel nightgown. *Thank God there is a bathroom on every floor.* Before I left for my nightly routine, I noticed the desk once more and was brought back to a pivotal memory. It was the day I had become a writer. Filled with life's tragedy, I sat huddled over the desk's wooden surface with my eight-year-old hands covering my face. I recalled fighting with my mother that day. About what, was lost to the annals of time. She and my aunt had sent me to my room as a consequence. An unfair punishment for fighting for my right to decide for myself.

I'd slammed the door and stomped around the hardwood floor for a few minutes, venting my anger and hoping to irritate them downstairs. But frustration and outrage soon gave way to an overwhelming feeling of powerlessness. It was then that I started writing to express my feelings. The end result was a rhyming poem about sadness and gladness. In writing it, I felt resolved and complete. At that moment, I had worked out one of life's mysteries by using the written word. Such clarity... and yet, the overall tale blurred. Smiling like Mona Lisa, I headed for the bathroom and realized I had just begun unraveling the stories contained within the house's walls.

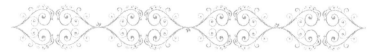

QUEEN ANNE'S AMULET

Demi Stevens

Celine Vranic's head still throbbed from the abrupt time travel back from the 1941 party to her wife Julia Boisseau's waiting arms. She reached for the phone to call her grandmother, Estella, and share the news that they had recovered the lost amulet rumored to have gone down with Blackbeard's ship.

The diamond and ruby-encrusted jewel was even more stunning than her *báka* had indicated. Surely it would fetch enough money to save the house from demolition. Celine cradled it inside a silk handkerchief while she dialed.

"*Báka*," she shouted when the older woman answered. "We found it!"

"What?" Estella asked with a voice scratchy from sleep. "What have you found, *unuka*?"

"The missing amulet," Celine purred as Julia wrapped a supportive arm around her and motioned her to a seat on the sofa.

She felt bad about prying up the floorboards in front of Shell House's fireplace, but the two of them had been careful and were sure a gifted craftsman would be able to replace them seamlessly.

"*Unuka*, that is wonderful news," her grandmother sighed. "I always knew you would be the one to solve Bertram's riddle. You... and that magical wife of yours."

The breath caught in Celine's throat. "Bertram." She remembered the faithful butler who had guided her to the secret hiding spot during her encounter back in time. "I met him. He's the one who hid the amulet for safekeeping and showed me where to find it."

"Ah, such a kind soul," Estella said. "We had a brief fling before I met your grandfather."

Celine gasped. "*Báku!* That must have caused a scandal!" She could only imagine how racial prejudices of the time would have driven a wedge in the relationship, even if it was just between two servant families.

The old woman just laughed. "No more than anything else going on in Shell House in those days. That Louisa Carpenter and her infamous parties, not to mention the soirees hosted there back during Prohibition..."

Celine's eyebrows lifted and she found herself leaning hard into Julia's shoulder.

"Such sweet memories," Estella sighed. "Dear Bertram was the one who hinted to me that the jewel had been secreted away for its protection. But I never knew he was the one who hid it. I always sensed a bit of *mojo* about him."

"*Mojo*," Celine repeated. "That's what he called Jules's magic that transported me back in time. It was as if he could see and hear me even though I wasn't physically present in the room."

"He had the gift, for sure. He used to enchant me with stories about ghosts who roamed the halls, secret passages through magical mirrors, and even other hidden treasures of Shell House."

Celine thought of the vanity mirror from the master bedroom, surrounded by mosaic tile pieces. When she'd been photographing the home in preparation for Julia's spell, she could've sworn she'd looked into its surface and seen an Eastern woman seated cross-legged with some strange instrument in her lap. But when she blinked and looked back, the image was gone.

"Well," Celine exhaled slowly. "I guess now we need to figure out how to use this amulet to rescue the mansion. But..."

"But what, *unuka*?"

Celine's thoughts were racing. "Bertram didn't seem to think its value would be able to save Shell House. He said it could help in other ways though. What do you suppose he meant?"

Celine clutched the locked case with clammy hands as she stood before Eli Jackson and Frannie Clark. "My grandmother thinks your historical society will be able to use something I found in Shell House while doing research." She wished Julia had been able to accompany her, but her wife had been called to a climate conference of lightworkers on the West Coast to lend her special magic.

A twinkle lit the woman named Frannie's eyes. "You mean you discovered one of Shell House's mysterious secrets, too?" She nudged Eli in the ribs and smiled broadly. "I'd love to write about whatever it is you've discovered. I'm working on a memoir of sorts, about the house and all its quirky owners and history."

Eli's face brightened as the woman spoke. "Frannie is a wonderful writer," he proclaimed. "She's going to make us all so very proud." He turned to Celine and said, "So what is it that's brought you here? And who is your grandmother?"

"Estella Vranic," Celine supplied. "Her family came over from what's modern-day Croatia and worked for a neighboring family back in the 1940s. She's been telling me stories about Shell House ever since I was a little girl."

"Where are my manners?" Frannie said. "We should have a little food and drink before settling into heavy discussion. Plus I'll want to fetch my notebook and a pen."

She invited them into the kitchen and pulled out a platter from the refrigerator containing half a pineapple upside down cake. Eli grasped a bottle of champagne and stemware while Celine opened drawers and cabinets in search of forks and dessert plates, still clutching the black case tightly in the crook of her left arm.

The three traipsed outside to the patio and sat under a spreading tree on the right, facing the ocean. Eli popped the cork ceremoniously and poured while Frannie served up generous slices of cake.

"When Eli and I met here," Frannie blushed, "I'd just found a bottle washed up on shore. It contained a map to a hidden safe in the pantry, along with ingredients and a card that had some sort of mystical looking symbol on top with a recipe for pineapple upside down cake."

"Since then," Eli picked up the tale, "I reached out to Frank White, the general contractor, and president of the historical society. I convinced him to talk to the buyer. It seems Frank had some similar sort of experience of finding a lost treasure here in Shell House during the recent hurricane, and he was hot to delay the demolition, too."

Celine released her breath. The tension she'd been holding in her chest subsided just a bit, though her shoulders still ached. She made a conscious effort to slow her inhales, looking up at the tree that offered them shade. *Palm trees in Delaware? Who knew?* Something shifted and caught her attention, like a weird emblem being written on the bark itself of the nearest tree. She shook her head and focused again, but whatever appeared had vanished as quickly as it came.

"And there's some sort of movement going on," Frannie said. "It's spearheaded by the daughters of the police chief and the local judge—Lacey and Sondra, I think their names are. They've rallied a bunch of people together to try to convince the buyer not to destroy the house."

Eli topped up their glasses. "Frank told me in secret that the guy—Brice somebody-or-other—reached out to the National Register of Historic Places, in addition to our local historical society." He raised his champagne flute in toast. "Seems he wants to explore options on preserving Shell House."

The three clinked glasses and Celine couldn't help but marvel at how Bertram's prediction had come to pass. The amulet couldn't save Shell House... but now it wouldn't need to. What had he meant when he said it could help in other ways?

Celine took a delicate sip of champagne then polished off her cake. "This is delicious," she said. "You found the recipe in the pantry?"

Frannie nodded. "The ingredients, too. It was written by someone named Molly, and we also found another recipe card from a woman called Penelope who appears to have taken over as head cook in later years. Something about potatoes and a quiche for the CIA. I couldn't make heads or tails of it, but..."

Eli let out a chuckle. "It's always something unusual here at Shell House. This place has seen hearts broken, lives lost, séances with the dead... Hell, I bet someday even aliens will visit and leave artifacts of their own."

Celine suppressed a giggle at the thought. No doubt if Bertram had been pressed to describe her arrival back in 1941, he might have resorted to referring to her as an alien rather than trying to make people believe in time travel.

She retrieved the black case from where she'd stashed it at her feet beneath the patio table. "My grandmother is the one who actually should get the thanks for this Shell House miracle," she began. "I'm hoping one of you can connect me with someone who will be able to help document the find and use it to assist in some way with the restoration or preservation of the property."

With a flip of two magnetic locking mechanisms, Celine opened the case to reveal the diamond and ruby-encrusted amulet, which sparkled like a thousand miniature suns in the fading light of day.

"Holy mother of..." Eli's eyes were as wide as the *palacinke*, the Croatian pancakes Celine's *báka* used to make on weekends.

"It's... it's..." Even the self-proclaimed writer couldn't find words to speak. Frannie simply stuttered and nodded like a life-sized bobblehead, pushing aside her dessert plate to start scrawling on the legal pad in front of her.

"I'm told this necklace was recovered from the *Queen Anne's Revenge* before Blackbeard's ship purportedly sank," Celine said. "It passed down through generations to be hidden somewhere inside Shell House just before World War I. My wife Julia and I were able to get an initial appraisal from a guy in New York who claimed it would fetch something in the way of five to ten million dollars.

Not nearly as valuable as 'The Heart of the Ocean,' if you saw *Titanic*, but still... that amount of money ought to be able to help in some way."

Eli reached for his iPhone and was fumbling to dial while Frannie made a credible sketch of the necklace, stretching with her left hand to shift the box on the table to catch the now diminishing rays of an otherwise spectacular sunset.

Celine heard Eli say, "Max, I've got an inside scoop for your paper. How's about you gather up your editor, and the mayor and police chief and that guy Brice who's been directing the action on Penn Street lately. Bring everyone here to Shell House. We've got a doozy of an announcement to make!"

Some forty-five minutes later, Celine found herself surrounded by chatty locals plus one seriously rich dude named Brice McDougal who'd made his fortune in real estate and had the police chief's daughter in tow, her left ring finger sporting a diamond nearly the size of a gumdrop.

"My caretaker here, Eli, seems to believe you have something we'll be interested in," Brice said to Celine with a smile, squeezing the hand of his fiancée Lacey who was as giddy as a prom girl.

"Sondra's going to be miffed she isn't here to find out firsthand," the woman named Lacey said. "Brice just told me yesterday that he's started paperwork to donate Shell House to the town, and my friend and I will become the executors. We have plans to turn the property into a gorgeous event space where the whole region can enjoy it for weddings and other celebrations, catered with menus inspired by the two fantastic cooks who worked here over the years. We might even do some sort of rotating display with the antique furnishings that Mr. Connor retained from the original home, along with guided tours of the property and maybe historical talks about the various mysteries we've unraveled about the many, many families who've stayed at Shell House."

After introductions to the newspaper reporter and local officials, the group gathered in Shell House's formal sitting room. Celine shared the contents of the black case and the amulet's history as she understood it.

"Well, I'll be," said the police chief. "Lacey, I expect some of those old-timers your friend Sondra works with might be able to corroborate parts of this story. Maybe fill in some missing details."

The girl was already speed-dialing her friend and began shouting into the phone, "Oh my gawd, Sondra! Remember that story Mrs. Morgan the nanny was telling the other day about some lost heirloom necklace? You're never gonna believe this but..."

Others crowded tightly around Celine for a peek.

"Maybe the light would be better in the hall under the chandelier," Celine offered.

The group followed her like pups, almost salivating at the reflection of sparkles emanating from the jewels.

"I never noticed before," Celine began, pointing from the velvet box in her arms up to the light fixture directly above her, "but the shape of the necklace mirrors the crystals at the center of this chandelier."

"I just don't understand," said Eli. "I'm a big history buff and remember all the hullabaloo in 2011 when they finally verified the boat discovered off North Carolina's coast was really the *Queen Anne's Revenge*."

Frannie nodded. "That's right," she said. "I wrote up a Top 10 list of pirate names for babies that autumn," then blushed.

"I'm pretty sure the ship sank sometime back in the 1700s," Eli continued. "How did a necklace from the recovered wreckage get here?"

Celine felt her skin heat. She couldn't exactly tell them about her and Julia's part in the amulet's retrieval, so she hedged. "My grandmother worked in one of the neighboring houses when she was young. There were already rumors of it back in the 1940s... so um..." she cleared her throat and added, "it's pretty much a mystery how the necklace was brought here. But it certainly wasn't after the wreckage was discovered off the Carolina coast."

Frannie slipped her hand through the crook of Eli's elbow and stared up at him. "Maybe you and I could sleuth it out for our book. What do you think?"

It was clear from the way he patted her hand and locked onto her gaze that the two were smitten. To keep further questions at bay, Celine volunteered, "I'll set up a call for you with Grandma Estella. I'm sure she'd be thrilled to reminisce about the good ol' days here at the shore."

Brice stepped in front of Celine and held out his palms. "May I?" he asked.

She handed him the black case and watched as he turned it appreciatively to catch every facet of the light. "You say you've already had it appraised?"

Celine couldn't help but notice Brice's deep tan, offset by his white linen shirt, rolled to the elbows and untucked. She answered cautiously, "Just a cursory inspection. Nothing formal yet."

"Fine," he said. "I've got a specialist on staff with contacts at Sotheby's. I'll have them research it and draw up all the necessary authentication documents. And of course I'll take care of any associated costs, plus insuring the amulet."

Celine felt relief that she wouldn't have to figure out how to best use this heirloom to help Shell House. The mayor had already hopped on his own call to work out a secure place in the bank vault to store the necklace until its appraisal could be arranged. The police chief was deeply ensconced in conversation with Lacey, who turned out to be his daughter, and was making notes on a tiny pad with names of Rehoboth residents for Sondra to interview.

Celine used the time to look around the house, noticing the wallpaper that had been changed out from the floral patterns that graced the walls of Shell House during her 1941 "mystery" visit. It almost appeared that one of the patterns did a little cartwheel and winked at her. Celine blinked and shook her head. Clearly she needed more sleep.

She backed away from the group and headed to the sitting room. A large painting dominated the space—a green-eyed sailor in uniform. According to the plaque his name was Samuel Wright and he had died more than a century earlier.

Celine collapsed on the love seat and pulled out her cell phone. A message from her wife Julia was waiting...

Conference is great! Met a lady named Liv who says she stayed at Shell House a few years ago. Wants you to say HI to her "magic palm tree"... whatever that means.

Celine smiled, thinking of the weird palm grove where she'd shared pineapple upside-down cake with Frannie and Eli. Time had a way of bringing people together in this lovely Delaware beach town, in this historic home. Shell House was full of mysteries, and she had a sense the story was far from over...

CONTRIBUTORS

LORRAINE DONOHUE BONZELET is a graduate of Steven's Institute of Technology, The Institute of Children's Literature, Dr. Mira Reisberg's Children's Book Academy, and a long-time member of the Society of Children's Book Writers and Illustrators. Lorraine is a picture book enthusiast and mindful writer. She has a nonfiction article and photographs published in *Boys' Quest* magazine, *Unusual Sports*. She's also published in the Mindful Writers Retreat Anthologies: *Into the Woods*, *Over the River and Through the Woods*, and *Love on the Edge*. Lorraine and her husband have no need for an alarm clock, for their two cats rally them out of bed before sunrise. Lorraine loves nothing more than spending precious time with her two daughters and vacationing with family. Her story, "A Shell for a Shell," was drafted while mindfully breathing in the salty air at Rehoboth Beach. Lorraine reverts to a giggly-giddy little girl when near large bodies of water, for that's where her imagination soars, stories unfold, and dreams really do come true!

GLORIA BOSTIC lives in York County, Pennsylvania, with Lee, her husband of thirty-four years. Her greatest joy is spending time with family, especially her three sons, four grandchildren, and sister. Bostic is an active member of the American Legion Auxiliary who prays for peace, supports our troops and serves our veterans who have sacrificed so much for our freedom. Since retiring from her career as a special education teacher, supervisor, and psychologist, Bostic has published one children's picture book and seven inspirational romance novels, all of which can be found on Amazon and in several local libraries.

Facebook @gkbostic

DEBORAH HETRICK CATANESE, a lifelong Pittsburgher and avid traveler, holds a BA in English and an MS in Information Science from the University of Pittsburgh. She has worked as a counselor, systems analyst, importer of South American handicrafts, and owner of printing and real estate businesses. Her writings have been featured in the *Pittsburgh Post-Gazette*, Project Motherhood, Carlow University's Voices in the Attic, Beautiful Cadaver project, Ekphrastic Review, and *But You Don't Look Sick* by Indie Blu(e). Her poem "Love's Remains" received First Place in Pennwriters' Annual Contest in 2021, along with a number of poetry awards from Konect E-zine. Deborah's books include *The Green Turtle Cookbook, Gilda's Club Presents Zelda's Kitchen*, and *ACK Poetically*, a poetry collection by her late friend Del Wynn.

JENNIFER D. DIAMOND is a speech therapist turned international award-winning author. When she's not reading, writing, or paddle-boarding, Diamond enjoys boating with her husband and rescue pup in the heart of Pennsylvania. jenniferddiamondwriter.wordpress.com

Facebook @Jennifer.D.Diamond.writer

Instagram @jennifer_d_diamond_writer

JUDY ENGLAND-McCARTHY is both an author and professional storyteller. Her creative intention is to entertain and transform people through her stories. Judy's professional career as a storyteller commenced in 2009 and as an author in 2013. One of her poems was presented in video format for "The Just Listening Project" and another poem won 1st place at Fanstory.com. Her book *Amazing Petunia's Adventures* is being made into an animation. Other books by this author are *Twas Midnight* and *Why Oh Why Did the Witch Swallow a Fly?* This is her fourth anthology and her second with Mindful Writers Retreat Series. Beginwithastory.com

PHIL GIUNTA's novels include the paranormal mysteries *Testing the Prisoner, By Your Side,* and *Like Mother, Like Daughters.* His short stories appear in such anthologies as *A Plague of Shadows, Beach Nights, Beach Pulp,* the ReDeus mythology series, and the Middle of Eternity speculative fiction series, which he created and edited for Firebringer Press. As a member of the Greater Lehigh Valley Writers Group, Phil also penned stories and essays for *Write Here, Write Now, The Write Connections,* and *Rewriting the Past,* three of the group's annual anthologies. He is currently working on a science fiction novel while plotting his triumphant escape from corporate America where he has been imprisoned for over twenty-five years.
www.philgiunta.com, Facebook: @writerphilgiunta, Twitter: @philgiunta71

KIMBERLY KURTH GRAY was born and raised in Baltimore where she finds daily inspiration for her writing. The winner of the William F. Deeck-Malice Domestic 2009 Grant for Unpublished Writers and a 2017 Hruska Fellowship, she is a member of Sisters in Crime, Guppies, and Pennwriters. Her short stories have been published in Cat and Mouse Press and Level Best Anthologies. In addition to working on a historical novel and writing short stories, she writes The Detective's Daughter on the blog Scenes from a Baltimore Kitchen at www.baltimorebound.me.

HILARY HAUCK is an Italian-speaking Brit living in the U.S. Dubbed "an extraordinary novel" by The Midwest Book Review, her debut novel, *From Ashes to Song*, was inspired by the true story of three Italians who immigrated to Pennsylvania ninety years before she did. As a young adult, Hilary moved to Italy from her native UK where she mastered the language, learned how to cook food she can no longer eat, and won a national karate championship. After meeting her husband, she moved to the U.S. in 2002, where she learned the craft of writing, the art of leadership, and at last lay her imposter syndrome to rest. Her stories and poems have appeared in anthologies in the Mindful Writers Retreat Series, *Like Sunshine After Rain*, *The Ekphrastic Review*, *Balloons Lit Journal*, and *Centered* magazine. Hilary lives on a small patch of woods in rural Pennsylvania with her husband and a cat with a penchant for laundry. Visit her at www.hilaryhauck.com.

LARRY IVKOVICH's speculative fiction has been published in over twenty online and print publications. He's been a finalist in the L. Ron Hubbard's Writers of the Future contest and was the 2010 recipient of the CZP/Rannu Fund award for fiction. His four-part urban fantasy series, The Spirit Winds Quartet, is published by IFWG Publishing, and the first two books in his independently published science fiction series, The Magus Star Trilogy, are available on Amazon. Larry is a member of the Pittsburgh SF group Parsec, the writing/critique group WorD, Pennwriters, the Mindful Writers East and North, and the Taoist Tai Chi Society of the USA. He lives in Coraopolis, PA with his beautiful, multi-talented wife Martha and wonder cat Milo.

STEPHANIE KEYES is the author of over a dozen young adult and romance titles, including the award-winning books *The Spellbinder's Sonata* and *The Internship of Pippa Darling*. Keyes is a technical writer and content strategist by day, and currently pursuing her master's degree in Clinical Mental Health Counseling at night. She lives in Pittsburgh with her husband, two boys, and a fashion-conscious goldendoodle named Duncan MacLeod.

Whether journeying in a fantasy world of her own making or voyaging the universe, SHARON M. KRAFTCHAK is passionate about discovering unique characters and chronicling their heartfelt stories to share with readers. She loves sunrise on the beach, sunsets in the mountains, and portraying Elizabeth Tudor. Working at the library and being surrounded by books ignites her passion to write. She has two dogs who talk and a ghost cat who still comes to the kitchen at dinnertime. She also has three awesome daughters and a husband who is her best friend, her harshest critic, and her most fervent supporter. Facebook @smkraftchak   smkraftchak.com

CINDY MOLDOVAN was born and raised in the tropical paradise of Belize, Central America, until the age of seventeen, when she moved to Houston, Texas. In her memoir, *Growing Up Third World*, Cindy wrote about her experience moving from Belize to the United States and often shares funny and real stories of what it was like growing up in a large family with ten siblings. She attended Lee College of nursing in Baytown, Texas, and worked in Houston for twenty-five years until she retired from the medical field of nursing. She followed her passion for writing and is now a published author. The proud mother of three adult daughters and grandmother of four, she is passionate about her family, often visiting them in Texas and South Carolina for long conversations, priceless hugs and kisses, and sweet stories from any of her four grandchildren.

AMY MORLEY is an author and accidental poet living in northwestern Pennsylvania. Her writing has been published in all previous volumes of the Mindful Writers Retreat Series anthologies. Her work is also featured in *The Ninth Room*, a narrative in verse told through the collective minds of ten different authors which debuted at #1 New Release in June 2021. Amy is currently co-writing a children's book and a cookbook with her writing partner/husband, Michael Morley. Aside from writing, her most important role is spending time with her family of Yorkshire terriers. www.an-accidental-poet.com, Facebook @AmyMorleyAuthor

With an ambition for reading anything with words, from alphabet soup to highway billboards, MICHAEL MORLEY never dreamed of becoming an author. Hailing from Germany, he grew up in West Palm Beach until his family eventually settled into small-town living in a city north of Pittsburgh. A decorated athlete, who eventually found his way working in corporate America, Michael realized he was not living his American Dream, so he ventured west to Ohio where he found his home as a Penguin at Youngstown State University. But it wasn't until he took a Children's Literature course as an elementary education major that inspired him once again to switch gears, and he began writing his own stories. Three years, three manuscripts, and three writing awards later, *Say Hello to Henry* is his fiction debut.

JAMES ROBINSON, JR. hails from Pittsburgh, PA. He has written both fiction and nonfiction. His first book, *Fighting the Effects of Gravity: A Bittersweet Journey into Middle Life*, is a humorous look at midlife filled with autobiographical anecdotes. *Gravity* won an Indie Book Award. His fiction consists of a three-book series chronicling the life of The Johnson Family. Mr. Robinson's book, *Death of a Shrinking Violet,* consists of thirteen humorous essays.

Dr. LARRY "Rock 'n' Roll!!!" SCHARDT is on a journey of discovering and sharing the power of living a life of happiness and "Success That Rocks!" Larry's passion is people. He's been studying human behavior since he was a boy. As the oldest of eight, he's had lots of practice. He co-coordinates the popular Mindful Writers Retreats. Bestselling author of *James Conner: Legend of a Football Hero* and the newly released *My Runaway Summer*, his inspiring stories appear in the *Chicken Soup for the Soul* books: *Find Your Happiness, The Power of Gratitude, The Best Advice I Ever Heard,* and *Your 10 Keys to Happiness.* Larry writes a daily Facebook blog to entertain, celebrate, share, and pay forward the good things in life. He loves the outdoors, walking, reading, skiing, and music that rocks... from classical to Rock 'n' Roll. Facebook @Larry.Schardt; Twitter & LinkedIn @LarrySchardt; Larry@SuccessThatRocks.com

CAROL SCHOENIG lives in Cranberry Township, Pennsylvania, with her husband of fifty-four years and a golden doodle named Millie.

Bestselling author, KATHLEEN SHOOP, holds a PhD in reading education and has more than twenty years of experience in the classroom. She writes historical fiction, women's fiction, and romance. Shoop's novels have garnered various awards in the Independent Publisher Book Awards (IPPY), Eric Hoffer Book Awards, Indie Excellence Awards, Next Generation Indie Book Awards, Readers' Favorite, and the San Francisco Book Festival. Kathleen has been featured in *USA Today* and the *Writer's Guide to 2013.* Her work has appeared in *The Tribune-Review,* four *Chicken Soup for the Soul* books, and *Pittsburgh Parent* magazine. Kathleen coordinates Mindful Writing Retreats and is a regular presenter at conferences for writers. She lives in Oakmont, Pennsylvania, with her husband and two children. www.kshoop.com, Facebook @Kathleen Shoop.

DEMI STEVENS, CEO of Year of the Book Press, has personally assisted in the production of more than 500 titles by 150 authors, ranging from children's picture books to sizzling romance, award-winning mysteries, and bestselling business books. She holds degrees from West Virginia University, Capital University, Northwestern, and Ohio State University, and has served on the faculties of Ohio State and Delaware Valley University, and as Director of Paul Smith Library. Each year she coaches a limited number of writers one-on-one through the entire drafting, editing, and publishing process. YOTBpress.com

LISA VALLI, a certified financial planner and benefits consultant, has been featured in *INC Magazine* and Who's Who of American Women for her professional achievements. But she also enjoys exercising her "right brain" by creating stories. She is a member of various writers' organizations and is currently working on a story inspired by her trips to nearby Deep Creek Lake, Maryland. She resides in Venetia, Pennsylvania, with her husband, two daughters and their little dog, Crosby (named after Sidney, of course).

Founder of the Mindful Writers Groups and Retreats, MADHU BAZAZ WANGU's skillful Writing Meditation Practice combines meditation, journaling, walking, and reading. Dr. Wangu is a multi-award-winning author whose works have won Writer's Digest, Readers Favorite, Indie Excellence, Next Generation Indie Book, and TAZ awards. She is also the Pennwriters 2020 Meritorious Award winner. Dr. Wangu serves as a board member for Books Bridge Hope which promotes reading, writing, and literacy to the community living in shelters and on streets. She is a frequent workshop presenter at Pennwriters Annual Conferences and was a featured author for Beaver County Book Fest in 2017. Her inspiring CDs *Meditations for Mindful Writers I, II & III* help cultivate focus, increase flow and productivity. Practice with her at Online Mindful Writers Group at: tinyurl.com/MindfulWriters

DENISE WEAVER, a *summa cum laude* graduate of the University of Pittsburgh, is a former library director. A love of sharing food and stories, along with a penchant for photography and research, make a winning combination that inspires her to write. She has more than 250 nonfiction articles published in local and regional magazines and is delving into the world of short stories. She once conquered her fear of public performances and sang on-stage at Carnegie Hall. Denise and her husband split their time between the beautiful Laurel Highlands of Pennsylvania and the irresistible pull of the Sunshine State. www.deniseweaver.com

MICHELE SAVAUNAH ZIRKLE, MA, PhD, is a published author, high school teacher and holistic energy practitioner who enjoys sharing innovative ways to break through writing barriers and to live a creative life. She is the author of *Rain No Evil*. In addition to hosting "Life Speaks," on Appalachian Independent Radio, Michele leads meditations and healing events, inspiring partici-pants to live with passion and purpose. Her short stories have appeared in *Mountain Ink Literary Journal* and vignettes in *The Journal of Health and Human Experience*. She presents writing workshops for West

Virginia Writer's Inc. and Northern Appalachia Writer's Conferences. She is a graduate of Concord University, Marshall Graduate School, and The Institute of Metaphysical Humanistic Science. www.michelezirkle.com Facebook @ZirksQuirks

ALSO BY

MINDFUL WRITERS RETREAT AUTHORS

Into the Woods (Book 1)
Short stories, poems, essays, music, and one walking meditation. Each piece is unique in tone and genre and the result is that the collection captures the fascinating, frightening, fun, healing, and fantastical wonder of time spent in the woods. The twenty-six contributors who attend Mindful Writers Retreats in the mountains of Ligonier, Pennsylvania, are donating one hundred percent of the proceeds to support the research and work of The Children's Heart Foundation.

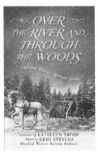

Over the River and Through the Woods (Book 2)
A holiday pastiche from the authors of Mindful Writers Retreat, sure to light your festive candles! From a Thanksgiving snowstorm that mends old feuds... to the family misunderstandings that fuel new ones... a quirky elf and some romantic stardust will get you ready to go *Over the River and Through the Woods* on a journey through time!

Love on the Edge (Book 3)
From love in the time of war to love at first sight and long walks in the snow... to sparks flying because of nosy neighbors... *Love on the Edge* reveals the essence and evolution of human relationships, written in a time when we're all searching for deeper meaning and connection.

CPSIA information can be obtained
at www.ICGtesting.com
Printed in the USA
LVHW011924150822
725987LV00002B/153